Praise for *Boys, Bea*

"Sam Miller is my hero: a fearless vi
once vivid, electrifying, brutal, and full of heart. Un, the rest
of them."
—Sarah Pinsker, author of *A Song for a New Day* and *Sooner or Later Everything Falls into the Sea*

"This is the collection you are looking for. Explosive, careening, shape-shifting tales . . . haunting and defiantly tender."
—Ben Loory, author of *Tales of Falling and Flying*

"The stories in this collection offer a nuanced and beautiful exploration of masculinity and the many faces of love, touching on romance, desire, family, and friendship, all presented through the lens of the fantastic—with literally mind-altering drugs, resurrected dinosaurs, near-future worlds in post-environmental collapse, and of course, monsters."
—A. C. Wise, *The Kissing Booth Girl and Other Stories*

"Miller's sheer talent shines through in abundance. . . . *Boys, Beasts & Men* is an outrageous journey which skillfully blends genres and will haunt you with its original, poetic voices as much as its victims, villains, and treasure trove of leading actors."
—*Grimdark Magazine*

"The very best horror in all its ghoulish, glorious humanity."
—Deborah Miller, two-time winner of the PEN Syndicated Fiction Award (and also Sam's mom)

"Even in the darkest of these perfectly crafted stories, Sam Miller's tragic boys yearn to be good instead of bad, strong

instead of weak, whole instead of broken. May your heart ache with love for every doomed one of them; I know mine did."
—Andy Davidson, author of *The Boatman's Daughter*

"Loneliness, manhood, and ferocious queer joy . . . thick with both the tenderness and ugliness of imperfect relationships."
—*Publishers Weekly*

"In these stories Sam J. Miller writes about people on the margins and in transition, both capturing a sense of uncertainty and horror while immersing us in these worlds with sensitivity and care."
—Carrie Vaughn, author of *The Immortal Conquistador*

Praise for Sam J. Miller

"[Miller] will tear your heart in two and then gently place the pieces back inside your chest—while reminding you to have a sandwich and love yourself."
—*NPR*

"Sam J. Miller has proven himself a force to be reckoned with."
—Barnes & Noble

"Sam J. Miller has cemented his status as one of the most visionary fiction writers of his generation."
—Kass Morgan, *New York Times* bestselling author of *The 100*

"Like Clive Barker, Miller has a great talent for creating interesting characters and building up quiet dread."
—*San Francisco Chronicle*

Praise for *The Art of Starving*

★"A dark and lovely tale of supernatural vengeance and self-destruction."
—*Kirkus*, starred review

★"Miller's creative portrait of a complex and sympathetic individual will provide a welcome mirror for kindred spirits."
—*Booklist*, starred review

★"Matt is a master at suppressing his urges, but there is nothing romantic about debut novelist Miller's portrayal of anorexia."
—*Publishers Weekly*, starred review

"Funny, haunting, beautiful, relentless and powerful."
—*Book Riot*

"As gritty with salted wounds as are all great fairytales, *The Art of Starving* is *The Outsiders* with superpowers."
—Maria Dahvana Headley, bestselling author of *Magonia*

Also by Sam J. Miller

The Art of Starving (2017)
Blackfish City (2018)
Destroy All Monsters (2019)
The Blade Between (2020)

BOYS
BEASTS
&
MEN

SAM J. MILLER

TACHYON • SAN FRANCISCO

Cover art by Jennifer O'Toole
Interior and cover design by Elizabeth Story
Author photo by Kalyaní-Andrí Sánchez

Tachyon Publications LLC
1459 18th Street #139
San Francisco, CA 94107
415.285.5615
www.tachyonpublications.com
tachyon@tachyonpublications.com

Series editor: Jacob Weisman
Project editor: Jaymee Goh

Print ISBN: 978-1-61696-372-9
Digital ISBN: 978-1-61696-373-6

Printed in the United States by Versa Press, Inc.

First Edition: 2022
9 8 7 6 5 4 3 2 1

for Walead Esmail Rath
and Deborah Miller

my first short-story heroes

CONTENTS

INTRODUCTION
by Amal El-Mohtar

THE FIRST TIME I met Sam J. Miller he was cosplaying Aang from *Avatar: The Last Airbender*—dressed in orange and yellow, a wide blue arrow painted on his forehead. He appeared before me like a vision, an intrusion of fantasy into reality in the already surreal space of a midwestern science-fiction convention.

The second time I met Sam J. Miller he was dressed in a silver lamé jumpsuit—at the same convention—with fuchsia-coloured hair: a study in contrasts, smiling at the intersection of glamour and gleam.

Until it came time to write this introduction, I had mashed these two meetings together in my memory, blended the shimmering silver outfit and the Airbender's arrow. Only browsing back through snapshots from those events did I find that they'd occurred a year apart, that I was mixing my impressions of Sam and his work into my recollections of our encounters, weaving them into a story that better suited my overall sense of him. No single traditional element can embody that sense: instead, when I think of Sam I think of water mixing with fire, deep wells of compassion lit by a hungry, brilliant spark. I think of his fiction and imagine him wielding a shining, liquid silver between his hands, an infinitely shapable fluid force.

In order to talk about Sam's writing in this collection I find I also want to talk about his photography—another kind of blending of water and fire, liquid and light. His photos are always instantly recognizable to me in the chaotic torrents of social media timelines. Sam's gaze turns a subject inside out, perceives it like a chisel perceives stone, breaks it open into startling, devastating beauty. A rusted pipe on a mountainside, its ceiling eaten away into sky, looms up like the ribs of an impossible whale; a railway trestle over the Hudson forms a delicate, skeletal backdrop to the foregrounding of two great circular metal slabs, dislocated from origin and function, their stamped surfaces frosted over with verdigris into hieroglyphic fragments. Meanwhile a peony bud, tight as a fist and dropleted in rain, suggests the sleek, tender eroticism of human skin. His subjects always feel arrested in motion, tense and dynamic, straining, in sharp lines and fulsome colours, against the static of a frame.

In 2014, Sam launched an art series titled "Intrusions," in which he'd sketch manga-influenced drawings over original photography in order to "highlight and comment on the way visual narratives like comics and cartoons help us make sense of the real world in all its ugliness, beauty, and banality." Shirtless men ride dinosaurs near trestle bridges, or twist their limbs against the webby tangles of yellow Transit Authority tape; a young woman joyfully brandishes a katana as she leaps over a broken chain-link fence, folded over itself like a dog-eared page.

These intrusions, more than anything else, evoke for me the experience of reading Sam's fiction. Sam writes alternate presents and shadow futures, turning our world inside out, breaking its ugliness into beauty, its banality into wonder. Whether set in revolutionary Russia or small-town America, these are profoundly queer stories: stories about men loving and being loved, the difficult bonds between parents and children, the gifts and burdens of inheritance. They are stories less about coming out than of coming *in*: stories of parents and siblings struggling towards understanding the extraordinary secret selves of their children and brothers, reckoning with the effects of that new-found knowledge on their own lives.

In what follows, you'll find reality and fantasy dancing together like light and silver, illuminating and exposing each other in the darkroom of Sam's mind—and in your own. As you thumb your way through imprisoned megafauna, pyro-kinetics, and the heart-broken souls of empty homes, you'll find another presence surrounding the stories, introducing them to each other with more tenderness and danger than I could hope to achieve here. If you've encountered these stories in magazines or on the shortlists of awards, you'll find them transformed by their proximity to each other, bound together by left-handed stitches of text in a sly voice that intrudes and unites like a needle.

On the internet Sam often goes by the name "sentencebender," which—appropriately—bends several meanings into itself. A sentence can be a complete textual unit, a tool with which to communicate—and it can be a punishment, a consequence. When I think of Sam as a bender of sentences I think of his fiction, but I also think of his activism, his organizing, his devotion to collective action as the means to confronting vast and vicious systems. I think of how assumptions and prejudices are types of sentences, their grammars muddy and opaque, and how he bends light into them through unexpected angles of perspective and inquiry. I think of how both water and fire have nourishing and destructive aspects, like love. It's been an honour and a privilege to watch him develop his art over the years—to see him steep his stories in that heady suspension of hope and memory that makes new worlds bloom in the dark.

i.

Eye contact; flash of animal panic.

He locks his gaze to mine, this man three bar stools down, and even though it's what I came here hunting for I can feel my insides quiver with the existential terror of any prey animal.

Worse: he grins. His smile holds so many scenarios: sex, murder, a back room or a dark alley or decades of marital bliss. Stories inside of stories.

"Hey, boy," he says.

ALLOSAURUS BURGERS

Our teacher Mrs. Strunt said the allosaurus coming to Hudson Falls was the best thing that ever happened to Hudson Falls, but the worst thing that ever happened to the allosaurus. She herded us onto the bus looking mad about it, trying to keep us from seeing she was just as excited as we were. The bus was freezing and we had all the windows fogged up in five minutes. Other boys drew curse words. I wrote F-U-C and then flinched, imagining my mother finding out, so I wiped it away and drew an allosaurus.

"The poor thing," Mrs. Strunt said. "Wherever it came from, it's got to feel terribly lonely and lost and scared."

The roads were all madness on the way to the farm. Barely a day since Mr. Blecher made his big announcement, and everyone in the world was coming to Hudson Falls. Scientists and men with giant cameras, and lots of soldiers with lots of guns, but not the mean soldiers and scientists from movies. Everyone I saw had a smile so big it could have been their birthday. *Everyone is coming to Hudson Falls,* I thought.

And then: a treacherous, wicked, horrible thought.

Maybe my dad will come.

Where had it come from—*dad*—that foul, forbidden word? I sucked in my cheeks like making a fish face and closed my teeth on as much flesh as I could, and bit down hard. And then harder. Punishing myself. Until I felt the same hot smothering rage that rises up in my mother every time I say that word.

I thought my mother was God, then. Six-foot-something, all flesh and freckles, she towered over our neighbors in church and at the supermarket. She came home from the slaughter-house smelling like blood. I was nine then, and she could still pick me up, hoist me into the air. Not even the fathers of the other boys my age could do that. She wasn't afraid of anything.

At breakfast that morning my mother had said, "Day after tomorrow, the army's going to take it away, and I personally think it can't happen soon enough."

I finished my milk and Mom poured me more, which I did not want, which I drank. Mom is certain that the government wants to take our stuff. Mostly our guns. She has a lot of guns and a lot of stickers on her car about them and her *cold dead hands*. So now I wondered why she wanted them to take the allosaurus.

"Woulda taken it right away, only it'll take 'em forty-eight hours to scrounge up the right equipment."

I nodded. Mom drank from the jug and put it back in the fridge.

"Blecher's going to make out okay, though. Heard he's got a million in TV deals lined up." She likes Mr. Blecher because he's an old, old man, but he can still get over on her once in a while in arm wrestling. "And he's hidden away some of its droppings to sell to the companies."

"What kind of companies?"

Mom frowned. "How the hell would I know something like that?"

I wondered what they would do with dinosaur poop. Could you clone something from its poop? Could something so gone forever come back so easily? And if poop worked, what else would? I thought of my father's baseball cap, the one Mom didn't know I had, the one that still smelled of his sweat when I crawled to the back of my closet late at night and in total darkness buried my nose in it.

Mom never sits at mealtimes. She made anxious circles through the tiny kitchen, moving refrigerator magnets and removing expired coupons and straightening the cat and dog figurines I could never stop forcing to fight each other. It was a Tuesday morning, which is when my sister Sue calls from college. Waiting for the call always made Mom a little tense.

"What?" she said, kicking me lightly. "Why the face, like I just killed a puppy?"

I shrugged.

"You want me to be excited about it. But that thing ain't right. They got scientists out combing that corner of Blecher's farm, but mark my words they won't find nothing. This is something bigger than science."

"At church yesterday, Pastor said it's a creature of God," I spoke carefully, not contradicting, just seeking clarity. I could no longer swing my legs when I sat at the kitchen table. This was a recent development, one I'd been looking forward to that had turned out to be pretty crummy. My feet rested resentfully on the cold tiles. A draft came from under the door.

"Pastor'll say what needs to be said to help Mr. Blecher out and to get people to come and spend their money in town. Creature of God, my foot."

Church was the most important thing in my mother's life, but I don't think she believed in God. The Hudson Falls Evangelical Lutheran Church gave her lots of things, like friends and a full social calendar and a reason not to go to the liquor store. God didn't offer her anything extra. Mostly she just liked what Pastor said: the sermons full of blood, fire, and the devil and impending doom, about a world gone haywire and full of sinners and about to be punished.

She heaped bacon on my plate, five then six then seven slices. "'Fore you know it, there'll be bunches of them things, running riot over all the world. Eating us all up."

"It's locked up, Mom."

"I know you saw *King Kong*, because I saw you crying at the end of it—" and she thumped me on the arm, not hard, because I saw her cry too when the big ape fell— "so I know you know they had Kong tied up good and proper, and he still got loose."

My sister Sue called then. Mom talked to her for a little while, not sounding super-excited. Mom handed me the phone while Sue was in a sentence.

"Hi," I said, interrupting her.

"Matt? Hi! Exciting stuff, right? A dinosaur in stupid little Hudson Falls! It's on *all* the news channels."

"Yeah."

"Have you seen it?"

"No," I said. "We go today."

"I wish I could come see it, but it'll be gone soon, right? Did you read the dinosaur books I sent you?"

"No."

"Why not?"

I shrugged.

"Did you just shrug? You can't shrug over the phone."

"I don't *know*," I said.

"Do you not like dinosaurs anymore?"

I shrugged again. Then I remembered about shrugging. "I don't know."

But I did know. Starting around the time I turned seven, Mom frowned when I talked about dinosaurs. "You get too excited about those things," she'd say. "Loving something too much is dangerous." So whenever I got the urge to pick up a dinosaur book or toy, I bit down hard on the inside of my cheek.

The allosaurus was different, of course. It was something you couldn't ignore or pray away.

"I talked to Dad," Sue said. Mom was making a lot of noise putting the dishes in the sink. "He's coming to town to see the allosaurus. He begged his editor to give him the assignment."

"Oh."

"Do you remember your dad?"

"No." There was nothing to remember. Some phone calls, sometimes, some letters, and once a box with a birthday present. Mom set it on fire without opening it. Sadness-anger tightened my stomach. I bit my lip to banish it.

"Mom's . . ." Sue spent a while figuring out where to go with that one. "Mom's not always thinking straight, when it comes to him." She knew she had to be careful. After she screamed bad things at Mom, I refused to speak to her for the whole week before she went to college. "I know it seems like Mom's the toughest chick on two legs, but she's afraid of lots of things."

The being-mad-at-Sue didn't really go away until we clambered down from the bus at Blecher's Farm. I had been a million times, for church picnics and farm field trips, but had never seen it so full of strangers, people on cell phones, slinging weird devices. The inside of the barn was full of new gates and doors and walls, built quick by the army while they waited for the elephant cage to come from San Diego.

The allosaurus was as tall as two of my mother when it reared up to its full height, but it rarely did. Its usual leaning-forward walk placed it at just the right level to look Mom in the eye. It looked the way it did in books and movies, a tyrannosaurus but smaller, only it had something the movies don't: a personality. Curious and mistrustful, not particularly smart, a little like a seagull that wants to steal your food.

"The poor thing," Mrs. Strunt said, looking up at it. It bobbed its head as it walked.

I was glad Mom wasn't there. I could stand there staring at the thing with what Mom calls my "gape-mouthed imbecile look."

The allosaurus was anti-camouflaged, wine-colored with long, wide, yellow streaks down the flank. It didn't need to hide from anyone. The claws were a weird marbled grey I hadn't imagined. Blood and hay covered the floor. It had been eating; its arms and face were messy from it. It didn't look lonely or lost or scared. It looked proud of itself, like it had lucked into a lot of food and was waiting to see how things played out.

Mr. Blecher took us on a personal tour, his hands heavy on the heads of the kids he knew from church.

We stood at the edge of the barn, beside the steep railing that penned it in. The allosaurus came closer and someone screamed. Its nostrils snorted smoke into the chilly air. The barn had been there since forever, but the sawdust-and-cement smell of the air gave the place a freshly-built feel that was not reassuring. Only raw wood and new nails kept it away from us. It nudged a bar with its head, its claws a yard from my face, and a whole bunch of someones screamed. Maybe including me. The arms are what make an allosaurus so much better than a tyrannosaurus. Tyrannosaurus is way bigger, but they have stupid stumpy little arms with two claws. Allosauruses have long, muscular, useful arms with *three* scary claws.

Mrs. Strunt asked, "What are they going to do with it?"

"Rent it out to movie studios," Blecher said. "Take its DNA and make little ones. Bottle its spit and sell it for engine grease. Honestly ma'am, I have no idea."

He took us around to the adjoining cages, where the goats had been crammed. He gripped the lever that would release a goat into the allosaurus pen, and grinned and said, "You kids want to see what happens when I pull this?"

We all screamed yes, but Mrs. Strunt said no. She said it loud and weird so Mr. Blecher didn't.

"Sure wish I could keep it, but they won't let me. It was all I could do to get them to camp down the hill with their whole security rigmarole, not keep me up all night with their noise."

I watched the allosaurus. Mr. Blecher was telling the story about how he found it on bear patrol in his John Deere Gator Utility Vehicle, and how everyone always told him he was crazy to bring the harness and the tranquilizer cannon like he could shoot down a grizzly and bring it home. Didn't he do them one better? . . . except that he had to call up five of his friends to bring *their* Gators to help drag it back.

In my head I broke the allosaurus down into the cuts Mom taught me, from the picture of the cow. Thick rib, thin rib. Silverside. Brisket. Chuck. Blade. Drumstick? Cows don't have drumsticks. Probably the allosaurus was closer to a chicken, but Mom doesn't work with chickens. That's a separate slaughterhouse. That's a whole set of words she doesn't know.

"So?" Mom said. "How was it?"

"Neat," I said, sitting down at the kitchen table. She blinked and smiled like she'd been praying, or napping. Her hands were raw, bright pink. Winter's tough at the slaughterhouse. The meat gets cold fast. Mom doesn't do the killing. The room where they hang the cows to empty out, after they've been killed but before Mom comes through to turn them into smaller pieces, isn't heated. By the time she gets there they're barely above freezing.

"Is it true they don't know if it's a boy or a girl?"

I nodded.

"Well shoot, you'd think that'd be easy to figure out."

"You should come," I said.

"What'd Rebecca have to say about the thing?"

I shrugged. Mom hates Mrs. Strunt. They went to school together, but Mrs. Strunt went to college after and Mom went to the slaughterhouse, and now Mrs. Strunt makes more money than Mom does. Not *much* more, Mom says, but the fact that Mrs. Strunt doesn't have to spend the whole day standing up and lifting heavy things really rankles.

"Why don't you want to come see it?"

"Lord, Matt, I don't know."

"Stanley's parents let him stay home from school today. They said it was because they're Catholics and the Pope hasn't spoken on the allosaurus yet, so they don't know whether it's demonic or not. But really it was because Stanley was scared."

I held my fists to my chest right after I said it, steeling myself for what might come, but Mom just smiled. "You think maybe I'm scared of that big brute? He don't scare me. All it is is meat."

She stood up and I heard something pop. Mom said one bad word, then, and spent a long time saying it. She put both her hands on her back.

I stood up, but didn't go closer. Lately I'd been hearing that popping more and more. Once the pain passes she usually moves on to being mad. But this time she shut her eyes and her lips moved, and when she opened them the fierceness had gone out of her face.

"Is she a good teacher? Rebecca?"

"I guess," I said.

"Do you like her?"

I nodded.

"Good. You need to do well in school." She looked at me, smiled at whatever she saw. "Somebody ought to make that dinosaur into steaks, is all I'm saying. Or burgers. Eat it before it eats us." Then she elbowed me. "Would you eat allosaurus burgers, kid?"

I said I would. She said she would too. We laughed about it more than maybe we meant to, but laughing felt good.

Much later that night the phone woke me up. I sat at the top of the stairs so I could hear Mom's side of the conversation.

"No."

"No. Uh-uh."

"Don't."

So it was Dad.

"Really, Max? That's all it is? And if they shipped the dinosaur out to Texas or it died tomorrow, you wouldn't come?"

"You're a damn liar."

"No."

"No. Why would you ask me that?"

"Why all of a sudden do you care about him now?

"You're the one who chose to live way the hell down there. And we're doing fine, him and me."

"No."

"Don't."

"Please, Max. Please don't."

I cried a lot when Mom got drunk and burned the box with my birthday present from Dad, but only because I was five. I wouldn't cry now.

Things started to get bad between Mom and Sue around the same time Sue called Dad.

"She's taken him back once before," she had told me, not long after she snuck out of the house and took a train to see him without telling Mom, and not long before she decided to go to college in Plattsburgh because that would put her just a six-hour bus ride from where Dad was. "I was nine when he came back. He stuck around for a month or two."

Sue is nine years older than me.

"You should see him. He's a big, strong, tough guy. Like you'll probably be."

I wouldn't rise to the bait.

"He's smart too. Also like you'll probably be."

I thought about him a lot. But I'd learned not to ask about him ever. Mom had lots to say.

"Why . . ." I said, back then, to Sue—but I needed to be careful if I was going to say out loud the things I barely dared think. The things that would break my mother's heart to hear. "Why does she hate him so much?"

"She can't say to no to him," Sue said. "That's why Mom goes to church so much. Because she's not nearly as strong as she wants people to think."

I said something, probably not nice.

"The only reason they're not together is that he hated Hudson

Falls. Said he could never live there. And you know what? She was going to leave everything, to move to the city with him. Quit her job, sell the house, leave her friends and church and family. And then at the last minute—like, the night before—she got blind drunk, stole his car, drove it one block and then deliberately crashed it into a pole, walked home, told him she hated his guts and to get the hell out of her town and her life."

"You're lying," I said. "That's stupid. Mom's not stupid."

"I'm not lying. She can either have him or be in control of her life, and she chose to be in control. And she doesn't care who gets hurt because of it."

I didn't understand Sue then, didn't know what she was saying, but when Mom hung up on Dad, I heard the cabinet above the refrigerator open and the bottle and glass clink against the counter.

Mom left her bedroom and then made a lot of noise in the garage and I knew right away what she was up to, where she was going. I dressed fast in the dark and was outside by the time she was halfway down the block. She wouldn't risk taking the car. People would see it and know she had been there. I followed her from a distance. She was dressed in black for stealth and carried a bulging backpack—mine.

The walk to Mr. Blecher's farm was way too long. She walked like people walk on TV when they drink too many drinks. She paused a quarter of the way there, and it was like I could hear every thought as it went through her head. This is stupid. I should turn back. I can't do this. *I can do this. I have to do this.* Finally she took the bottle out and took a long time drinking from it before she started up walking again.

The quiet out at the farm was weird, after how noisy it had been in the daytime. The army had put up cameras and Mom put her hood up when she got close. There was a new metal door to the barn, with a complicated lock. Mom spent a while looking at the keypad. I was amazed when she guessed at the passcode and got it right the first time.

Here I thought my luck might not hold, but I would not be turned back. Church was the most important thing in both Mom and Mr. Blecher's lives, so I figured that was where the password came from. I tried the zip code of the church, but that didn't work. My second guess was the last four digits of the church phone number, which Mom made me memorize because it's where I could always find her if she wasn't home or at work. That's what it was.

I crept in quiet as a cartoon ninja. Mom stood in the middle of the barn, looking in to where the allosaurus was. She fumbled for a light and found one, but it was at the far end of the barn and barely lit one corner. We watched the darkness together, apart. We couldn't see the allosaurus; it was asleep or maybe watching from a corner. Mom hollered, but the allosaurus didn't holler back. She set the backpack down and opened it up and took out two of her biggest guns and put them together and put the backpack back on. Then she climbed up onto the high new door of the pen, and said, "Hey!"

The allosaurus rose out of nothingness and took one-two-three tiny steps forward.

I walked around to the adjoining cages. I didn't hurry. My mouth was full of blood from biting my cheeks. I never prayed in church, but I was praying then. She still had time to decide not to do it. From that far away I could watch her and pretend what I was watching wasn't happening. I put both hands on the lever that would open the goat pen gate, ready to save the allosaurus from my mother. Goats grumbled in the dark beside me.

Sue is wrong, I thought. *Mom is not afraid of the allosaurus. She doesn't do dumb things out of fear. She does them out of fearlessness.*

She raised the gun, and wobbled. The allosaurus tilted its head to see her better. They were ten feet apart. It stood up straight, so it was looking down on her, which Mom clearly did not like. She pulled herself up higher, to stand on the top tier of wood. She held her hands out to steady herself, but did not do a good job of it. The edges of the bars were dented and splintered where they connected to the frame. I imagined the allosaurus whacking its tail or head against them all night long, trying to get out, or trying to get the goats it smelled just out of sight.

The wood cracked. Mom fell. In.

It looked down at my mother. Its claws flexed. It lowered its head, and took a step toward her. Mom didn't move. Her back was to me and I was glad I could not see her face. The thing took another tentative step, then walked purposefully toward her. Only when I saw it stand over her, mouth open and eyes wide, did I realize just how big and beautiful and scary it was.

I pulled the lever as hard as I could. The cage gate swung open and a goat darted into the pen, bleating its excitement, conditioned to believe there would be food when it got there. And there would be, except it would *be* the food.

At the goat's bleat, the allosaurus turned its head. The goat was a little further from it than my mother, and a little smaller, so the allosaurus took another step toward Mom. I jumped down into the goat cage and shoved a second goat into the pen. It balked, either out of contrariness or fear. The goat was warm, smelly, and I could feel its muscles unclench as it gave in and trotted forward. I felt bad for it. And then I hunched and prayed in the dark where my mother could not see me.

The goats stood still, looking stupid until they caught the smell of the allosaurus. They scattered. This swiftly-moving meat made the allosaurus let loose a machine screech and stomp after them.

Mom climbed up and out, slowly. Safe on the other side, she sank to the ground. She held her back with both hands. The goats were making an ungodly noise, but I owed it to them to watch, to see what I had done. Blood went absolutely everywhere.

Mom had her head between her knees and her arms around her head. I watched her for a minute and that hurt worse than watching the goats.

I didn't leave the dark stinking cage till Mom staggered out into the night. I wanted to help her up off the floor, but I knew not to. I listened to the allosaurus eat. It saw me when I stood up. It lowered its head to get a better look. And then it turned and stalked back to the barn-corner shadows. The allosaurus wasn't a demon or a bad-ass movie monster. It was only an animal. It obeyed laws it did not understand and had no hand in making, just like me.

I followed Mom home much later and snuck into my bed. In the morning I came down to bacon for breakfast. She poured orange juice and I asked for coffee, like I always did, and she smiled when she said I was too young for it. I was glad to see her smile. She didn't need to know she would never be the same size again.

ii.

His voice unspools something in my stomach, black and heavy inside as the feel of this cheap bar whiskey. The words don't matter. All I hear is the feral groan of it, the animal wilderness inside. His beard is a wolf pelt, his teeth canine. He calls me Boy *and he is clearly* Man, *although we seem to be about the same age. The dividing line between us is something different: an experience; a way of walking in this world; something he possesses that I lack. He leans in to whisper* wanna go for a stroll *and I follow him out of the bar with no idea what kind of tale I'm stepping into.*

57 REASONS FOR THE SLATE QUARRY SUICIDES

1. BECAUSE IT WOULD TAKE the patience of a saint or Dalai Lama to smilingly turn the other cheek to those six savage boys day after day, to emerge unembittered from each new round of psychological and physical assaults; whereas I, Jared Shumsky, aged sixteen, have many things, like pimples and the bottom bunkbed in a trailer and clothes that smell like cherry car air fresheners, but no particular strength or patience.

2. Because God, or the universe, or karma, or Charles Darwin, gave me a different strength, one that terrified me until I learned what it was, and how to control it, and how to use it as the instrument of my brutal and magnificent and long-postponed vengeance.

3. Because I loved Anchal, with the fierceness and devotion that only a gay boy can feel for the girl who has his back, who takes the *Cosmo* sex quiz with him, who listens to his pointless yammerings about his latest crush, who puts herself

between him and his bullies so often that the bullies' wrath is ultimately re-routed onto her.

4. Because after the Albany Academy swim meet, while I was basking in the bliss of a shower that actually spouts hot water—a luxury our backwoods public school lacks—I was bodily seized by my six evil teammates, and dragged outside, and deposited there, in the December cold, naked, wet, spluttering, pounding on the door, screaming, imagining hypothermia, penile frostbite, until the door opened, and an utterly uninterested girl let me in and said *Jeez, calm down.*

5. Because it's not so simple as evil bullies in need of punishment; because their bodies were too beautiful to hate and their eyes too lovely to simply gouge out; because every one of them was adorable in his own way but they all had the musculature and arrogance of Olympic swimmers, which I lacked, being only five-six of quivery scrawn; because I loved swimming too much to quit the team, the silence of the water and how alone you were when you were in it, the caustic reek of chlorine and the twilight bus rides to strange schools and the sight of so much male skin; and because of those moments, on the ride home from Canajoharie or Schaghticoke or Albany, in the rattling short bus normally reserved for the retarded, with the coach snoring and everyone else asleep or staring out the window watching the night roll by, when I was part of the team, when I was connected to people; when I belonged somewhere.

6. Because I had spent the past six months practicing; on animals at first, and after the first time I tried it on my cat she shrieked and never came near me again, but my dog was

not so smart, and even though while I was working him his eyes showed raw animal panic he kept coming back every time I took my hand away and released him, and pretty soon working the animals was easy, the field forming in the instant my fingertips touched them, their brains like switches I could turn off and on at will, turning their bodies into mirrors for my own, but I still couldn't figure out a way to harm them.

7. Because once, while she slept, in my basement, engorged on candy and gossip and bad television, I tried my gift on Anchal, and it was much harder on a human, because she was so much bigger and her brain so much more complex and therefore more difficult to disable, and even though I tried to only do things that would not disturb her, her eyes fluttered open and then immediately narrowed in suspicion and fear, the wiser animal part of her brain recognizing me as a threat before the dumb, easily-duped mammalian intellect intervened and said, *no, wait, this is your friend, he would never do anything to hurt you,* and she smiled a blood-hungry smile and leaned forward and said, "How the hell did you do that?"

8. Because Mrs. Burgess assigned us Edgar Allan Poe's "Hop-Frog" for English class, which helped my vengeance take shape, and because none of them read it.

9. Because Anchal did read it, and came to me, after school, eyes all laughing fire at the ideas he gave her—Hop-Frog, that squat, deformed little dwarf who murdered the cruel king and his six fat ministers in a dazzling spectacle of burned flesh and screaming death, and her excitement was infectious, and we worked on my gift for hours, until turning

her into a puppet was as easy as believing she was one.

10. Because *Carrie* came on television that same night.

11. Because I am an idiot, who still hasn't learned how stories and movies mislead us, showing us how things ought to end up, which is never how they do; and because stories are oracles whose prophecies we can't unravel until it is too late.

12. Because Anchal worked long and hard on the revenge scenario, sketching out all the ways my gift could be used to cause maximum devastation, all the ways we could transform our enemies into an ugly spectacle that would show the whole world what monsters they truly were.

13. Because I didn't listen, when she said we would have to kill them, that they were *sick sons of bitches and would never stop being sick sons of bitches*. Because I still believed that they would be mine.

14. Because Anchal, equal parts Indian and Indian—Native American and Hindu—always smelled like wood smoke, lived with her Cherokee mom in a tiny house barely better than a cabin, and so I thought that she was invincible, heiress to noble, durable traditions far better than my own impoverished Caucasian ones, and that she could survive whatever the world might throw at her. And because she was beautiful; because she was smart and strong; because boys flocked to her; because she knew that if there was one sure thing we could depend upon, it was that teenaged boys were a lot more likely to make dumb decisions when lust was addling their brains.

15. Because Spencer, alone among my swim teammates, would smile at me for no reason, and speak to me sometimes when the others weren't around, and because tiny things gave me hope that he too was gay, and that one day he would be mine.

16. Because Rex, on the other hand, an ogre of rare and excellent proportions, thick-headed but shrewd when it came to cruelty, served as the ringleader, and just as they had all obeyed him in his plan to pour Kool-Aid into Anchal's locker as punishment for stopping them from stomping my skull in, so I knew that *he* was the linchpin, the only one I would need to work, and that once I had him, the others would fall.

17. Because Coach was sick that day, and our next meet wasn't for a week, so they gave us the day off from practice, an unheard-of gift of free time, and I knew that here was our shot, and we couldn't waste it, so I texted Anchal *We are go* and then after school, while Rex was alone in the weight room, I stood outside in the hallway and called her, and said in a maybe-a-little-bit-too-loud voice, *Hey, so, I got a couple hours to kill, wanna meet me by the slate quarries in an hour, maybe bring some of your mama's vodka?* and she said *Yes*, and I said *Great*, and whistled while I walked away.

18. Because I hid myself in a darkened classroom where I could watch the weight room through the window in the door, and I saw how Rex called them all into a huddle when they arrived from their own classes, and they rubbed their hands or licked their lips or punched each other in the arm in glee, and then they left, as one, and I knew the bait had been taken.

19. Because they had their bicycles and I had mine, and after they left, I let five minutes go by, and if I had stuck to that timeline everything would have gone exactly according to plan.

20. Because as I was about to unlock my bike I heard someone holler my name, and I swooned at the sound of it in Spencer's mouth, and I stopped, and saw him standing, sweaty and tank-topped, at the cafeteria window, smiling, nervous, looking exactly like he always did in the dreams where we finally told each other our separate, identical secrets, and said "Can I maybe talk to you for a minute?"

21. Because I have an easily-duped mammalian intellect of my own, and because if there's one thing you can depend upon, it's that teenaged boys are a lot more likely to make dumb decisions when lust is addling their brains.

22. Because I went to him, and said *Hey*, and he said *Hey*, and we stood there like that for a second, and his pale skin had the same faint green-blue tint as mine, from soaking in chlorine four hours a day for months, and his eyes were two tiny swimming pools, and somehow there wasn't a single pimple anywhere on him. And he said, "That Edgar Allan Poe shit was pretty fucked up, wasn't it?" and I laughed and said that yes, it was, and my heart was loud in my throat and it had hijacked my brain and I could not disobey it, through several minutes of small talk, even while I knew what it meant for Anchal.

23. Because he smiled and said *Do you think I could, I don't*

know, come over some time, and I grinned so hard it hurt, and said *Yeah, Yes, Sure, That'd be great,* while my mind scrolled through a zoetrope of blurry images, heavy petting on the bean bag chair in my basement, pale skin warming pale skin, us walking hand-in-hand through the hallowed, horrible halls of Hudson High, me and Spencer against the world, my heinous, monastic celibacy broken.

24. Because his phone buzzed, then, and he took it out and looked at it and then looked at me and said *Yeah, uh, so, I should be going,* and I saw at once that my plan had been seen through, my timeline tampered with, and I knew what even these few moments of delay might mean for Anchal—and I left him in midsentence, and ran for my bike and pedaled as hard as I could, heading for the slate quarries.

25. Because the long, rocky road in to the quarry was littered with giant, jutting slabs of slate, obscuring my view and slowing me down, so I didn't see her, or any of them, until I arrived at the top of the quarry and saw Anchal standing her ground, the five of them in a semicircle around her, but nothing between her and a drop to the jagged rocks and quarry lagoon below, and her face was bruised and bleeding but she was still on her feet and holding something in her hand, and she turned, and saw me, and saw Spencer coming close behind, and knew what I had done, how my weakness had hurt her, how only her own strength had saved her from the horrific fate I abandoned her to, and she knew, in that moment, exactly what I was, and what I was was a sick son of a bitch.

26. Because Rex had taken off his jacket, and his sweater, and his shirt, even though it was mid-December twilight, and

freezing, and goosebumps armored his torso, and he turned and smiled when he saw me ride up, and said *Hold her there for a minute, boys, let me just take care of something first.*

27. Because I tossed my bike to the ground and advanced on him, unafraid, for once in my life, because guilt and shame over how weak I was had overpowered the fear of physical pain that usually held me back, and one of them laughed with surprise at my aggressiveness and said *Damn, Rex, look out*, and I yelled *Get away from her you pigs,* and Rex laughed and said *Or what? You'll take us all on? All six of us?*—for Spencer had taken Rex's spot in the semicircle—and I said *I'll kill you all*, and I knew, hearing myself say it, that it was true, that Anchal was right, that there was no way not to kill them, that being a threat was who they were, and only death would make them cease to be one.

28. Because Rex said *Come on then* and I reached out for him, and he evaded me, and I reached again with the other arm and he leapt back, and I wasn't throwing fists because all I had to do was touch him, bare skin to bare skin, to possess him.

29. Because the terrible thought occurred to me, when Rex had successfully dodged several of my grabs, and threw his arm out at me, not in a fist but in the same extended-finger grip as mine, *What if I'm not the only one with this gift?*

30. Because we looked more ballet than battle, ducking and leaping and flinging our arms out, and I was gaining ground, pushing him back toward the circle and the ledge, and his friends were laughing but in a nervous kind of way, and

because I knew that he was thrown off balance by trying not to make eye contact with any of his fellow thugs, but that so was I, in my efforts to avoid looking into Anchal's eyes, for fear of what I'd find there.

31. Because Anchal's arm shot out then, and sprayed the little mace canister in Rex's eyes, and he stopped like someone pushed pause, and I struck his bare shoulder with one triumphant palm.

32. Because his scream of pain was cut short in that instant, and we stood like that, frozen, touching, for a solid thirty seconds, while I battled Rex for control of his body, and I saw how ill-advised this plan had been, because only the pain and confusion caused by Anchal's mace kept him from easily turning my own gift back on myself, and if any of his friends had touched me, my control would have been broken and I'd surely have died that day.

33. Because none of them did touch me.

34. Because once I had Rex, the rest were easy.

35. Because I reached out my left arm and Rex reached out his in a precise mirror-motion, and touched it to the right arm of the boy standing beside him, and now when I reached out with my left arm *both* boys reached out with theirs, and touched the next boy, and so on, until all six boys, including Spencer, were linked hand to hand with me, and every move I made, they made.

36. Because my gift had established a field of control that no

longer depended on mere touch, and when I took my hand away the boys were my vassals, my puppets, unable to move or speak on their own, free will gone, their hearts pumping at precisely the same rate as mine, their lungs taking in and casting out air in perfect rhythm with my breath.

37. Because I, on the other hand, felt nothing at all, beyond the slight tension of the muscles that I always felt when I used my gift.

38. Because I raised my arms and they raised theirs; I jumped and so did they; I let loose a wolf call matched by six baying voices.

39. Because their eyes, I was surprised to learn, retained their autonomy, and the semicircle now showed me an impressive ocular display of hatred, fear, pain, anger.

40. Because Anchal stood up, and looked at me, and unlike my captive animals her eyes told me nothing, and she ran, silently, into the dark, and when I called her name those six boys said it too.

41. Because I let a long time pass, standing, listening, waiting for her to come back.

42. Because she didn't.

43. Because it is not a simple thing, to kill a man who mimics your every move.

44. Because Anchal chose the slate quarry for just that purpose.

45. Because I squatted, and they squatted, and I picked up a heavy rock, and their hands closed on nothingness, and I stood, and they stood, and I hoisted the rock over my head, and they raised their empty hands up just as high, and I threw the rock as hard as I could at Rex's head, and they made the same gesture.

46. Because Rex could neither flinch nor blink nor budge as the rock struck his face, nor even snap his head back to soften the impact by moving with the rock's inertia, and blood covered his face in seconds, and in the darkness we could smell the blood but not see the extent of the damage, and now every emotion other than terror was gone from those eyes.

47. Because I spoke, then—I shouted, and their screams formed around my words, a ghastly chorus of doomed men, echoing: *Once I dreamed of being one of you, of having your bodies, of moving so easily and fearlessly through the world, of belonging so effortlessly to a group of friends—but now that I can taste it for myself, now that I have your bodies, now that I am you, all of you, I see it for the horrid, meaningless thing that it is.*

48. Because the speech was not for them, and I'd spent a long time practicing it, and I was proud of it, but its intended audience was gone, fled, betrayed and hurt, by me.

49. Because suddenly my anger was gone, replaced by shame, and I had no more energy for our plan of a moment ago, of slowly but surely inducing them to bash each other to bits,

to leave a grisly mess for forensic scientists to spend decades puzzling over.

50. Because the water at the bottom of the quarry was still an eerie blue with the light from the sky, even though the sun had already slipped past the horizon.

51. Because they were all standing so much closer than I was to the uneven lip of the quarry, and I reached out my arms and clasped my hands on air, so they were linked up in a human chain, and I ran and leapt and they went over the edge but I still had another three feet of solid ground ahead of me.

52. Because I stepped forward and looked down and there they were, far below, their backs to me, waist-deep in water and looking down into it, still holding hands, some of them unable to stand on broken legs, and there was blood in the water.

53. Because it was more from weariness than anything else when I lay down on the ground, head pressed to the dirt, and I knew even though I couldn't see them that they were all fully underwater, and I opened my mouth and breathed in that sweet, cold December night air and then breathed it out, breathed it in and breathed it out, until the tension slackened in my muscles and I knew the field was broken, because they had drowned.

54. Because I got up off the ground knowing I had lost her forever, that she had seen straight through to the cold, twisted heart of who I was. And in seeing who I was, she had shown me myself.

55. Because I had been too dumb to see how this power, this privilege I didn't want but was stuck with, far from helping me to see, had blinded me to the truth of who we were.

56. Because Carrie's punishment for killing her foes was to die, and mine was to live.

57. Because Anchal knew what I did not: that we are what we are, and we act it out without wanting to, and only death can break us of the habit of being the bodies we're born into.

iii.

We walk. Two bodies, two wild separate beings. Sex tingles all through me: the hunger for it, for the joy that is more than just the pleasure of it, or the pride of being desired. Of connecting to someone on a profound and pre-human level. Of shedding the skin of your own unutterable separateness.

And still: the fear. A face like that—he'd spent his whole life knowing he could get whatever he wanted. Someone so beautiful—his hungers could easily become extreme. He could murder me. Drug me, chain me up in a basement, torture me for ages.

Or drunk jock bros could burst out of nowhere to bash us. Cops could bust our heads.

But this, too—this fear, this risk—is part of the joy.

WE ARE THE CLOUD

ME AND CASE MET when someone slammed his head against my door, so hard I heard it with my earphones in and my Game Boy cranked up loud. Sad music from *Mega Man 2* filled my head and then there was this thud like the world stopped spinning for a second. I turned the thing off and flipped it shut, felt its warmth between my hands. Slipped it under my pillow. Nice things need to stay secret at Egan House, or they'll end up stolen or broken. Old and rickety as it was, I didn't own anything nicer.

I opened my door. Some skinny thug had a bloody-faced kid by the shirt.

"What," I said, and then "what," and then "what the," and then, finally, "hell?"

I barked the last word, tightening all my muscles at once.

"Damn, man," the thug said, startled. He hollered down the stairs, "Goddamn Goliath over here can talk!" He let go of the kid's shirt and was gone. Thirty boys live at Egan House, foster kids awaiting placement. Little badass boys with parents in jail or parents on the street, or dead parents, or parents on drugs.

I looked at the kid he'd been messing with. A line of blood cut his face more or less down the middle, but the gash in his forehead was pretty small. His eyes were huge and clear in the middle of all that blood. He looked like something I'd seen before, in an ad or movie or dream.

"Thanks, dude," the kid said. He ran his hand down his face and then planted it on the outside of my door.

I nodded. Mostly when I open my mouth to say something the words get all twisted on the way out, or the wrong words sneak in, which is why I tend to not open my mouth. Once he was gone I sniffed at the big, bloody handprint. My cloud port hurt, from wanting him. Suddenly it didn't fit quite right, atop the tiny hole where a fiber-optic wire threaded into my brainstem though the joint where skull met spine. Desire was dangerous, something I fought hard to keep down, but the moment I met Case I knew I would lose.

Egan House was my twelfth group home. I had never seen a kid with blue eyes in any of them. I had always assumed white boys had no place in foster care, that there was some other better system set up to receive them.

I had been at Egan House six months, the week that Case came. I was inches away from turning eighteen and aging out. Nothing was waiting for me. I spent an awful lot of energy not thinking about it. Better to sit tight for the little time I had left, in a room barely wider than its bed, relying on my size to keep people from messing with me. At night, unable to sleep, trying hard to think of anything but the future, I'd focus on the sounds of boys trying not to make noise as they cried or jerked off.

On Tuesday, the day after the bloody-faced boy left his hand-print on my door, he came and knocked. I had been looking out my window. Not everyone had one. Mine faced south, showed me a wide sweep of the Bronx. Looking out, I could imagine myself as a signal sent out over the municipal wifi, beamed across the city, cut loose from this body and its need to be fed and sheltered and cared about. Its need for other bodies. I could see things, sometimes. Things I knew I shouldn't be seeing. Hints of images beamed through the wireless node that my brain had become.

"Hey," the kid said, knocking again. And I knew, from how I felt when I heard his voice, how doomed I was.

"Angel Quiñones," he said, when I opened the door. "Nick-named Sauro because you look a big ol' Brontosaurus."

Actually my mom called me Sauro because I liked dinosaurs, but it was close enough. "Okay . . ." I said. I stepped aside and in he came.

"Case. My name's Case. Do you want me to continue with the dossier I've collected on you?" When I didn't do anything but stare at his face he said "Silence is consent.

"Mostly Puerto Rican, with a little black and a little white in there somewhere. You've been here forever, but nobody knows anything about you. Just that you keep to yourself and don't get involved in anyone's hustles. And don't seem to have one of your own. And you could crush someone's skull with one hand."

A smile forced its way across my face, terrifying me.

With the blood all cleaned up, he looked like a kid. But faces can fool you, and the look on his could only have belonged to a full-grown man. So confident it was halfway to contemptuous, sculpted out of some bright stone. A face that made you forget what you were saying mid-sentence.

Speaking slowly, I said: "Don't—don't get." Breathe. "Don't

get too into the say they stuff. Stuff they say. Before you know it, you'll be one of the brothers."

Case laughed. "Brothers," he said, and traced one finger up his very-white arm. "I doubt anyone would ever get me confused with a brother."

"Not brothers like Black. Brothers—they call us. That's what they call us. We're brothers because we all have the same parents. Because we all have none."

Why were the words there, then? Case smiled and out they came.

He reached out to rub the top of my head. "You're a mystery man, Sauro. What crazy stuff have you got going on in there?"

I shrugged. Bit back the cat urge to push my head into his hand. Ignored the cloud-port itch flaring up fast and sharp.

Case asked: "Why do you shave your head?"

Because it's easier.

Because unlike most of these kids, I'm not trying to hide my cloud port.

Because a boy I knew, five homes ago, kept his head shaved, and when I looked at him I felt some kind of way inside. The same way I feel when I look at you. Case.

"I don't know," I said.

"It looks good though."

"Maybe that's why," I said. "What's your . . . thing. Dossier."

"Nothing you haven't heard before. Small-town gay boy, got beat up a lot. Came to the big city. But the city government doesn't believe a minor can make decisions for himself. So here I am. Getting fed and kept out of the rain while I plan my next move."

Gay boy. Unthinkable even to think it about myself, let alone ever utter it.

"How old? You."

"Seventeen." He turned his head, smoothed back sun-colored hair to reveal his port. "Well, they let you make your own decisions if they'll make money for someone else."

Again, I was shocked. White kids were hardly ever so poor they needed the chump change you can get from cloudporting. Not even the ones who wanted real bad to be *down*. Too much potential for horrific problems. Bump it too hard against a headboard or doorframe and you might end up brain damaged.

But that wasn't why I stared at him, dumbfounded. It was what he said, about making money for someone else. Like he could smell the anger on me. Like he had his own. I wanted to tell him about what I had learned, online. How many hundreds of millions of dollars the city spent every year to keep tens of thousands of us stuck in homes like Egan House. How many people had jobs because of kids like us. How if they had given my mom a quarter of what they've spent on me being in the system, she never would have lost her place. She never would have lost me. How we were all of us, ported or not, just batteries to be sucked dry by huge faraway machines I could not even imagine. But it was all I could do just to keep a huge and idiotic grin off my face when I looked at him.

The telecoms had paid for New York's municipal wireless grid, installing thousands of routers across all five boroughs. Rich people loved having free wireless everywhere, but it wasn't a public service. Companies did it because the technology had finally come around to where you could use the human brain for data processing, so they could wave money in the faces of hard-up people and say, *let us put this tiny little wire into your brain and plug that into the wireless signal and exploit a portion of your brain's underutilized capacity, turning you into one node in a massively-distributed data processing center.* It worked, of course. Any business model based around poor people making bad decisions out of ignorance and desperation always works. Just ask McDonald's, or the heroin dealer who used to sell to my mom.

The sun, at some point, had gotten lost behind a ragged row of tenements. Case said: "Something else they said. You're going to age out, any minute now."

"Yeah."

"That must be scary."

I grunted.

"They say most guys leaving foster care end up on the street."

"Most."

The street, the words like knives driven under all my toenails at once. The stories I had heard. Men frozen to death under expressways, men set on fire by frat boys, men raped to death by cops.

"You got a plan?"

"No plan."

"Well, stick with me, kid," Case said, in fluent fake movie gangster. "I got a plan big enough for both of us. Do you smoke?" he asked, flicking out two. I didn't, but I took the cigarette. His fingers touched mine. I wanted to say *It isn't allowed in here,* but Case's smile was a higher law.

"Where's a decent port shop around here? I heard the Bronx ones were all unhygienic as hell."

"Riverdale," I said. "That's the one I go to. Nice office. No one waiting outside to jump you."

"I need to establish a new primary," he said. "We'll go tomorrow." He smiled so I could see it wasn't a command so much as a decision he was making for both of us.

My mother sat on the downtown platform at Burnside, looking across the elevated tracks to a line of windows, trying to see something she wasn't supposed to see. She was so into her voyeurism that she didn't notice me standing right beside her, uncomfortably close even though the platform was bare. She didn't look up until I said *mother* in Spanish, maybe a little too loud.

"Oh my god," she said, fanning herself with a damp *New York Post*. "Here I am getting here late, fifteen minutes, thinking oh my god he's gonna kill me, and come to find out that you're even later than me!"

"Hi," I said, squatting to kiss her forehead.

"Let it never be said that you got that from me. I'm late all the time, but I tried to raise you better."

"How so?"

"You know. To not make all the mistakes I did."

"Yeah, but how so? What did you do, to raise me better?"

"It's stupid hot out," she said. "They got air conditioning in that home?"

"In the office. Where we're not allowed."

We meet up once a month, even though she's not approved for unsupervised visits. I won't visit her at home because her man is always there, always drunk, always able, in the course of an hour, to remind me how miserable and stupid I am. How horrible my life will become, just as soon as I age out. How my options are the streets or jail or overclocking; what they'll do to me in each of those places. So now we meet up on the subway, and ride to Brooklyn Bridge and then back to Burnside.

Arm flab jiggled as she fanned herself. Mom is happy in her fat. Heroin kept her skinny; crack gave her lots of exercise. For her, obesity is a brightly colored sign that says *NOT ADDICTED ANYMORE*. Her man keeps her fed; this is what makes someone a Good Man. Brakes screamed as a downtown train pulled into the station.

"Oooh, stop, wait," she said, grabbing at my pantleg with one puffy hand. "Let's catch the next one. I wanna finish my cigarette."

I got on the train. She came, too, finally, hustling, flustered, barely making it.

"What's gotten into you today?" she said, when she wrestled her pocketbook free from the doors. "You upset about something? You're never this," and she snapped her fingers in the air while she looked for the word *assertive*. I had it in my head. I would not give it to her. Finally she just waved her hand and sat down. "Oh, that air conditioning feels good."

"José? How's he?"

"Fine, fine," she said, still fanning from force of habit. Fifty-degree air pumped directly down on us from the ceiling ducts.

"And you?"

"Fine."

"Mom—I wanted to ask you something."

"Anything, my love," she said, fanning faster.

"You said one time that all the bad decisions you made—none of it would have happened if you could just keep yourself from falling in love."

When I'm with my mom my words never come out wrong. I think it's because I kind of hate her.

"I said that?"

"You did."

"Weird."

"What did you mean?"

"Christ, honey, I don't know." The *Post* slowed, stopped, settled into her lap. "It's stupid, but there's nothing I won't do for a man I love. A woman who's looking for a man to plug a hole she's got inside? She's in trouble."

"Yeah," I said.

Below us, the Bronx scrolled by. Sights I'd been seeing all my life. The same sooty sides of buildings; the same cop cars on every block looking for boys like me. I thought of Case, then, and clean, sharp joy pushed out all my fear. My eyes shut, from the pleasure of remembering him, and saw a glorious rush of ported imagery. Movie stills; fashion spreads; unspeakable obscenity. Not blurry this time; requiring no extra effort. I wondered what was different. I knew my mouth was open in an idiot grin, somewhere in a southbound subway car, but I didn't care, and I stood knee-deep in a river of images until the elevated train went underground after 161st Street.

WE ARE THE CLOUD, said the sign on the door, atop a sea of multicolored dots with stylized wireless signals bouncing between them.

Walking in with Case, I saw that maybe I had oversold the place by saying it was "nice." Nicer than the ones by Lincoln Hospital, maybe, where people come covered in blood and puke, having left against medical advice after spasming out in a public housing stairwell. But still. It wasn't *actually* nice.

Older people nodded off on benches, smelling of shit and hunger. Gross as it was, I liked those offices. All those ports started a pleasant buzzing in my head. Like we added up to something.

"Look at that guy," Case said, sitting down on the bench beside me. He pointed to a man whose head was tilted back, gurgling up a steady stream of phlegm that had soaked his shirt and was dripping onto the floor.

"Overclocked," I said, and stopped. His shoulder felt good against my bicep. "Some people. Sell more than they should. Of their brain."

Sell enough of it, and they'd put you up in one of their Node Care Facilities, grim nursing homes for thirty-something vegetables and doddering senior citizens in their twenties, but once you were in you were never coming out, because people ported that hard could barely walk a block or speak a sentence, let alone obtain and hold meaningful employment.

And if I didn't want to end up on the street, that was my only real option. I'd been to job interviews. Some I walked into on my own; some the system set up for me. Nothing was out there for anyone, let alone a frowning, stammering tower of man who more than one authority figure had referred to as a "fucking imbecile."

"What about him?" Case asked, pointing to another guy whose hands and legs twitched too rhythmically and regularly for it to be a dream.

"Clouddiving," I said.

He laughed. "I thought only retards could do that."

"That's," I said. "Not."

"Okay," he said, when he saw I wouldn't be saying anything else on the subject.

I wanted very badly to cry. *Only retards.* A part of me had thought maybe I could share it with Case, tell him what I could do. But of course I couldn't. I fast-blinked, each brief shutting of my eyes showing a flurry of cloud-snatched photographs.

Ten minutes later I caught him smiling at me, maybe realizing he had said something wrong. I wanted so badly for Case to see inside my head. What I was. How I wasn't an imbecile, or a retard.

Our eyes locked. I leaned forward. Hungry for him to see

me, the way no one else ever had. I wanted to tell him what I could do. How I could access data. How sometimes I thought I could maybe *control* data. How I dreamed of using it to burn everything down. But I wasn't strong enough to think those things, let alone say them. Some secrets you can't share, no matter how badly you want to.

I went back alone. Case had somewhere to be. It hurt, realizing he had things in his life I knew nothing about. I climbed the steps and a voice called from the front-porch darkness.

"Awful late," Guerra said. The stubby man who ran the place: Most of his body weight was gristle and mustache. He stole our stuff and ate our food and took bribes from dealer residents to get rivals logged out. In the dark I knew he couldn't even see who I was.

"Nine," I said. "It's not. O'clock."

He sucked the last of his Coke through a straw, in the noisiest manner imaginable. "Whatever."

Salvation Army landscapes clotted the walls. Distant mountains and daybreak forests, smelling like cigarette smoke, carpet cleaner, thruway exhaust. There was a sadness to the place I hadn't noticed before, not even when I was hating it. In the living room, a boy knelt before the television. Another slept on the couch. In the poor light, I couldn't tell if one of them was the one who had hurt Case.

There were so many of us in the system. We could add up to an army. Why did we all hate and fear each other so much? Friendships formed from time to time, but they were weird and tinged with what-can-I-get-from-you, liable to shatter at any moment as allegiances shifted or kids got transferred. If all the violence we visited on ourselves could be turned outwards, maybe we could—

But only danger was in that direction. I thought of my mom's man, crippled in a prison riot, living fat off the settlement, saying, drunk, once, *Only thing the Man fears more than one of us is a lot of us.*

I went back to my room, and got down on the floor, under the window. And shut my eyes. And dove.

Into spreadsheets and songs and grainy CCTV feeds and old films and pages scanned from books that no longer existed anywhere in the world. Whatever the telecom happens to be porting through you at that precise moment.

Only damaged people can dive. Something to do with how the brain processes speech. Every time I did it, I was terrified. Convinced they'd see me, and come for me. But that night I wanted something badly enough to balance out the being afraid.

Eyes shut, I let myself melt into data. Shuffled faster and faster, pulled back far enough to see Manhattan looming huge and epic with mountains of data at Wall Street and Midtown. Saw the Bronx, a flat spread of tiny data heaps here and there. I held my breath, seeing it, feeling certain no one had ever seen it like this before, money and megabytes in massive spiraling loops, unspeakably gorgeous and fragile. I could see how much money would be lost if the flow was broken for even a single second, and I could see where all the fault lines lay. But I wasn't looking for that. I was looking for Case.

And then: Case came knocking. Like I had summoned him up from the datastream. Like what I wanted actually mattered outside of my head.

"Hey there, mister," he said, when I opened my door.

I took a few steps backward.

He shut the door and sat down on my bed. "You've got a Game Boy, right? I saw the headphones." I didn't respond, and he said, "Damn, dude, I'm not trying to steal your stuff, okay? I have one of my own. Wondered if you wanted to play together." Case flashed his, bright red to my blue one.

"The thing," I said. "I don't have. The cable."

He patted his pants pocket. "That's okay, I do."

We sat on the bed, shoulders touching, backs against the wall, and played *Mega Man 2*. Evil robots came at us by the dozen to die.

I touched the cord with one finger. Such a primitive thing, to need a physical connection. Case smelled like soap, but not the Ivory they give you in the system. Like cream, I thought, but that wasn't right. To really describe it I'd need a whole new world of words no one ever taught me.

"That T-shirt looks good on you," he said. "Makes you look like a gym boy."

"I'm not. It's just . . . what there was. What was there. In the donation bin. Once Guerra picked out all the good stuff. Hard to find clothes that fit when you're six six."

"It does fit, though."

Midway through Skull Man's level, Case said: "You talk funny sometimes. What's up with that?" and I was shocked to see no anger surge through me.

"It's a thing. A speech thing. What you call it when people have trouble talking."

"A speech impediment."

I nodded. "But a weird one. Where the words don't come out right. Or don't come out at all. Or come out as the wrong word. Clouding makes it worse."

"I like it," he said, looking at me now instead of Mega Man. "It's part of what makes you unique."

We played without talking, tinny music echoing in the little room.

"I don't want to go back to my room. I might get jacked in the hallway."

"Yeah," I said.

"Can I stay here? I'll sleep on the floor."

"Yeah."

"You're the best, Sauro." And there were his hands again, rubbing the top of my head. He took off his shirt and began to make a bed on my floor. Fine black hair covers almost all of me, but Case's body was mostly bare. My throat hurt with how bad I wanted to put my hands on him. I got into bed with my boxers on, embarrassed by what was happening down there.

"Sauro," he whispered, suddenly beside me in the bed.

I grunted; stumbled coming from dreams to reality.

His body was spooned in front of mine. "Is this okay?"

"Yes. Yes, it is." I tightened my arms around him. His warmth and smell stiffened me. And then his head had turned, his mouth was moving down my belly, his body pinning me to the bed, which was good, because God had turned off gravity and the slightest breeze would have had me floating right out the window and into space.

"You ever do this before? With a guy?"

"Not out loud—I mean, not in real life."

"You've thought about it."

"Yeah."

"You've thought about it a lot."

"Yeah."

"Why didn't you ever do it?"

"I don't know."

"You were afraid of what people might think?"

"No."

"Then what *were* you afraid of?"

Losing control was what I wanted to say, or *giving someone power over me*, or *making a mess*.

Or: *The boys that make me feel like you make me feel turn me into something stupid, brutish, clumsy, worthless.*

Or: *I knew a gay kid, once, in a group home upstairs from a McDonald's, watched twelve guys hold him down in a locked room until the morning guy came at eight, saw him when they wheeled him toward the ambulance.*

I shrugged. The motion of my shoulders shook his little body.

I fought sleep as hard and long as I could. I didn't want to not be there. And when I knew I couldn't fight it anymore I let myself sink into data—easy as blinking this time—felt myself ebb out of my cloud port, but instead of following the random data beamed into me by the nearest router, I *reached*—felt my way across the endless black gulf of six inches that separated his cloud port from mine, and found him there, a jagged, wobbly galaxy of data, ugly and incongruous, but beautiful, because it was *him*, and because, even if it was only for a moment, he was mine.

Case, I said.

He twitched in his sleep. Said his own name.

I love you, I said.

Asleep, Case said it, too.

Kentucky Fried Chicken. Thursday morning. For the first time, I didn't feel like life was a fight about to break out, or like everyone wanted to mess with me. Everywhere I went, someone wanted to throw me out—but now the only person who even noticed me was a crazy lady rooting through a McDonald's soda cup of change.

Case asked, "Anyone ever tell you you're a sexy beast?" On my baldness his hands no longer seemed so tiny. My big, thick skull was an eggshell.

"Also? Dude? You're *huge.*" He nudged my crotch with his knee. "You know that? Like *off the charts.*"

"Yeah?"

I laughed. His glee was contagious and his hands were moving down my arm and we were sitting in public talking about gay sex and he didn't care and neither did I.

"When I first came to the city, I did some porn," Case said. "I got like five hundred dollars for it."

I chewed slow. Stared at the bones and tendons of the drumstick in my hand. Didn't look up. I thought about what I had done, while clouddiving. How I said his name, and he echoed me. I dreamed of taking him up to the roof at night, snapping my fingers and making the whole Bronx go dark except for Case's name, spelled out in blazing tenement window lights. It would be easy. I could do anything. Because: Case.

"Would you be interested in doing something like that?"

"No."

"Not even for like a million dollars?"

"Maybe a million. But probably not."

"You're funny. You know that? How you follow the rules. All they ever do is get you hurt."

"Getting in trouble means something different for you than it does for me."

Here's what I realized: It wasn't hate that made it easy to talk to my mom. It was love. Love let the words out.

"Why?" he asked.

"Because. What you are."

"Because I'm a sexy mother?"

I didn't grin back.

"Because I'm white."

"Yeah."

"Okay," he said. "Right. You see? The rules are not your friend. Racists made the rules. Racists enforce them."

I put the picked-clean drumstick down.

Case said, "Whatever" and the word was hot and long, a question, an accusation. "The world put you where you are, Sauro, but fear keeps you there. You want to never make any decisions. Drift along and hope everything turns out for the best. You know where that'll put you."

The lady with the change cup walked by our table. Snatched a thigh off of Case's plate. "Put that down right this minute, asshole," he said, loud as hell, standing up. For a second the country-bumpkin Case was gone, replaced by someone I'd never seen before. The lady scurried off. Case caught me staring and smiled, *aw-shucks* style.

"Stand up," I said. "Go by the window."

He went. Evening sun turned him into something golden.

Men used to paralyze me. My whole life I'd been seeing confident, charismatic guys, and thought I could never get to that place. Never have what they had. Now I saw it wasn't what they *had* that I wanted, it was what they *were*. I felt lust, not inferiority, and the two are way too close. Like hate and love.

"You make me feel like food," he said, and then lay himself face down on the floor. "Why don't you come over here?" Scissored his legs open. Turned his head and smiled like all the smiles I ever wanted but did not get.

Pushing in, I heard myself make a noise that can only be called a bellow.

"Shh," he said, "everyone will hear us."

My hips took on a life of their own. My hands pushed hard, all up and down his body. Case was tiny underneath me. A twig I could break.

Afterwards I heard snoring from down the hall. Someone sobbed. I'd spent so long focused on how full the world was of horrible things. I'd been so conditioned to think that its good things were reserved for someone else that I never saw how many were already within my grasp. In my head, for one thing, where my thoughts were my own and no one could punish me for them, and in the cloud, where I was coming to see that I could do astonishing things. And in bed. And wherever Case was. My eyes filled up and ran over and I pushed my face into the cool nape of his sleeping neck.

My one and only time in court: I am ten. Mom bought drugs

at a bodega. It's her tenth or hundredth time passing through those tall, tarnished-bronze doors. Her court date came on one of my rare stints out of the system, when she cleaned up her act convincingly enough that they gave me briefly back to her.

The courtroom is too crowded; the guard tells me to wait outside. "But he's my son," my mother says, pointing out smaller children sitting by their parents.

I am very big for ten.

"He's gotta stay out here," the guard says.

I sit on the floor and count green flecks in the floor. Dark-skinned men surround me, angry but resigned, defiant but hopeless. The floor's sparkle mocks us: our poverty, our mortality, the human needs that brought us here.

"Where I'm from," Case said, "you could put a down payment on a house with two thousand dollars."

"Oh."

"You ever dream about escaping New York?"

"Kind of. In my head."

Case laughed. "What about you and me getting out of town? Moving away?"

My head hurt with how badly I wanted that. "You hated that place. You don't want to go back."

"I hated it because I was alone. If we went back together, I would have you."

"Oh."

His fingers drummed up and down my chest. Ran circles around my nipples. "I called that guy I know. The porn producer. Told him about you. He said he'd give us each five hundred, and another two-fifty for me as a finder's fee."

"You called him? About me?"

"This could be it, Sauro. A new start. For both of us."

"I don't know," I said, but I *did* know. I knew I was lost, that I couldn't say no, that his mouth, now circling my belly button, had only to speak and I would act.

"Are you really such a proper little gentleman?" he asked. His hands, cold as winter, hooked behind my knees. "You never got into trouble before?"

My one time in trouble.

I am five. It's three in the morning. I'm riding my tricycle down the block. A policeman stops me. *Where's your mother/ She's home/ Why aren't you home?/ I was hungry and there's no food.* Mom is on a heroin holiday, lying on the couch while she's somewhere else. For a week I've been stealing food from corner stores. So much cigarette smoke fills the cop car that I can't breathe. At the precinct he leaves me there, windows all rolled up. Later he takes me home, talks to my mom, fills out a report, takes her away. Someone else takes me. Everything ends. All of this is punishment for some crime I committed without realizing it. I resolve right then and there to never again steal food, ride tricycles, talk to cops, think bad thoughts, step outside to get something I need.

Friday afternoon we rode the train to Manhattan. Case took us to a big building, no different on the outside from any other one. A directory on the wall listed a couple dozen tenants. *ARABY STUDIOS* was where we were going.

"I have an appointment with Mr. Goellnitz," Case told a woman at a desk upstairs. The place smelled like paint over black mold. We sat in a waiting room like a doctor's, except with different posters on the walls.

In one, a naked boy squatted on some rocks. A beautiful boy. Fine black hair all over his body. Eyes like lighthouses. Something about his chin and cheekbones turned my knees to hot jelly. Stayed with me when I shut my eyes.

"Who's that?" I asked.

"Just some boy," Case said.

"Does he work here?"

"No one *works here.*"

"Oh."

Filming was about to start when I figured out why that boy on the rocks bothered me so much. I had thought only Case could get into my head so hard, make me feel so powerless, so willing to do absolutely anything.

A cinderblock room, dressed up like how Hollywood imagines the projects. Low ceilings and Snoop Dogg posters. Overflowing ashtrays. A pit bull dozing in a corner. A scared little white boy sitting on the couch.

"I'm sorry, Rico, you know I am. You gotta give me another chance."

The dark scary drug dealer towers over him. Wearing a wife beater and a bicycle chain around his neck. A hard-on bobs inside his sweatpants. "That's the last time I lose money on you, punk."

The drug dealer grabs him by the neck, rubs his thumb along the boy's lips, pushes his thumb into the warm wet mouth.

"*Do* it," Goellnitz barked.

"I can't," I said.

"Say the fucking line."

Silence.

"Or I'll throw your ass out of here and neither one of you will get a dime."

Case said, "Come on, dude! Just say it."

—and how could I disobey? How could I not do every little thing he asked me to do?

Porn was like cloudporting, like foster care. One more way they used you up.

One more weapon you could use against them.

I shut my eyes and made my face a snarl. Hissed out each word, one at a time, to make sure I'd only have to say it once.

"That's." "Right." "Bitch." I spat on his back, hit him hard in the head. "Tell." "Me." "You." "Like it." Off camera, in the mirror, Case winked.

Where did it come from, the strength to say all that? To say all that, and do all the other things I never knew I could do? Case gave it to me. Case, and the cloud, which I could feel and see now even with my eyes open, even without thinking about it, sweet and clear as the smell of rain.

"Damn, dude," Case said, while they switched to the next camera set-up. "You're actually kind of a good actor with how you deliver those lines." He was naked; he was fearless. I cowered on the couch, a towel covering as much of me as I could manage.

What was it in Case that made him so certain nothing bad would happen to him? At first I chalked it up to white skin, but now I wasn't sure it was so simple. His eyes were on the window. His mind was already elsewhere.

The showers were echoey, like TV high school locker rooms. We stood there, naked, side by side. I slapped Case's ass, and when he didn't respond I did it again, and when he didn't respond I stood behind him and kissed the back of his neck. He didn't say or do a thing. So I left the shower to go get dressed.

"Did I hurt you?" I hollered, when ten minutes had gone by and he was still standing under the water.

"What? No."

"Oh."

He wasn't moving. Wasn't soaping or lathering or rinsing.

"Is everything okay?" Making my voice warm, to hide how cold I suddenly felt.

"Yeah. It was just . . . intense. Sex usually isn't. For me."

His voice was weird and sad and not exactly nice. I sat on a bench and watched him get harder and harder to see as the steam built up.

"Would you mind heading up to the House ahead of me?" he said, finally. "I need some time to get my head together. I'll square up things with the director and be there soon."

"Waiting is cool."

"No. It's not. I need some alone time."

"Alone time," I smirked. "You're a—"

"You need to get the hell back, Angel. Okay?"

Hearing the hardness in his voice, I wondered if there was a way to spontaneously stop being alive.

"I got your cash right here," the director said, flapping an envelope at me.

"He'll get it," I said, knowing it was stupid. "My boyfriend."

"You sure?"

I nodded.

"Here's my business card. I hoped you might think about being in something of mine again sometime. Your friend's only got a few more flicks in him. Twinks burn out fast. You, on the other hand—you've got something special. You could have a long career."

"Thanks," I said, nodding, furious, too tall, too retarded, too sensitive, hating myself the whole way down the elevator, and the whole walk to the subway, and the whole ride back to what passed for home.

When the train came above ground after 149th Street, I felt the old shudder as my cloud port clicked back into the municipal grid. Shame and anger made me brave, and I dove. I could see the car as data, saw transmissions to and from a couple dozen cell phones and tablets and biodevices, saw how the train's forward momentum warped the information flowing in and out. Saw ten jagged blobs inside, my fellow cloudbounds. Reached out again, like I had with Case. Felt myself slip through one after another like a thread through ten needles. Tugged that thread the tiniest bit, and watched all ten bow their heads as one.

Friday night I stayed up till three in the morning, waiting for Case to come knocking. I played the Skull Man level on *Mega Man 2* until I could beat it without getting hit by a single enemy. I dove into the cloud, hunted down maps, opened up whole secret worlds. I fell asleep like that, and woke up wet from fevered dreams of Case.

Saturday—still no sign of him.

Sunday morning I called Guerra's cell phone, a strict no-no on the weekends.

"This better be an emergency, Sauro," he said.

"Did you log Case out?"

"Case?"

"The white boy."

"You call me up to bother me with your business deals? No, jackass, I didn't log him out. I haven't seen him. Thanks for reminding me, though. I'll phone him in as missing on Monday morning."

"You—"

But Guerra had gone.

First thing Monday, I rode the subway into Manhattan and walked into that office like I had as much right as anyone else to occupy any square meter of space in this universe. I worried I wouldn't be able to, without Case. I didn't know what this new thing coming awake inside me was, but I knew it made me strong. Enough.

The porn man gave me a hundred dollars, no strings attached. Said to keep him in mind, said he had some scripts that I could "transform from low-budget bullshit into something really special."

He was afraid of me. He was right to be afraid, but not for the reason he thought. I could clouddive and wipe Araby Studios out of existence in the time it took him to blink his eyes. I could see his fear, and I could see how he wanted me anyway for the money he could make off me. There was so much to see, once you're ready to look for it.

Maybe I was right the first time: It *had* been hate that made it easy to talk to my mom. Love can make us become what we need to be, but so can hate. Case was gone, but the words kept coming. Life is nothing but acting.

I could have:

1. Given Guerra the hundred dollars to track Case down. He'd call his contacts down at the department; he'd hand me an address. Guerra would do the same job for fifty bucks, but for a hundred he'd bow and *yessir* like a good little lackey.

2. Smiled my way into every placement house in the city, knocked on every door to every tiny room until I found him.

3. Hung around outside Araby Studios, wait for him to snivel back with his latest big, dumb, dark stud. Wait in the shower until he went to wash his ass out, kick him to the floor, fuck him endlessly and extravagantly. Reach up into him, seize hold of his heart and tear it to shreds with bare, bloody, befouled hands.

The image of him in the shower brought me to a full and instant erection. I masturbated, hating myself, trying hard to focus on a scenario where I hurt him . . . but even in my own revenge fantasy I wanted to wrap my body around his and keep him safe.

Afterwards I amended my revenge scenario list to include:
1. Finding someone else to screw over, some googly-eyed blond boy looking to plug a hole he has inside.
2. Becoming the most famous, richest, biggest gay porn star in history, traveling the world, standing naked on sharp rocks in warm oceans. Becoming what they wanted me to be, just long enough to get a paycheck. Seeing Case in the bargain bin someday; seeing him in the gutter.
3. Burning down every person and institution that profited off the suffering of others.
4. Becoming the kept animal of some rich, powerful queen who will parade me at fancy parties and give me anything I need as long as I do him the favor of regularly fucking him into a state of such quivering sweat-soaked helplessness that childhood trauma and white guilt and global warming all evaporate.
5. Finding someone who I will never, ever, ever screw over

Really, they were all good plans. None of it was off the table.

Leaving the office building, I ignored all the instincts that screamed *get on the subway and get the hell out of here before some cop stops you for matching a description!* Standing on a street corner for no reason felt magnificent and forbidden.

I shut my eyes. Reached out into the cloud, felt myself magnified like any other signal by the wireless routers that filled the city. Found the seams of the infrastructure that kept the flow of data in place. The weak spots. The ways to snap or bend or reconstruct that flow. How to erase any and all criminal records; pay the rent for my mom and every other sad sack in the Bronx for all eternity. Divert billions in banker dividends into the debit accounts of cloudporters everywhere.

I pushed, and when nothing happened I pushed harder.

A tiny *pop,* and smoke trickled up from the wireless router atop the nearest lamppost. Nothing more. My whole body dripped with sweat. Some dripped into my eyes. It stung. Ten minutes had passed, and felt like five seconds. My muscles ached like after a hundred push-ups. All those things that had seemed so easy—I wasn't strong enough to do them on my own.

Fear keeps you where you are, Case said. Finally I could see that he was right, but I could see something else that he couldn't see. Because he thought small, and because he only thought about himself.

Fear keeps us separate.

I shut my eyes again, and reached. A ritzy part of town; hardly any cloudbounds in the immediate area. The nearest one was in a bar down the block.

"What'll you have," the bartender said, when I got there. He didn't ask for ID.

"Boy on the rocks," I said, and then kicked at the stool. "Shit. No. Scotch. Scotch on the rocks."

"Sure," he said.

"And for that guy," I said, pointing down the bar to the passed-out overclocked man I had sensed from outside. "One. Thing. The same."

I took my drink to a booth in the front, where I could see out the window. I took a sip. I reached further, eyes open this time, until I found twenty more cloudporters, some as far as fifty blocks away, and threaded us together.

The slightest additional effort, and I was everywhere. All five boroughs—thousands of cloudporters looped through me. With all of us put together I felt inches away from snapping the city in two. Again I reached out and felt for optimal fracture points. Again I pushed. Gently, this time.

An explosion, faraway but huge. *Con Edison's east side substation,* I saw, in the six milliseconds before the station's failure overloaded transmission lines and triggered a cascading failure that killed all electricity to the tri-state region.

I smiled, in the darkness, over my second sip. Within a week the power would be back on. And I—we—could get to work. Whatever that would be. Stealing money; exterminating our exploiters; leveling the playing field. Finding Case, forging a cyberterrorism manifesto, blaming the blackout on him, sending a pulse of electricity through his body precisely calibrated to paralyze him perfectly.

On my third sip I saw I still wasn't sure I wanted to hurt him. Maybe he'd done me wrong, but so had my mom. So had lots of folks. And I wouldn't be what I was without them.

Scotch tastes like smoke, like old men. I drank slow so I wouldn't get too drunk. I had never walked into a bar before. I always imagined cops coming out of the corners to drag me off to jail. But that wasn't how the world worked. Nothing was stopping me from walking into wherever I wanted to go.

iv.

No one is stopping us. We can do anything. We reach the water's edge, the manicured, modern park that replaced the raggedy piers with their falling-down buildings and the constant thrum of illegality.

"Get on your knees, boy," he barks, the voice too loud for this dark, silent space. And I do, and I'm shocked, as I always am, at our wild, lonely freedom in this world. I'm fumbling at his belt buckle and the ebb-tide river is sloshing beneath the boards I kneel on and the moon is in the sky and the sea is in my veins and half of me feels like a helpless animal tugged by distant bodies and savage instinct and the other half of me is prostrate before the ragged terrifying reality of free will:

We can do whatever we want.

And anything might happen to us, after.

CONSPICUOUS PLUMAGE

SUMMER MEANT FREEDOM, and freedom was terrifying. Every window was open; every curtain billowed in the breeze. Darkness came and the street went on forever. I sat on the porch and hugged my knees, watched where Trench Street vanished into the gloom. Who was to say who or what might come walking up that street, into my life, and what terrifying things they might bring? Worse—who was to say where I could go, and what might happen to me when I got there?

Certainly not Mom and Dad. My parents were frozen solid, all summer long. Ice froze their tongues at dinner time. They said nothing to each other; nothing to me. My questions got cold brittle looks and ice-shard answers. Even the television stayed turned down low, as if too much sound might shatter the icicle palace their grief had built.

Sometimes I couldn't handle the ice, the silence, and I'd do something dumb, something I knew I shouldn't, like someone might stand at the edge of a cliff and scream even though they know it'll cause an avalanche and they might get crushed, because anything is better than freezing to death.

For example: "You never make spaghetti anymore"—because

spaghetti was my brother's favorite.

Or: "We should watch *Ed Sullivan* tonight," because my brother always made us watch it, and somehow, always, through the sheer magnitude of his enthusiasm, made us enjoy it.

"Taylor Elizabeth," my mother would say, when my father got up suddenly and fled to the upstairs bathroom.

When I was little, my parents only used my first and middle names together when I was being very bad. Now it's all they call me.

My brother's hands became birds when he danced. Mere metaphors at first, the blur of motion and grace making them into something emblematic of freedom, and then—birds. Two of them, sometimes, his hands having broken free of his body and the miserable fixed limits of flesh, and sometimes a whole flock swooping and whirling around him. Sometimes, in his most inspired moments, like the time he and his friends staged a show in the gutted strip-mall shell of where the ballet school used to be, by the end of his dance he'd be nothing but birds. We still have photos. Look close and there is no Cary. Only starlings, grackles, owls, robins, whip-poor-wills, Cary's favorite— an ornithologist's nightmare of interspecies cooperation.

I saw the body. My parents wouldn't. Movies make ID'ing a corpse into this big traumatic thing where moms weep and dads vow revenge, but really it doesn't have to be a parent, doesn't even have to be family. Two people who knew the person well. One, in some cases, but for Cary it was two, because the town is small and the funeral parlor guy was a family friend who'd seen my brother go from gangly fireball child to the solid, handsome body that landed on his table.

Blue lips. Purple patches all over his body. Black where the skin had broken. Dried blood mostly cleaned up, but still visible in crusty streaks here and there. All terrible, I know; all signs of the violent end he met, but beautiful too, in a way Cary would have appreciated. Like he'd transformed into something else. Conspicuous plumage, the anti-camouflage effect of brightly colored feathers found in predatory birds. Creatures too terrifying and magnificent to need to hide from anyone.

Did he freeze to death, beaten into a coma and left in the woods in flannel and jeans in awful North Country February? Did he die of his injuries? Bleed to death? Hard to say, our funeral parlor friend said, and even though the cops did their own autopsy they didn't dig too deep. Guys turn up dead along the Northway sometimes. It's just a thing that happens. When it's a drug dealer or a gay guy or some other segment of the population that police believe is especially prone to ending up dead, they don't spend too much time looking for cause of death. Because they already know it. Dude made bad decisions, is what they figure, and this is what happens.

Pterodactyls and tigers prowled the bowling alley parking lot. Elvis thumped from car speakers. Hank Williams. Boys, everywhere, squatting on fenders or leaning back behind the wheel. Blowing cigarette smoke lewdly in my direction. Streaks of fire circled me as I walked. Blue, green, and white, beautiful in their way, but nothing I wanted to stop and look at.

Inside was better. Beer and cigarette stink; the sharp, fake vanilla of the spray they use on the rental shoes. Old men and women, and middle-aged ones, with no particular need or desire to display.

"Hey," I said to Hiram Raff, who was right where I thought he'd be, polishing shoes in a corner where hardly anyone ever looked. Off the high school baseball field Hiram was all awkward stammers and intentionally poor posture, ashamed and afraid of the adulation he had unwillingly earned.

"Hey," he said, a little nervously, like *what does this person want from me?*

"How you doing?" I asked, fingers rubbing at an invisible spot on the counter.

"I'm all right," he said, and his pretty face said he most certainly was not. I felt awful, like I was frightening a small animal for selfish reasons, but I could not stop now.

"I heard you can make people see things," I said.

Lines appeared between his eyes, and at the edges of his mouth. Poor boy looked close to bursting—into tears, maybe, or, simply bursting. I was a monster, I knew, but I had to say what I'd come here to say. I owed it to my brother.

"Can you help me? Can you come on a road trip with me?"

I had two pieces of information about Hiram Raff, both of them ill-gotten, gossip-derived. Common knowledge. Things he was deeply, irrationally ashamed of, for reasons that were his own. The first was what I'd already said: that under certain circumstances he could cause visions—of the past, of the future, of fictional scenarios that had never been and would never be, and whether he or anyone else could tell the difference was subject to much conjecture. The second was that he had a congenital, terminal case of politeness. Hiram was a boy who could never tell anyone No.

Which is why instead of fleeing from my invasive request, as he clearly wanted to, he frowned down at the plastic shoe in his hands and said:

"When?"

Our house used to be alive with color. Walls would shift from blue to red without warning; the black-and-white beginning of *The Wizard of Oz* would be as bright and technicolor as the rest of it; my father's eyes could change from emerald to gold. On nights when my mom and dad were getting ready to go out without us, the air around us would dance with a kind of small-scale aurora borealis. When we were little, my brother and I would run through the hallways playing with it, flapping our arms and blowing hard to watch the dancing clouds react.

My parents were seventeen when Cary was conceived, eighteen when he was born. Cary was eighteen when he died. They're young, someone said, at the funeral, too young for something so awful, and I wondered when in your life it became okay for terrible things to happen to you.

Since then, the colors in our house are dead. Stuck. Static. Our pea-green bathroom wallpaper will not become anything else. Mom could make them change and dad could make them move, but now they do neither.

"Hey Dad," I said, the morning I was going to meet Hiram. August already, and hot. Dad was on the porch, as he often was, watching the end of the road. Not drinking. Drinking was another thing that had stopped.

"Hey," he said, and scooted over to make room on the porch swing for me.

"I'm going to the movies," I said.

"Okay."

Not With who, not When will you be back. Having a father who let you do whatever you wanted was nowhere near as great as I'd thought it would be.

I sat. Waited. He didn't put his arm around me. Didn't say a word.

I stood up. He tried to smile and did not entirely succeed. I kissed his forehead. Turned to go. I wanted to shake him, scream, stomp my feet, howl, but I knew none of those things would make a difference. Dad was frozen solid, in there, somewhere. It would take something truly brutal to thaw him out.

Hiram waved when he saw me. For a second he was a little boy, his smile wide and his motions impulsive, uncontrollable. He bounded down the steps and got into the car and my heart felt happy, light, like I was getting somewhere, like something would happen today, like a box had opened.

"Hi!" he said.

"Hey, Hi," I said.

"Do you like rock?" he asked, fiddling with the radio before his seat belt was buckled.

"Sure," I said, and remembered my brother the first time he heard Fats Domino. How his whole body moved, even while standing still. He'd been thirteen, then, and me eleven, and it was the first time I ever saw the birds. Three of them, ravens, probably, or no real bird at all, just a fledgling expression of the man my brother was becoming, and then they were red, and then they were green, and Mom was in the doorway laughing.

Hi turned the knob slowly, navigating through the sea of static, landing on something mild and empty.

"Pat Boone," I said. "Gross."

"You don't like him?"

"He didn't write this song. My brother said the only reason

anyone knows who the hell Pat Boone is is because most of the radio stations in this country won't play the guys who actually wrote these songs."

"Why not?"

"Whites only," I said. Cary was forever sending in for the things advertised in the backs of magazines down at the library, getting pamphlets and books in the mail. My brother knew things no one else in town knew.

Hiram was silent. "I didn't know that," he said, and frowned, and began to turn the knob again.

"Route 9," I said, "and then head for the Northway."

Only terrible music was on the radio. He turned it off when we arrived back at Pat Boone.

"I'm sorry about your brother."

"Thank you," I said. Our windows were down and we were leaving our town behind and it almost didn't hurt to hear someone mention him.

"Is that where we're going?"

"It is."

I don't want revenge. This is not that kind of story. Even if I could find out who did this to my brother, there's nothing I want to do to them. Living life after doing something like that is its own kind of punishment, and if he's (they're?) the kind of person (people?) who could kill somebody as beautiful as my brother, well, then, being that broken will cause him/them far more pain in future than puny Taylor Elizabeth could ever dish out.

What I want is to know how it happened.

What I want is to know how to make it not happen to me.

"What can you do?" Hiram asked, and when I didn't answer: "What's your . . . gift?"

Dead things whizzed past the car. Houses; trees; boulders. A whole frozen world of things, baking in the summer heat. Things that might have danced, once, but would never dance again.

"I don't know," I whispered. "I'm afraid to try."

"Yeah," Hiram said, and his voice sounded as thin and fragile as mine did. "That's smart."

Driving, Hiram looked very sincere and thoughtful. His face relaxed and he didn't seem anxious or frightened the way he always did when he spoke, so I let a long time go by without saying anything.

The river was fat, sluggish, still. Even the plumes of black smoke from the factories we passed just hung there, as motionless as the columns they came from.

"How did you know?" he asked. "What I can do?"

There was no safe answer. Nothing that wouldn't hurt him. Nothing that wouldn't crack that lovely face down the middle. I'd been about to say something like *I don't know, it's just something I overheard someone saying*, but I saw now that this would hurt him even more. Even if it was the truth. To be reminded that he was gossiped about, to hear again how the stories were passed from stranger to stranger, would be too devastating for fragile, private, little Hiram Raff.

"Sharon told me," I said, thinking fast.

On the median, between the north and southbound lanes,

was a willow. Beside it slept a mammoth, big as the tree itself, long tusks and dense brown wool. Beside that sat a man, ragged and guitar-wielding. A traveler, a vagabond. A hitchhiker who couldn't find a ride. What might that mammoth do, if he caught sight of me?

A mile passed, maybe five. Then Hiram said: "What did she tell you?"

I looked out my window. "Hardly anything. Just what you could do. I'd been asking around. To see who might be able to help me."

"And what exactly do you want me to help you *with*?" he whispered.

I said nothing. I wasn't entirely sure myself. My plan was flimsy, poorly-plotted. A child's plan. My brother would have known how to do this right. My brother had skills he was not afraid to use. And while I hadn't planned on telling Hiram, that seemed like the best way not to have to talk anymore about what had happened between him and Sharon, and what she did afterwards.

It wasn't Hiram who Sharon wanted. His big brother Herk was the one who wore the mantle of sports star the way it was supposed to be worn. Hard-drinking, friends with everyone, dumb in an attractive sort of way. Quick to anger, eager to sleep with any girl who looked his way, and more than a few that did not. When Herk went away to college, all of Mohawk High grieved.

Under their father's brutal tutelage, both boys had become baseball prodigies—but while Herk accepted and embraced that violent masculinity, Hiram balked at it. So he wasn't prepared to stand outside of his brother's shadow, least of all when it came to the women who'd flocked to him for the multitude of social perks that hooking up with him provided, and who now looked to Hiram to fulfill the same function.

And while Hiram could avoid the beer-soggy parties and evade the post-game advances of most of Mohawk High's would-be popularity opportunists, he was no match for Sharon Baranchik.

Who said:

"I saw . . . I don't know what I saw. The whole time, it was like the sky was pure CinemaScope. People I've never seen before, but who looked totally familiar. Like maybe they were me, in the future, or . . . I don't know, a past life or something. And his eyes did this adorable scrunched-up thing—"

She went on like that, to anyone who would listen, her story so full of details that they must have mostly been made up. Nobody believed all of it, but enough people believed enough of it that Hiram was so upset he stayed home sick from school for three days.

I'd always believed that this had broken him. Watching him drive, now, I was fairly certain he'd been broken long before that, probably by something tiny, or not even a something, but a nothing, a missing piece, some tiny but crucial ingredient in the cake that was a fully-functional human being. And I thought of my brother, who dedicated whole dance cycles to trying to figure out why it was that he liked boys when most boys liked girls, and I thought of how hard it must be to end up completely normal, and whether I had, and whether I'd know it if I hadn't.

"I want to go to where it happened," I said. "Where my brother was murdered. And I want you to show me what actually happened."

"Oh, Taylor," he said, his voice like a boy about to cry. "That's a terrible idea."

"I know," I said. "I need to see it. Are you with me?"

Hiram said nothing, because Hiram was still a boy who could not say no.

"It doesn't work like that," he said. "I can't control what people see. The chances that you'll see what you want to see . . ."

"I'll help you," I said.

"How will you do that?"

"I have no idea," I said, and laughed, and so did he. The Northway was narrowing by then, as we left behind the grimy little cities that surround the state capital. Nothing ahead of us but tiny, dead, frozen-solid summer towns, all the way to Canada.

"And if *you* do manage to see? Wouldn't that be worse?"

"Yes."

I believe Cary's birds are what killed him. People are afraid of beautiful things. They hate how they make them feel. The loss of control, the emotion that overwhelms. Cary danced, and people felt things.

Of course college was where he blossomed. Where he found the people who would love him as much as we did. Where he'd no longer be a swan among ducklings. He would have tasted that freedom and lost his mind. Every boy would have been desperate to have him, and he'd have been only too happy to be had. He'd only been away at school for six months when he was killed. He flew straight into the sun the first chance he got.

Was it a jilted boyfriend? Or some macho man who saw his show and felt things inside that he'd spent his whole life fighting? Maybe another dancer, someone who moved in clouds of smoke or schools of fish and saw Cary's magnificence and knew she'd never be half as good, a third as beautiful?

Whatever it was, his birds were at the bottom of it.

And once I knew how, once I could connect the dots of how his gorgeous gift got him killed, I could be certain that mine, whatever it was, never would.

We got out of the car. Stretched. Stood there, stunned, turned to stone by the staggering heat of the August sun.

"Do you know where," Hiram asked, but didn't know how to end the sentence. Finally he settled on, "Where we're going?"

"I think so," I said, but did not move.

During the semester the place would be packed, full of anxious, energetic boys and girls finally out from under the thumbs and watchful eyes of mothers, fathers, small-town busybodies, churches, synagogues . . . during the semester the place would be enchanted and exciting, but now it was just as dead and frozen as the place we'd come from. I took a few breaths but couldn't detect what Cary had told me about on the phone, *the way the whole world smells different here.*

A week before he died, Cary performed. A recital, at the campus's brand-new, hog-ugly performing arts center. That's where Hiram and I went. It wasn't where he died, but it was the first stop I had to make.

The performance was a smash success. Everyone fell in love with Cary then. He called us glowing, drunk on success, from a backstage pay phone. Behind him was a sea of laughter. Happiness. Mom and Dad were out, when he called. Back then they still went out. We talked, my brother and I, until someone drunk on actual alcohol took the receiver out of his hand and said to me *He's got to go now, everyone wants to pet him.*

Hiram and I went inside. No doors were locked to us. No one was guarding anything. We sat in the front row; we climbed up on stage; we went behind the curtain and into the dressing rooms. We found the pay phone he had called me from. I held it to my ear, listened to the dial tone, that single note of hope and possibility, that could connect me to anyone anywhere in the world, and maybe even ring up the past or the future, if I only knew the right number to dial, I might reach my brother, seventeen, in our kitchen, still considering what college to go to, still exploring the edges of his gift, and tell him never to go anywhere, to stay in the town he hated, and never do anything with the thing that made him happiest, the thing that made him the most beautiful.

I listened, and I felt: nothing. Not the love and joy and warmth of his presence; not the hate and fire and brutal metal rods of his destroyers. I hung up the phone. I pressed both hands to my face.

The ice wasn't in the world. It was in me.

Hiram picked up a chair. He swung it at the wall, hard. It fell to the ground undamaged.

"What the heck?" I asked him.

"Thought it might be one of those stage chairs," he said. "You know. The breakaway kind. The one they smash for dramatic effect."

"Dramatic effect," I said, and felt bad for being surprised, for not having imagined Hiram Raff capable of using phrases like that. "Try that bottle."

He picked a whiskey bottle up off the table, held it by the neck and swung it at the fallen chair. Something about the swing of his arm sent a little wave of warmth into me.

The bottle broke beautifully. He stooped to pick up a shard of glass, and then giggled.

"Look!" he said, a little boy again, and handed it over. "The edges!"

They were smooth, brittle, harmless.

"Come on," I said, and took his hand in mine, the glass shard pressed between our palms. "I know where it happened."

I didn't know where it happened; only where they found him. But maybe they were the same place. And if they weren't, maybe Hiram could show me how to trace back the steps of whoever dumped his body there.

Behind the performing arts center, we followed a paved walkway. Down a hill, around a pond. Over a bridge. To the edge of the woods, where the walkway petered out and the pavement stopped. A flimsy trail cut between the trees, and we followed that.

They'd said it was one of those spots, where kids went when they wanted to do things no one should see. Smoke dope, presumably, or drink, or have sex when the roommate would not leave and would not fall asleep. The walk wasn't long. Whatever privacy it provided would be risky, fraught with imminent discovery by other kids coming in search of some privacy of their own.

Pine trees ringed the clearing. In February they'd have been as green and thick and soft as they were right now. Two logs, covered in paint and carved initials, converged near the center.

The highway rumbled, not far away. The Northway; the road

that could have taken him home. Dying, he would have heard the cars whispering away from him.

Hiram let go of my hand. And laughed again. "The glass—it melted." He licked his palm. "Sugar!" he said.

I licked mine. Sugar.

Real broken glass glittered at our feet. I stepped forward, and saw: birds.

Hundreds of them. Origami cranes and taxidermied crows; cute stuffed eagles and drawings on paper. Chicken feathers. Some were soggy with rain and melted snow. Some had almost dissolved, while others looked brand new.

"Oh my god," Hiram whispered. "Taylor."

"I know," I said.

"People loved your brother," he said.

"I know," I said.

He was crying. I couldn't cry, so how was he?

Boys don't cry, I thought, a hateful ugly thought I did not believe, but that somehow lived inside my head, and instantly everything made sense. Why he hated the gossip, hated the attention from the girls. Hated what Sharon Baranchik had done to him, what his brother, what his father had tried to do. Hiram had a whole beautiful universe inside his head, but the world was determined that he be nothing but a body. Something to play baseball, something to sleep with.

Just like it had done its damnedest to make me anything *but* a body. To make me afraid. To convince me not to dance, the way my brother had danced, or change the colors of things, the way my mother could.

Wind stirred the trees.

I hadn't had a plan. Hadn't known what to do; how I would draw Hiram's gift out and find a way for it to do what I needed it to do. Maybe I hadn't even believed anything at all would happen. Maybe the trip itself was what mattered, one more attempt to break the ice I saw everywhere but inside me.

I stepped closer to him. He hugged me, clutching for me the way a hurt child clutches at a parent. I hugged him back. Felt his heat. Let it in.

Our heads turned toward each other. Our noses knocked. We laughed, and then I kissed him. His muscles tightened, all up and down his body, but only for a second. He breathed out like someone letting go of a breath he'd been holding for years.

"Sugar," he said, licking his lips, and smiled.

We saw: everything.

"I'm so sorry," Hiram said-sobbed. Both our faces were red and wet. Our hands clasped. The ground was cool against our bare backs where our shirts had been pushed up, but warming. "I wish I hadn't shown us that."

"I wanted you to," I said.

At least it had been silent. Hiram's skill didn't extend to sound. Mouths had screamed wordlessly; bones had broken with no more noise than the whoosh of the Northway.

"It's never worked like that," he said. "The things I've shown have always been . . . weird, broken, scary, disjointed. How did you . . ."

I kissed him again, and hoped it would be explanation enough. Some things are simultaneously too obvious and too ridiculous to say out loud.

"Are you . . . okay? Did it hurt?"

"Barely," I said. "It was nice."

"Yeah," Hiram said, shocked into smiling. "It really was." His hand clasped mine.

I let myself smile, too. I let myself feel. Frozen things want to melt; motionless things want to move. They felt good, the things I'd tried not to feel, the things I'd been afraid to do.

I'd watched my brother do what Hiram and I had just done. There on the ground, on a bank of February snow, with a boy he cared about. I'd seen the beauty of the act; seen his flocks of birds unfold in colors and sizes more magnificent than anything nature could make. Love wasn't terrifying. Sex hadn't killed him. Bad men had done that, overgrown boys pink with beer and rage over a football game that hadn't gone the way they wanted, who'd stumbled upon something wonderful that their own ugliness saw as ugly. The other boy escaped. The other boy abandoned him.

I shut my eyes and saw my kitchen, my parents. The ice. The ice I could melt. How easy it was to make things move, when you weren't afraid to grab hold of them.

"Watch," I whispered to Hiram.

There were hundreds of birds in that clearing. Paper, plush, and cardboard. Gifts from people who loved my brother. Pieces of him; physical expressions of what he'd made them feel. I thought about that.

We watched those birds rise into the air. We watched them fly.

v.

Sex is still sacred, even now, even here. Flesh mingles, merges. Boy, beast, man: we are one thing. Breath syncs up. Flashback to first times, adolescent fumblings, orgasms that shattered sidewalks, shook dungeons, sundered chains.

SHATTERED SIDEWALKS
OF THE HUMAN HEART

STRANGE THAT I DIDN'T SEE who she was when she stood in the street, arm upraised, headlights strobing her like flashbulbs, exactly as she'd appeared in the publicity stills that papered New York City for one whole summer. Only when she got in the cab and told me where she was going and slumped back in the seat, and I looked in the mirror and saw the look of utter exhaustion and emptiness fill her face—only then did it click.

"You're her," I said, breath hitching.

"I'm somebody," she said, weary, clearly gut-sick of having this conversation, but I couldn't stop myself.

"You're Ann Darrow."

"The one and only."

And maybe I *had* recognized her, on some unconscious level, because I hadn't meant to pick up any passengers when I got in my cab and started driving. Friday nights I'd sometimes hit up the Ziegfeld, the Palace, drive in circles to see the movie stars arriving at their premieres, and, later on, leaving, and later still staggering out of their afterparties. Purely recreational, usually, but that night it was downright medicinal. I needed that glamour, those sixty-karat smiles, the wonder in the eyes of the crowd. The lie of a beautiful world.

Bombs were falling, four thousand miles away. Crematoria were being kindled.

I pulled away from the curb. One of her posters was framed on the wall of the room I rented. The only decorative touch that had followed me through all five of the boarding houses I'd lived in since getting kicked out of the house. Ann Darrow, eyes wide with terror, arm upraised to fend off something monstrous. A massive black outline hulked behind her. Art deco lettering beneath her blared KONG: THE EIGHTH WONDER OF THE WORLD.

"You Jewish?" she asked.

"I am," I said, tracing my profile in the rearview mirror. "The nose gave it away?"

"The eyes," she said. "The only people who look really scared today are Jewish."

It took me an awful long time to say, "That's because most people have no idea what horrible things human beings are capable of," and even once I said it it wasn't quite right, didn't quite capture the rich flavor of my fear, my rage.

"Some of us do," she said. "Some of us know exactly."

"I'm Solomon," I said.

"That why your radio's switched off, Solomon?"

"Yeah, sorry. Couldn't stand to hear it one more time. I can turn it back on if you want to listen to something."

"No," she said. "That's one of several things I'm trying not to think about tonight."

September 1st, 1939. At 4:45 that morning, Germany had invaded Poland. Word was, England and France would be declaring war within the week. Not that anyone expected them to lift too many fingers to save the millions of Jews in Poland.

"I'm sorry," I said. "Forgot to ask—where you heading?"

"Just drive," she said. "I'll figure something out."

"You coming from a movie premiere?"

"Yeah," she said. "*The Women.* It had its moments. They love to have notorious floozies and disgraced politicians show up on the red carpet. Who am I to turn down free food and alcohol?"

Normally, my New York City cabdriver cool prevailed. Even with only five years driving under my belt, I'd already had more movie stars in my backseat than there were cross streets in Manhattan. But this was no movie star. No fraudulent sorcerer, whose magic was made up of lighting and make-up and special effects and screenwriting. This was *Ann Darrow.* This was someone who knew what magic was. Who'd been held in its hand. Who'd been lifted high into the sky by it, and then watched it die.

"Let me guess," she said, catching my repeated mirror glances. "You were there that night. You were in the theater. You're a baby, you would have been, what, twelve?"

"Twelve exactly," I said, startled. Most people pegged me for far older. I'd been driving a cab on New York City streets since I was thirteen, and nobody'd ever batted an eyelash at it. "But I wasn't in the theater that night."

"I know," she said. "Somebody tells me they were, I know they're lying. Swear to god, you add up all the people who've told me they were there that night, there were a couple million people in the audience. Place only had a thousand seats, and half of them were empty. People make it seem like Denham was some kind of genius promoter, but that piece of shit was as bad at that as he was at everything else."

I had so many questions. For years I'd dreamed of this moment. Now my words were nowhere to be found.

"Let me guess," she said. "You want to know about . . . him."

"Yeah."

She rolled her eyes.

She wasn't that much older than me. She'd been twenty, when she traveled to Skull Island. But those events, and the six years since then, had accelerated her aging. From her purse, she pulled a bottle and a glass. Not a flask; a glass, in her purse. "You want a drink, Solomon?"

"Not while I'm driving."

"Where are your people from, Solomon?"

"Poland," I said.

She cursed, so softly I couldn't hear which one. "You got people over there still?"

"Three grandparents."

"Oh, honey," she said, one hand reaching forward to touch my shoulder.

She was kind. That much was true. I'd imagined her in the hold of the ship, comforting Kong in his chains and his seasickness. Backstage, calming him down while tiny men flashed cameras in his helpless face. Eighty stories up, pleading with him to pick her back up, trying to tell him that the airplanes wouldn't shoot him while he was holding her. Angry at him for not understanding her, or for understanding and not wanting to put her at risk.

"I never knew them," I said. "My parents came over in 1920. For a while their parents were happy to stay where they were, but since stuff's been getting scary over there we've been saving up money to bring them over. Now I can't really see that happening."

We both watched the next several blocks slide by. Street signals switching, red to green. Crowds throbbing. Laughter. Hunger. None of them carried what she carried, the secrets of something extraordinary.

No sense lying: I wanted something from her. I knew it was

wrong, to expect anything of a woman who'd spent six years with everyone clamoring for a piece of her, and I couldn't bring myself to ask, but I could hope. For something—anything—no one else knew. Some piece of him.

Ann Darrow tipped her head back, to down her drink. Saw something high above. "There she is," she whispered.

There she was. I didn't need to crane my neck to look to know what she was seeing. The Empire State Building, showing through the gap between buildings made by 37th Street.

"There were no people living on Skull Island," she said, and chuckled at my shocked expression. "Cannibal natives, that was another one of the lies Denham told the reporters, in the weeks before Kong's debut. He thought it added to the story. Savages menacing the virginal blonde. *People eat that shit up*, he said. Every time he told the story, it got bigger and crazier. Spiders the size of houses. Pterodactyls. The T. rex was real, but to hear him tell it she had horns and breathed fire and flew. Only Kong stayed the same size."

"Because he was bigger than anything that asshole could dream up."

"Exactly," she said, raising her glass again. "He never hurt me."

"Everyone knows that."

No New Yorker ever accepted the story Denham tried to spin: Kong the Monster. From the moment he fell he was myth, was legend, the hope and hero of everyone who ever tried to climb up from the grit and filth of our streets while the little people tried to drag them back down. He was ours. Every souvenir stand and tchotchke shop in the city sold Kong figurines, Kong toys. Every Halloween, he was the most popular costume. And practically half the city had one of those lockets around their neck, with a tuft of black fur purporting to be his.

All the property damage, all the people who died—no one blamed Kong for that. It wasn't his fault he was bigger than life, bigger than us, made for a better world than ours. You didn't blame the flames that burned down your house. You blamed the man who started the fire.

"Is it true you agreed to be in the movie?"

"Of course not," she said, snorting. "Denham told producers I was on board, but that was a lie."

RKO optioned the story, started preparing to make the movie, but the outcry had been immediate, and immense. The mayor flat-out refused to let them film in his city. Said it'd be like re-creating the Triangle Shirtwaist Factory Fire for film. People died. *Kong* died. And so, so did a part of us. Some things were sacred.

"So where were you, Solomon? That night."

"Home. Lower East Side. Six families, thirty people, one apartment. One radio. Everybody glued to it."

Even over the air, even as a thing described by strangers, our hearts were with him. Little boys pounding our chests. Imagining something strong enough to derail a subway car, to shatter the thickest chains . . . but still too small for this city, for its big buildings and its brutal cops, who had bullets where their hearts should be. Which one of us wasn't Kong, a king among ants even as they destroyed us?

When he started climbing the Empire State Building, I slowly backed out of the room. Nobody saw me. They weren't there; they were imagining Kong's ascent. No one heard me scamper down the stairs.

I was a kid. This was my city. I'd sprinted its length more times than I could count. I knew how long it would take me to make it to 34th and Fifth. But how fast could Kong climb to the top? He'd be slowed down by the beautiful woman he carried.

I never thought he would die. I didn't imagine it was possible.

Thick crowds kept me from getting onto Fifth Avenue, but I could still see him. A tiny spot so high above us. We heard the airplanes, a distant sound, getting nearer. We'd gasped, as one. We heard the gunfire.

I didn't tell Ann any of that. She'd think less of me, if she knew. I'd seen her when she came down to street level again. I'd seen the tears streaming down her face, and I'd seen her hate. "What is wrong with you?" she'd shrieked. No one answered. No one knew.

After Kong, Denham spent three years with his back up against the wall. He was still news for a little while, the *Herald-Tribune* running interviews headlined "Most Hated Man in New York City Speaks Out," but before long he was just another one of yesterday's villains, drinking himself to death beside all the other politicians and businessmen who never let a little thing like morality come between them and money. Everywhere he went, someone wanted to take a shot at him, and Denham's crippled manhood wouldn't let him back down from a single one. Until somebody cracked a rib, drove it into some important organ. Even in the hospital he was dialing up journalist numbers he'd committed to memory, offering them exclusives, and even when he told them he was dying they hung up on him.

"I hate this city," she said, watching the after-theater crowds spilling off the sidewalk onto the street.

"Me too," I said. "Even if I also love it."

Her eyes, on mine. "That's it. That's it exactly."

The block where Kong landed—they kept it closed off for weeks. Because of the body, at first—a ten-ton corpse was not so easy to cart off—and then because of the crowds. We came by the thousands. Paupers and newsies and dowager empresses gathered on the shattered sidewalk. We stood, alone with our wonder, and wept.

How much did he change us? Who would we be, if he'd never come blundering into our lives to show us how full of wonder the world could still be, and how full of cruelty we still were? Vegetarianism skyrocketed, it's true—papers said thirty percent of New Yorkers abstained from eating meat now, vs half of a percent before 1933—and the country passed laws to limit animal cruelty, stop medical testing on mammals, make sure meat animals weren't mistreated. Kong wasn't the only reason, he just made a handy symbol of all that was majestic and worthy of respect in animals.

But we'd changed in bad ways too. Plenty of people hated the big ape, especially after the city voided all lawsuits for injury and property destruction related to his rampage, calling Kong an "act of God." Someone shot the gorilla at the Bronx Zoo through the bars of her cage. Not to mention the backlash to the new laws, big business laying people off saying they couldn't make money now that they couldn't cram chickens into tiny cages and feed them shit, out-of-work slaughterhouse men butchering pigs in the streets in protest.

"I don't wanna take money out of your pocket," she said. "You can drop me off wherever, go pick up some actual passengers, instead of an old drunk feeling sorry for herself."

"No," I said, not wanting it to end, not ever. "I was done already."

Her eyes, on mine again.

"You still on the Lower East Side, Solomon?"

"Upper West," I said.

"You want to take me there?"

I could have said yes. I could have tried to do what she wanted. But I couldn't lie to her, not with my words and not with my body. And if I wanted her to share something meaningful with me, some secret she'd kept from everyone else, I couldn't very well keep any of my own.

"I'll take you wherever you want to go, Ann Darrow. I'd do anything for you—but if it's a lover you want, you could probably find plenty of better ones than me."

"Can't get it up?" she snorted, wounded pride vying in her voice with curiosity, at a man who'd make such an admission.

"Not for women, unfortunately."

She nodded. Looked out the window. An idiotic move, sharing that with her. Stupid of me to think that just because her empathy extended to monsters like Kong, it would reach all the way to monsters like me.

Central Park South; a line of tents that marked the entrance to a Hooverville. Men begged. Women walked up to horse-drawn carriages stopped in traffic, demanded money. Word was, only war would end the Depression, and wasn't that some shit right there? Rich men fucked up so bad they made millions of people poor, and the only way to fix it was to make millions of people dead.

"Go to the Bronx," she said. "Hunts Point. You can start the meter."

"No ma'am," I said. "You'll always ride free in my cab."

For a while we didn't speak. I tried to think of ways to do damage control, but my heart wasn't in it. We were what we were, Ann and I, and people treated us accordingly.

We crossed the Willis Avenue Bridge. Small houses sprouted all around us, and brand-new apartment buildings. Lots of my family members had moved up here. I'd have been able to afford a real place. But doing so would be giving up on any hope of finding love, finding sex, and I was eighteen years old and I wasn't ready to do that yet.

"Everybody wants something from me," she said. "Something I can't give them, because I don't have it myself."

"What's that?" I asked, knowing the answer, because it was what I wanted myself.

"They want Kong."

She guided me—left, then right, then left again. Deeper into the Bronx's weird, warped topography, so different from Manhattan's dependable grid. Finally we arrived at blocks and blocks of warehouses. She didn't know the address, and we got lost a couple times looking for the right one.

"Park here," she said.

I did.

"Follow me," she said. And I did. I knew it was stupid. For all I knew her brothers were waiting inside, burly dock worker types who at a word from their spurned sister would gleefully beat me to death. But she was Ann Darrow, and I was as helpless in her hands as she had been in Kong's, and I still held out hope that she could give me what I wanted.

And, anyway, would death be so bad? Who wanted to live in a world like this, anyway? A world getting its revenge on us, for all the damage we did, and damned if we didn't deserve it—dust storms stripping the skin off the country; Oklahoma's entire corn crop mysteriously blighted, according to the radio. A world where Germany invaded Poland and everyone else went about their business. A world that would kill Kong.

"This is where he kept him," she said. I climbed the steps after her. "Before the Broadway debut. Dumb-ass Denham—he either forgot or never even realized that he bought the whole damn warehouse. He was as bad with his backers' money as he was with his own. And after Kong he was so bogged down in debt and lawsuits that this was the least of his thoughts. He died without a will, without heirs. So I guess it'll stand here until it falls down or the city gets around to foreclosing on it for unpaid taxes."

"Kong was here?" I whispered.

"For three weeks." She rummaged in her purse. "I had a locksmith switch this out. I'm the only one with a key."

The air in the warehouse was rank, mammalian. Wild. The smell of something uncageable, and caged. I shut my eyes. Breathed deep.

"That's him," I said.

"That's him. Not as he was in the wild, of course. Chained, without access to the sea, he couldn't clean himself properly. And his spirit came damn close to breaking. You can smell that, too. A sourness. But he was stronger than us."

I stepped inside, with the same fear and humility as entering synagogue. The walls were blue. So was the floor. And the ceiling.

"What's . . ."

I looked down. The blue was a plant, a vine that had grown to cover every surface.

"Gorillas are vegetarians," she said. "Most people don't know that."

"I did." I'd read a lot about gorillas in the months after Kong fell. Dreamed of being a zoologist, except that you needed to be able to afford to go to college for that.

"Kong ate plants. So he had seeds, in his belly. Nobody but me noticed that something had sprouted from his dung. I potted it, kept it secret."

I nodded.

"I made clippings," she said, and gave me a small terra cotta pot. "This is for you."

Up close I could see spearhead-shaped leaves. Red veins spread out in curls and ripples. Vines trailed down the side, ending in fat seed pods. At the center of the pot the leaves curled inward, numerous and beautiful as the petals on a chrysanthemum.

A piece of him. Of Kong.

"Watch the center," she said. "And be very quiet."

I watched. I was quiet. I was patient. The pattern of the veins was so intricate. Hypnotic, almost. So much so that I could have sworn I saw one vine growing while I watched. But of course no plant grew so fast.

The leaf-petals parted, suddenly. Like an eye opening. And beneath the petals: an actual eye. Not human, but not far from it, either. All brown iris, and black pupil. It blinked, twice, twitched around as the eye scanned the sky. Then found mine. Held my gaze.

"Is that his?"

Ann nodded. "The plant took something, passing through him."

I held the pot in my hands. Reverent; apologetic. Unworthy.

"I planted some in a vacant lot next to my building," she said. "Near some kudzu. Came back that afternoon and it had totally swallowed up the kudzu. Would have covered the whole lot in a day if I hadn't clipped it back."

Her eyes were on me. Wanting something. "I—I don't . . ."

"We killed him," she said. "We saw him, this god, this king, and the only thing we could think to do was capture and chain and kill it. That's what people are. You see that, don't you? I know you do. It's why I brought you here."

"Yeah, of course," I said, looking back and forth between her eyes and the plant's. "But I don't . . ."

"Skull Island was rough. Anything that evolved to survive there would be the ultimate invasive species. It'd cover the earth, if it got the chance. Choke off all kinds of life."

And—I got it. I nodded. Said, "What a shame that would be."

"The money from my book deal—I spent that on a tour of the USA, and then Europe. Dropped a few seeds wherever I went."

"You spend any time in Oklahoma?"

"Just enough," Ann said. "Maybe you want to help."

"Thank you," I said, my hands occupied, unable to wipe the tears off my face. Wondering where so many had come from, so fast.

She hugged me. She smelled like alcohol and lilacs and I sobbed into her neck.

I drove back into Manhattan. Headed for the Ziegfeld again. By now the afterparties would be getting out; drunk movie stars needing rides home. Plenty of people hailed me, but I didn't stop. In the seat where Ann sat was a potted plant.

Kong was my passenger. He always had been. I'd carried him in my heart since the moment I watched him fall, felt the earth shake, the sidewalk shatter, my heart with it. All of our hearts.

On the corner of 54th and Seventh, I saw a woman leaning on a streetlamp. Dressed up; holding a high heel under her arm while she rubbed that stockinged foot. Her day had been long, and hard. She was angry. She was going to do something about it. Most people probably wouldn't be able to see it, but I could. Now. How mighty she was. What heights she could climb to. How she could shatter the world with the seeds she carried inside her.

vi.

He lights a cigarette, after. Smirks down at me. When he takes a drag the tip illuminates his face: still beautiful, but different, his perfection hardened by his orgasm, or softened by mine. Here is where he could whip out a hatchet to kill me quickly now, or a syringe full of sedatives to kill me slowly later.

He seems to be searching my face. Looking for something. Wondering whether I'm worthy—of what? A date? A reciprocal blowjob? Living to see another day? But the longer he looks the more he seems to be assessing whether or not he should offer me . . . something. Something he has, and wants to give away. His heart, maybe, or a million dollars, or vampiric immortality.

But really I don't know. Anyone at all could be inside that body.

SHUCKED

ADNEY HAD SEEN THE MAN staring well before he spoke to them. Two tables over, in the otherwise-empty restaurant loud with the sound of waves against the breakwater. Fifty-something; poor posture; took good care of himself. A tourist like them, she could tell by the clumsy way he'd conversed with the woman behind the bar. A guest at the hotel upstairs—hence he was unburdened by bags or backpacks like the ones at their feet.

It happened from time to time: people stared. One of the burdens of being with a boy as beautiful as Teek. This guy at least had the decency not to pretend she didn't exist. He was transfixed by her boyfriend, yes, but he was also assessing her. When he caught her staring back—when their eyes locked—he smiled affably. But was affable the right word? There was something else happening in his eyes, something less friendly. Conspiratorial, almost, like eye contact had made them complicit in something.

Teek was immersed in his phone, trying to decide what tourist-type spot to visit when they left the restaurant. She picked his camera up off the table and took a picture of him. When it flashed on the screen, she tried to see it as if he were a stranger to her. Black hair cropped close; olive skin darkened by a week of vacation sun; untamable stubble. Hazel eyes that seemed always to be aimed down. Slim. Slight. An overall sense of delicacy. Fragility, even.

In the background, out of focus: the man. Clearly staring. Maybe smiling.

To tell Teek or not? He'd find it funny, for sure, but might it also make him self-conscious? Or, worse, swell his ego so it tipped over into insufferable? They had not been dating long enough to know for sure, so she said nothing. The woman behind the bar was pouring water from one big glass pitcher into many smaller ones. She was old and stout and said little, but always had a smile for her. They'd come to the same place every night since they arrived in Amalfi. Teek had said last night that she was "super mean," and Adney was dazzled at how they had such different experiences of the same person.

She struggled with the oyster she was shucking. "Let me," Teek said, and she handed it over—and marveled at how effortlessly he sank the knife into the hinge, wobbled the hand that held the oyster until the blade made a full circumference. Peeled back the shell, severed the muscle that bound the meat to its hard, translucent platter. Where had he learned to do that? He'd come from a pathetic inland Jersey strip-mall exurb, same as she did. *A summer working in a fancy spot down the Shore*, she imagined, and could see it quite vividly. Teek in a white apron; Teek the apple of the eye of every man and woman at the country club.

"I always hated oysters," she said. "My father loved them. We couldn't afford to buy them hardly ever, and it was a big deal when we did. Once he'd shucked them, and when he wasn't looking, I'd dump them all out onto the ice and swap them back into the wrong shells. I thought I was getting away with something."

"That's . . . pretty dumb."

"Yeah," she said. "I was six."

"Why did you order them if you hate them?"

She shrugged. After that, the silence came flooding back in like the tide. She indulged in that thing everyone had been doing last semester: shut your eyes and you can hear your student-loan debt piling up. Cents per second, dollars per minute.

"The church has some amazing art, apparently," he said, holding up the phone to show a church not far from them. "Including a disputed Caravaggio."

"Is it free?" she asked.

He scrolled down, gave a thumbs-up.

"Let's do that," she said. They'd met in Art History, last semester, so that was one thing they could have a conversation about. This was the second mostly silent lunch in a row. *Two weeks is probably too long*, she thought, *for a vacation together so early in a relationship. Especially when neither one of us has any money. Outside of bed there is not so much of a spark, and there's only so long we can stay in bed.*

Even through the glass, the afternoon waves were very loud. She remembered the woman at the hostel explaining the complex system of bells used to signal the start and end of high and low tide. Amalfi was eerily empty of tourists that week. Everyone had a theory why.

Teek picked up his camera, pointed it at the water. Put it down without taking a picture. Lately he'd been doing that a lot. He was obsessed with photography and could talk endlessly about the work he wanted to do, the aesthetic he aspired to— grungy, gritty high fashion—but the actual taking of photographs rarely happened.

She watched waves punish the Amalfi jetty. Crashing against it, sending up spray in high glass curtains. *Like white elephants*, she thought, and rolled her eyes at herself. Last night they'd wanted to walk out along the breakwater, but she'd been too afraid.

"You're a lucky woman," the man said, startling them both.

"Am I," she said, not a question. Teek turned around and took the man in for the first time. Trying to determine whether he represented a threat.

"Obviously," the man said. "You're sitting with the most handsome man in this or any city."

Teek's face broke into a wide, self-conscious smile, and then swiftly reddened. Gratified, but embarrassed. His awkward happiness softened Adney's initial anger at the man's intrusion.

He got up, dragged his chair over. She smiled at him, aware that doing so was a kind of encouragement. But she was bored, and the break in their long, shared silence was not completely unwelcome.

"You're Americans?"

"We are," she said. "Don't hold it against us." He had an accent. She couldn't place it and didn't want to ask.

"Forgive my impertinence," he said. "I'm sorry to be so forward, but I believe it's best to cut right to the chase when it comes to strange offers."

"Offers," Adney said. Teek's blush deepened. "Strange ones."

From a briefcase she hadn't noticed, he took a massive stack of bills.

"I'll give you ten thousand dollars for one hour of your boyfriend's time."

No one said anything. The sound of the sea had dropped out entirely, replaced with the quickening thud of her own blood in her ears. Teek squirmed. She waited for him to reject the offer, but his mouth remained a rigid wobble.

She wondered what he was thinking. Feeling. Her own emotions were strangely absent. As ever, he was unreadable. Was he excited at the thought of being turned into a rent boy? Horrified? Humiliated that the offer was made to her and not to him, as if his own feelings on the matter were irrelevant? Or did that same fact arouse him? It was a constant source of frustration for her, how little Teek said about what was going on inside his head. How he was still a mystery to her, along with all his traumas and fears and hopes and funny stories.

Adney made herself laugh. "Get out of here," she said, because somebody had to reject the offer, and Teek wasn't.

The man turned to Teek. Teek's frown sharpened.

They both had outside hookups, sometimes. It was within the rules they'd fashioned for themselves. And Teek had been with boys. Since they'd started dating, even. Not his favorite thing. One of his friends, usually, drunk and pushy and pleading. Teek was good-natured like that. Eager to make someone happy, if he could.

There were no rules for this.

How had he known they needed the money? But of course they did. They were Americans. Americans were either obscenely rich or super poor, and they were obviously not the former.

"One hour . . . doing what?" Teek asked.

The man put both hands on the table. They were big, coarse. Hairy. The sight of them thrilled her, as if she was the one he wanted to grab hold of. "We're not children here. I don't think I need to spell it out. I'll respect your boundaries, of course, but I'm not paying you to talk."

"Can we have some time to think about it?" Teek asked.

"You cannot," the man said, and this, too, was thrilling to Adney, and the thrill unsettled her. She imagined the most

degrading of demands being issued to her in that same impe-
rious, commanding tone. But of course it wasn't her he'd be
degrading.

Teek looked at her, pretty eyes wide, like, *What the fuck, this
is so bizarre*, but also like, *What do we do?*

A giddy tremor shivered through her. *He's waiting for me to
say Yes or No*, she realized. *This is up to me.*

It would mean eating dinner at all the restaurants they'd
had to pass by the last five nights. Moving from the precarious
cliffside hostel outside of town, high up the unlit hill, and into
one of the grand old hotels in town. Going on to Venice. Being
able to afford delivery, all semester long, when school started
back up. Making a dent in that mountain of loan debt.

They came so easily, the cold equations of pimping her boyfriend.

"Do it if you want to do it," she said, and he frowned, but she
could see the excitement in his eyes. Or at least that's what she
told herself she could see.

"Why the fuck not," Teek said.

The man handed her a stack. "That's half. I'll give him the
other half when he's finished."

He was handsome, she saw, for the first time. Sharp chin;
well-kept beard. Eloquent eyebrows. The slightest shabbiness
around the edges, overall, like he, too, came from a fallen place.

"Bye," Teek said, grinning. He stood, then stooped to kiss her.

"You're sure this is okay?" she asked.

"Of course!" he said, showing teeth. This was him, the eager
boyish thing she'd fallen for—but it was also not him, or not
the him she'd known. Another facet revealed: the fact that he'd
sell himself. Like when she learned he smoked. She liked it, she
thought. She hoped.

"Be careful," she said, and then they were gone.

The woman behind the bar smiled at her. *She knows*, Adney thought. *She saw it all in our faces.* But she knew that was illogical. If they had been in America, the woman would have come over, filled her coffee cup, but they weren't, so Adney had to get up to fetch another espresso.

A long, narrow mirror stretched along the back wall. Brand new, with beveled edges. Adney imagined an ancient one before it, broken in a brawl or tiny non-newsworthy earthquake. She watched their reflections, the old woman's and hers—two broad noses, one Roman and one pure New York—two survivors of shattered empires. One gone two thousand years, the other so recently most people hadn't noticed it yet. About the same height. Would her black hair go gray as spectacularly as this woman's had? Easy to imagine them as avatars of each other, or this woman with deft arthritic hands as a future version of herself.

Back at her table, she tried and failed several times to lose herself in the book she'd brought, but it was proving impossible to think of anything other than what was happening upstairs. Would the man want to fuck Teek, or would he want Teek to fuck him? Would it be vanilla, or very very not?

More worrisome was wondering how Teek would be, when he came downstairs. Would this push him back into one of his glum, silent, blue periods? Or would he return buoyed up, excited, energized in a way that sex with her had not been able to do for him lately? And which would be worse?

She took a cigarette out of the pack he'd left on the table. Held it up in the woman's direction; she shrugged. Adney lit it, sucked in smoke, held it in her mouth. Did not inhale. Blew it out in a slow, narrow billow.

An hour passed fast. Or maybe it wasn't that long at all. Maybe they finished far sooner. Teek came down alone, back pocket bulging. Walking with no discernible limp or other evidence of trauma. Smiling.

"Hey," she said when he lowered his face to her. She flinched, afraid of what his lips might taste like, and that made him laugh, and then he kissed her, and they tasted like nothing.

Teek smiled quizzically, possibly noticing she'd smoked. "Shall we go on to the church?" he asked.

He left a lot of money on the table and winked at the woman on their way out. For the first time, Adney noticed how she frowned at him.

Cold wind came off the water. Late afternoon by then. Dark clouds piling up over the ocean. He took her hand and they walked into the ancient, tattered city.

"Are you okay?" she asked.

"Sure am," he said, and squeezed her hand.

"How . . . was it?"

"Fine," he said.

"Did he—did you—"

"Cool if we don't talk about it right now?" Teek asked. "I mean, I get it, you have the right to know everything that went down and I'll totally tell you, just, not right now?"

"Of course," she said, and leaned in to rest her head on his shoulder. Something about it was off, though. Their heads did not fit together the way they normally did. His posture seemed somehow poorer.

"You're okay, though, right? Really okay?"

"Super okay." He kissed the top of her head.

Women watched them go, from several stories up. Clothes shook on laundry lines. Streets split, narrowed, became tunnels, opened up again. She wondered if she'd be able to tell whether the disputed Caravaggio was real or not. And whether it would be good, even if it wasn't real.

But the church was closed, in contradiction of the clearly posted hours, and with no sign to say why.

"Shit," she said, and sat down on a stone square that once helped men up onto horses. Already a smell of garlic frying in olive oil was filling the air. Dinnertime was close, and so was darkness. They'd have to climb up the steep road to the south, get their stuff from the hostel, come back to find a hotel. Her feet hurt from thinking about it.

"You're so beautiful when you're sad," he said, uncapping his camera. The compliment was uncharacteristic. Her face showed it, and she heard the shutter snap.

"I'm a world-famous photographer," he said, smiling, squatting. "And you're a supermodel who suddenly became a recluse at the height of her fame. This is your first shoot in two years."

A wide, warm smile shivered through her, but smiling would not have been in keeping with the character she'd been given. She forced herself to purse her lips. Pout. "How could I pass up the chance to work with you? In spite of your reputation. What's the shoot?"

"Cigarette ad," he said, tossing his pack to her.

The game was welcome, but it, too, was uncharacteristic. She shook one loose, held it in her fingers, extended her arm in front of her as elegantly as she could. Arched her back artfully. Shutter snaps came in quick succession and she moved her body slightly after each one. Curled a finger, cocked a smile. Raised an eyebrow. Flicked a foot.

It was like sex, a little. The way it warmed her up. When was the last time he'd made her feel that way, outside of bed? At a party, she recalled. At the end of the semester. He'd beckoned her over, told a semicircle of his friends about her print-making. Fake posters for fake seventies bands.

Where had it come from, this energy, this excitement? The

ability to take pictures, when he hadn't in so long? What had that guy done to him?

Adney should have been grateful, but she wasn't. In a slow unfurling, the tiny hairs along her spine stood up.

"There's a crocodile," he said.

"For the shoot," she said, good at this game. "Brilliant. Must have been costly."

He waved his hand. "The client is filthy rich with lung-cancer money. Let them pay to make our dreams real. To bring our brilliant art into the world."

"Where is it?" she asked.

"Out on the breakwater," he said.

"Really," she said, scared, excited. They headed back down the way they had come.

"Stop," he said, at a barrow overflowing with lemons, and had her pose there. Clasping one with both hands. Sfusato—the oversized Amalfi Coast lemons that local farmers had created over the course of centuries, breeding together local bitter oranges with tiny inedible lemons from Arab traders. The trees grew everywhere in the stone city and the high hills around it. Stalls sold soaps, candy, pastries, and pasta infused with lemon essence.

"Magnificent," he said, when she kissed it.

And that was when the thought came, bursting fully formed in her brain.

Preposterous. Irrational. But certain. The hairs standing on end all over her body said so.

This isn't Teek.

"Yessss," he said, at the way her face suddenly became something else. Thinking her horror wasn't hers; was the character's.

I've never heard him use the word magnificent *in all our time together.*

"Brilliant," said the boy with the camera as she stared past its lens and into the familiar green flecks of his hazel eyes.

They swapped bodies. That man pulled Teek out of his skin as easily as Teek shucked that oyster from its shell. Slid himself in. Young again; alive and energetic and beautiful.

It was easy, telling herself to stop being stupid. Things like that couldn't happen. She smiled, and he stepped forward.

"Goose bumps," he said, taking an extreme close-up of her shoulder.

"It's cold," she said.

"Crocodiles hate the cold," he said.

She succeeded in suppressing a shiver when he took her hand. Was his grip different? Tighter? Gentler?

They stopped for pictures along the way. She posed with ancient statues, steep staircase streets. She watched the water wrinkle in the distance. But she couldn't shake the thought now that it had entered her head. She laughed out loud at the absurdity of her certainty. But the certainty did not disappear when she laughed at it.

He didn't buy Teek's body for an hour with that money. He bought it for forever.

"Do you remember the first thing you ever said to me?" she asked.

"Of course," he said, smiling. "It was at that party, at the Chinese embassy in Moscow. Surrounded by despots and billionaire bureaucrat profiteers, and all their beautiful kept women and boys. Panthers in giant gilded birdcages. You still remember that?"

No, she wanted to say, *not in the game*. But she stopped herself. *I'll be free of this ridiculous suspicion soon enough. And I'll realize I'm stuck with the same Teek as ever, and I'd rather have the world-famous fictional photographer than the glum nonfiction one I've been with for most of the trip.*

He was performing, that was all. Putting on an act for her. One he was eerily good at. A skill set she'd never known about. Maybe neither had he. Maybe he could be a movie star. *Roll with it, Adney*. But the closer they got to the water the colder the wind became, and it stoked the fire of her fear.

"What's the plan?" she asked. "For the crocodile."

"You'll be sprawled across its back," he said. "Luxuriant. Regal. An empress."

"Like Avedon," she said, citing his favorite photographer. Trying to prompt a response from the Teek that she knew. "The famous photo, with the elephants. Dovima, arms out, bent, upraised, like the queen of the night."

"He's overrated."

They passed the restaurant, built into the side of the wall that had protected the city from sixteenth-century pirates. No sign of the man. Storm clouds bigger, closer. The woman was mopping. She waved to Adney.

They reached the breakwater way too soon. Waves high and loud against the rocks. His shutter snapped on her look of apprehension.

"Where's the crocodile?" she asked, stalling for time.

"Ugh," he said. "It's a whole thing, you would not believe. We spent seven thousand dollars on it, and my idiot assistant was unprepared for how hard it pulled. Yanked the leash right out of his hands. Escaped into the sea."

"Oh no," she said, sad for the imaginary crocodile. "It's so cold. It'll die for sure."

"Maybe," the photographer said. "But it might be glitchy from radiation or GMOs or something. Maybe it'll be very well suited to the cold Tyrrhenian Sea. Grow to immense size by snapping up sunbathing tourists. Be the scourge of the Amalfi Coast."

She nodded, then gestured commandingly to the breakwater.

Grinning—nervously—the photographer obeyed. Stepped onto the rocks.

When he had gone a short way out, she followed. It was slippery; she had to kick off her shoes. She aimed them into the sea.

"You won't need those again?" he asked.

"I'll buy more."

With my supermodel money.

With the money I got from whoring you out.

With the money I got from selling my boyfriend's body to a monster.

She stared into his eyes. He stared back. His expression softened. He smiled the slightest of smiles. It was trusting, wholesome. Innocent. Eager to please. Almost exactly like Teek's.

She lit a cigarette. Inhaled. Breathed smoke out into the darkening day. Waves soaked her. Soaked him. He held his camera up to keep it safe when the spray surged into them, then lowered it to keep taking pictures.

She finished her cigarette. Lit another one. A wave put it out and she tucked it behind her ear.

"Beautiful," he said, and her certainty faltered. The gentleness in his voice, the reverence—that was Teek, the Teek she only ever heard in bed.

Or was she hearing what she wanted to hear? Constructing a narrative where she was not a monster? Not an accomplice to an unfathomable crime. She saw the two of them on the beach for the next week. Clasping hands on the plane ride home. She saw the next semester, and all the ones after that. Life beyond college. The two of them, together, and she forever wondering whether it was really him in there.

Lightning struck, a long purple crack opening in the eggshell of the sky. So close, the thunder arrived almost immediately after.

"Teek," she gasped, fear forcing her out of character.

"Who's Teek?"

He's upstairs, she thought. *Gasping on the floor of a strange hotel room, trapped in a dying body. He's trying to call for help. I'm his only hope. And I'm out here with this monster, trying to tell myself I'm crazy.*

"You're ludicrous!" she shouted, not to him. He laughed, and so did she. There was that warmth again, in their laughing together.

Lights trembled, down the coast. Other cities, full of other lives. She turned to face them. Three-quarter profile; cigarette behind the ear aimed at the camera. Mouth open slightly in apprehension, maybe exhilaration.

That's the one, she thought, when she heard him (*whoever he is*) take the picture.

And soon we'll be back in the hotel room. And bright fluorescent lights will whisk all this stupidity out of my head. We'll make love and I'll know for sure that it's him. In the morning, we'll post these pictures. Add captions in the voices of our supermodel and superstar photographer.

But would sex truly answer her question? They were still new enough to have surprises up their sleeves, to try a new trick from time to time that might delight or disappoint. If he behaved differently, could she be certain?

Well, even if it doesn't convince me, in the morning the game will be over. I can quiz him, and he won't have a fictional photographer to hide behind. I'll find out if it's really Teek.

And what would she do if it wasn't? Or if she still wasn't sure?

Thunder rumbled, an impenetrable answer.

"You're magnificent," the photographer said, lowering the camera. Again, their eyes locked. Something conspiratorial kindled. Love meant walking beside someone you would never truly know.

Her mom would have a fit when the pictures were posted, seeing her out on the breakwater with those waves crashing all around her. *My helpless, innocent girl.* And her friends would all wonder how drunk she'd had to get to go out there. Strangers would comment on how her wet shirt clung to her.

They'll all see someone different, she thought, *but none of those women will be me.*

vii.

Who is looking out at me from those eyes? Who lives behind that beautiful face?

"If I tell you something, boy," he says, squatting so his eyes are level with mine, "will you promise to believe me?"

I can't promise that. But I do.

THE BEASTS WE WANT TO BE

Two things were wrong with the Spasskaya assessment. The first was the painting: a tiny square in a simple frame, something I barely noticed at the time, but which would go on to cause us so much suffering. The second was the woman.

Wailing greeted us when we arrived, almost at midnight. Assessment teams had to come without warning. Snow fell in great marching waves, helpless in the hands of the wind off the Moscow River. Barely three weeks old, the winter of 1924 seemed to know how desperate and hungry we were, and to be conspiring with the Western imperialists to slaughter us.

Twelve people lived in the Spasskaya mansion. Mere blocks from the Kremlin, big enough that thirty families would be moved in once we had stripped it. Our soldiers herded those twelve fat parasites into one room and encircled them while we did our work.

They had been expecting us, of course. Every aristocrat and landlord and other assorted enemy of the people could anticipate a visit from an assessment team. We came in the night, and we stole the things we could sell abroad.

Fabergé eggs and German expressionist sketches and errant Rembrandts passed through my hands; decadent filth that nonetheless could be turned into tens of thousands of rubles to feed the starving Soviet state. A watercolor by Kandinsky could buy us ten cows. The engagement ring of a century-dead empress could bring back two tractors. And these parasites, every one of them, actually believed they deserved these foul treasures bought with other men and women's sweat and blood. No matter where we went in the mansion, we could hear them wailing.

I didn't like it anymore, when they wept. Joy in the suffering of others was the first habit Apolek broke me of, sparing me a couple hundred hours in a Pavlov Box in the process. Class enemies saw us coming and attacked, or begged, or burst into tears, but I no longer singled them out for special brutality.

"Lenin says we need to punish the parasites," I had said, the first day I was assigned to Apolek's detail, when he urged restraint.

"Not with violence," he had said. "Not with cruelty."

Apolek was a blond and ruddy peasant, younger than me, the youngest assessment team leader in the Red Army. Soft-spoken, earnest, above human emotion. I was an illiterate, bloodthirsty street urchin, the son of steel workers who starved to death in the famine of 1910. Plucked out of the orphanage by the Ministry of Human Engineering, I was reconditioned into a species of man they said was "slightly smarter than a dog but just as vicious."

"They treated us with violence and cruelty," I said, pouting, plotting.

"Do it if you want," he said. "We'll see which one of us Volkov puts in a Box."

Back in the orphanage I'd beaten boys like him bloody on an almost daily basis, but his words were well-chosen. I'd just emerged from a Pavlov Box, suffering unending hours of electric shocks and chemical burns, pharmaceutical fumes and super-high-speed recordings, three times a day for months and months. And the mere possibility of escaping further torment was worth a try.

And Apolek was right, of course, as he would always be, about everything. I didn't understand it, how a man as savage as Commander Volkov would reward us for not being savage, but I didn't need to understand. I just had to do what Apolek told me.

"The Soviet Union needs beasts," he said, after that first assessment, carefully logging newly nationalized statues in the basement of the Kremlin Armoury. "It needs savage men to die in distant border skirmishes, or to torture kulaks. Is a beast what you want to be?"

"No," I mumbled, and in that moment I saw that I didn't want that at all.

"What do you want to be, Nikolai?"

I shrugged. I looked at Apolek, too dazed to hide the desperation on my face. I wanted him to answer my question for me.

"But not a beast," he said.

"No."

"We'll work on that, then."

I was nineteen and he was seventeen, but in that moment I gladly and wholeheartedly attached myself to him as his protégé. And while the lean and hairy Commander Volkov came sniffing around our unit several times a week, for a year and a half he never found a reason to Box me up again.

Eight of them accompanied us on our runs, to deal with the parasites when the parasites fought back. All of them Broken. Boys who'd been left too long in the Boxes, or test subjects who snapped beneath the weight of some new regimen of flashing lights and film strips and toxic fumes and prototype medicine. The Broken were useful for the terror they caused, and for the savage violence they would break into with the proper command from their conditioned leader. They were also useful as a constant warning to other revolutionary soldiers.

There was no more terrifying prospect, for those of us who had passed through a Pavlov Box, than the thought of being locked in one with no hope of reprieve. I dreamed of it endlessly. Probably it was programmed into all of us. Gnawing my lips open, screaming until I gagged on my own blood and puke and pounding my fists against spiked metal walls until the skin was all gone. Begging and pleading while the machines worked me over—and knowing that it would not end until my mind was completely gone.

I followed Apolek through the Spasskaya mansion, scuffing mud into carpet that had long ago ceased to be beautiful.

"Worthless," he said, after walking past ten gloomy paintings of Old Testament patriarchs.

"How so?" I asked. "They look nice to me."

"The names," he said. "The painters are not notable. Collectors in the West will only pay for the work of famous artists."

I never paid any attention to the signatures scrawled into the corners. Apolek probably told me that ten times before, but my Pavlov-Boxed brain had a hard time holding onto things. And a hard time concentrating, surrounded as I was by the smell of anger all the time.

No two men emerged the same from any one reconditioning regimen. People were too complex. Their own experiences conditioned them to respond to stimuli so differently.

Most reconditioned soldiers came away with "offshoots," unanticipated consequences that could be good or bad. Crippling fears of perfectly harmless sights and sounds, or a sudden faculty for foreign languages, and so on. The social engineers spoke openly of their desire to breed men who could read minds or move objects with only thought, but so far those men only existed in rumor.

I had an offshoot. I could smell violence. I could smell anger, could feel the heat of it wash over someone, before they said a word or even acted. No other emotion had any effect on me. Most of the time it was more of a liability than a gift; standing near an angry crowd could cripple me.

Apolek was a reconditioning marvel, a specimen who emerged from the Pavlov Box with astonishing strength and willpower. That's part of why Volkov gave him so much power so young. Apolek hinted he had conducted other missions, significantly less honorable ones, in which he had distinguished himself. "But that was the beast in me," Apolek said, "and if we are to succeed as men we must not feed the beast."

"I like the worthless paintings," he said tonight. "Especially when they're good. If they're worthless, they'll stay here. It's shortsighted to sell our most beautiful art to the countries that wish us all dead."

"Beauty can't feed people," I said, surprised I needed to spout Bolshevik clichés at him. "'A good pair of boots is worth more to a peasant than all of Shakespeare.'"

"On the contrary," Apolek said, stooping to retrieve something hidden behind a curtain, propped up on the sill of a tall window. "Beauty is as necessary as oxygen. And don't scowl so much, Nikolai. You look like an angry black bear when you do that."

I tried to smile, but Apolek did not see me. He held up a tiny painting, and his eyes widened.

"Jesus," Apolek whispered, reverent as any Old Believer. I stood on tiptoe to see, but it meant nothing to me. Two human-shaped stretches of bare white skin. Tears filled his eyes and then overflowed, and I looked again, but still saw nothing.

A woman watched us from a doorway across the hall, older than us but not by much, dressed all in black. Why was she not with the others? Apolek did not see her. When he took the painting, his lips trembled. Hers went white.

The Broken found her, and brought the woman with the rest of her family to the camps. The Spasskaya assessment was otherwise without incident. No heroics, no bloodshed, and only a handful of art objects worth selling.

I shuffled through my weekend the way I always did: miserably, unsure even of the ground I stood on. My dreams were all of Pavlov Boxes.

Apolek always told me I was lucky to even have a weekend, and I suppose he was right. Soldiers in totalitarian armies rarely get time off, especially in the bloody hunger chaos of the capitol, but Apolek actually treated his team like human beings. To me, a lowly grunt who had been told his whole life that savagery was his only strength, he gave a shocking amount of liberty. And a secretary. He took a big risk in doing all that. Apolek said he saw something in me.

My nightmares had been getting worse. This time I dreamed I was inside a Box, my whole body spasming from electric shocks, and one of them caused my jaw to slam shut with such force that I woke myself up—and found that I had shattered a tooth.

But then, Monday morning, when Apolek normally banished the darkness, I arrived at the Kremlin Armoury and he was not there. This had never happened before; every other day he arrived well before me, to study books on foreign art, or keep up on the latest social engineering successes. Sometimes he slept under his desk.

No one knew the last time he was there. Not even the guards, who barracked there all weekend, remembered seeing him.

I tried to do work. I had assessment deployments to plan out, backlogged incident reports to complete and submit, all the orderly, rational work that Apolek said would help me tame my inner beast. And none of it worked.

I did something I had never done before. I went down to the basement, alone, and consulted the logbook. An entry for every assessment, describing each item seized and a brief notation of the plans for it. I was proud of myself, heaving it down off the high shelf with only a glimmer of suspicion what I was chasing.

Besides the ten worthless Bible scenes, there were no paintings registered under the Spasskaya assessment.

Memory was not an important thing for a grunt, so my own reconditioning had not encouraged it. As a result my mind did not hold memories well, although my body did: weapons work, martial arts, even plumbing and mechanics came easy and stayed. Apolek had tried hard to help me reclaim my memory, by telling me things again and again. Stories. Fairy tales. Dirty jokes. Things that happened to him when he was a child. Some things had stayed. I could hear his voice in my ear, soothing and wise:

"It's a legend. No one knows if it's true or not. One day, an assessment officer found a painting that was simply priceless. A Leonardo thought lost, or something else that any Western museum would ransom half its collection for. Well, the assessment officer who discovered it, he told his commanding officer what he had. And the man murdered him, and erased the painting from the logbook, and fled to Paris. Remember, our superiors are no further from being beasts than we are. Some are a lot closer."

Apolek would never have concealed a painting. If it wasn't there, it was because someone removed it. And maybe removed Apolek as well.

I did not think about it for long. Apolek would have coun-
seled caution, but he was not there to do so. I climbed the stairs
to Volkov's office two at a time. I girded myself for a fight, prepared to barrel past guards and secretaries, but the officer sat
alone in a small room with no door.

"Comrade," he said, eyeing me suspiciously.

"Commander," I said, saluting. "It's Apolek, sir. He's gone."

Volkov frowned. "Barely noon on a Monday," he said. "I am
sure he is merely—"

"No," I said, and stamped my foot. "He's never late. We found
something Friday night. A painting. And it's not in the logbook.
And now he's gone. I think something terrible happened to
him. I think someone—"

His face showed no surprise. Why should he be surprised?
Apolek would have told him about the painting.

"That will be all, Comrade. My men will investigate. I will let
you know if we find anything."

Confronting him had been foolish, I now saw. But without
saying a word, Volkov had already told me everything I needed to
know. Because when I told Volkov that I knew about the painting, and about Apolek's disappearance, the sudden whiff of
anger was so strong it singed my nostrils.

The women's reconditioning camp stank. I don't know why I was
surprised, considering how bad the men's camp smelled. I guess
I thought women were different. It was noisier, too, more full
of anger, more likely to burst into violence. I found her easily
enough. They kept the new arrivals separate for a week, to minimize the spread of infectious disease.

From the bottom drawer of Apolek's desk, precisely where he

had repeatedly told me they would be in the event I ever needed them, I had stolen a stack of command forms upon which he had forged Volkov's signature. I requested an office to myself, and demanded they bring her to me.

"You," the Spasskaya woman said, when she saw me.

I didn't know what to say. Or do. Bow? Shake hands? Apologize? Back at her mansion her beauty had not impressed me, but now it made my hands fidget deep in my pockets.

"I need your help," I said.

The woman tilted her head, as if there must be more to me than she was seeing. Then she nodded. "The painting," she said. "Something happened to it. It's gone."

"How did you know that?"

The woman shrugged. I stepped closer.

I said, "Tell me about the painting."

Somehow, in all the filth and sickness and hunger of that camp, she did not stink. My offshoot, my nose for violence, was not bothered by her. The fear and anger of the place was overwhelming, the rage of thousands of women slowly dying for crimes like being born rich. The stink of it ruptured something in my nose, dripping blood into my gaping mouth.

But the woman smelled like funeral incense, clean and cold and tragic. I had come to interrogate her. Ask her some questions, extract some answers, with steel tools if necessary, and depart. Instead, I wanted terribly to take her with me.

I said, "I know you have no reason to help me. I know you probably hate me. But I need your help. And if you don't come, you'll die in here. And soon."

"I'll come," she said.

Another of Apolek's most important lessons: whatever you do, you should be able to explain why you're doing it. And ask yourself—is this a noble and revolutionary act, or something less honorable? More beastly?

In this case I could ask myself the question, but I couldn't answer it.

Why was I bringing her?

I produced another command form, signed paperwork, and Zinaida Spasskaya was officially my problem. I took her through the tall gates and into a Moscow already bled dry of sunlight.

Did I want to help Zinaida? Did I want her to help me? Did I want to throw her down and tie her up and do terrible things to her? Punish this enemy of the people?

Yes and yes and yes and yes. Apolek was still with me, a faint voice in my ear, but getting fainter. I had to find him fast.

Belorusskaya Station was thick with the screams of metal and men. Food coming in, and soldiers going out. Wheat for the starving millions in the capital, and men to die defending the Polish border. We did not have enough of either.

"Where are we going?" Zinaida asked.

"Stop asking," I said, maybe not so nicely, feeling frustrated because I didn't have a very good answer to her question myself.

Zinaida Spasskaya: thirty-one years old. Widow of Lieutenant Anatoly Spassky, killed in his home in March of 1921. No children.

Why was I bringing her? These were the answers I had come up with:

1. She knew the painting, what it was and what could be done with it;
2. I felt sorry for her, and what would certainly happen to her in the camps;
3. She was beautiful, and I wanted her.

I visited the Red Army guard station, and used their telephone to call the Kremlin Armoury. I'd been away from work for three days and I needed a cover story. This much, Apolek had also taught me. The fact that he didn't have one of his own was another sign that something terrible had happened to him.

"I'm going to Elektrograd," I told my secretary, a shriveled older man who feared me enough to be useful. "I have to oversee the processing of a particular piece of art. Please arrange and submit all the paperwork for me."

"Yes, sir," he said.

"I'd be very grateful for any help you can provide in not allowing Commander Volkov to know anything about this," I said.

"Volkov isn't here," he said. "He left the same day you did."

Elektrograd was the middle ground, where assessment officers met with museum lackeys and middlemen, where papers were signed and money changed hands. It was also where Apolek had his secondary office, where he was most likely to be—if Volkov had not already killed him.

Killed. Merely thinking it made me feel close to cracking.

Zinaida and I huddled together in a darkened boxcar, surrounded by the stink of livestock. I was shocked at how willingly she had come with me, how fearlessly she threw herself into each new leg of the journey. I must have been a slavering vicious brute to her, and yet she was kind to me.

There was a new item on my list of reasons why I took her:

4. Because Zinaida had his softness. His gentleness. His eye for art.

"It's a piece of a larger painting," she said, as I was about to fall asleep. Darkness and the clanging rhythm of the rails had made me drowsy.

"What happened to it?" I asked.

"Someone cut it to shreds."

"Why?"

"Men broke in," she said. "My husband commanded a brigade that was loyal to the Kronstadt rebels. On the night before the Uprising, Bolsheviks got wind of the rebellion and came to take him. He thought they were robbers. He held the painting to his chest, told them if they killed him they'd kill the painting. A soldier with a bayonet sliced them both up."

"Why are you telling me this?"

"I loved my husband," she said. "That painting . . . it's what's left."

Russia rolled by beneath us, changed and twisted.

Elektrograd was empty. A Potemkin village: an instant city constructed on scorched earth in under six months, with no purpose beyond the art sale summits. We arrived between sessions. No Apolek; no painting; no Volkov. A handful of fey museum men haggled over scraps with bleary-eyed assessment officers.

And everywhere we went were red-faced reconditioned soldier lads, conducting extensive inspections of our papers and bumbling attempts at interrogation. I wasn't afraid of them. These boys were soft. They did not know how it was in the capitol. Their hunger weakened them, while ours made us more vicious.

They did not have Volkov's violent voice whispering in their ear as I did. Normally Apolek's real-life voice could drown it out, but now I was alone with my most violent, vile thoughts. Bayonets plunged through eye sockets. Guts spilled. Zinaida spread wide for me.

"What now?" she said, sitting with me on the train platform. Benches had not yet been brought in. The day was almost over. I wanted to punch the concrete until it or my hands shattered.

"Is there someone you can call? At the Ministry?" Zinaida asked.

I frowned into my filthy hands. It would have been so easy to drag her off into the dark and destroy her. I made a list of reasons not to, and it wasn't long.

"Someone from his family, perhaps?"

"He has no one," I said, startled at how fast and hot my hate had risen. I hooked my hand into my belt, to keep from reaching for the dagger that hung there. "No one but me."

"Most ministries have dachas," she said. "Fancy cabins far from the city, to reward their workers with occasional vacations."

"How the hell would you know?"

"Maybe Apolek went to one of those," Zinaida said.

I hated the sound of his name in her mouth. How had she managed to preserve so much class, so much dignity, after all she had been through? Even in the tattered black dress from the women's camp, whose past several occupants had almost certainly died terribly in it, she looked noble. Apolek said that lust and violence were the beast in us. I felt them both, every time I looked at her.

"What did you do with your art?" I asked, pulling myself back. "Apolek said you must have had an incredible collection, yet we found nothing of value."

"We gave most of the paintings away," Zinaida said. "To our servants. I know you think we were heartless oppressors, but we loved them, and we wanted to give them something invaluable."

I thought of Apolek, wanting the great art to remain in Russia. These were impulses I could not grasp, like why the girl in the fairy tale touches the spindle even though it will obviously prick her finger and make her fall asleep. I was missing something. Something important.

"What would you do with it?" I asked. "If you could get it back?"

"Never let it out of my grip," she said. "Never stop staring at it.

Do you know the story of Narcissus? He died, wasted away, staring into a pool of water at his own reflection. That would be me."

"What makes it so valuable?"

"You looked at it," she said. "I saw you. In the home you stole from me. What did you see?"

I shrugged. "People. Naked. Or something."

Zinaida looked at me. "Who is your favorite painter?"

Twilight softened her grief, made her more beautiful. I made my hands fists, to keep from seizing her. "I don't have one."

"Then I cannot explain to you what made that painting what it was."

Time passed. I said: "Please?"

I waited till she was asleep to call the Kremlin Armoury. I left Zinaida where she lay, curled on the cold cement, and there was comfort in her helplessness.

Midnight. Elektrograd was silent except for the cockroach-clicking of the telegraph machine inside the station.

You broke me, I whispered to the wind, to Apolek.

The station agent did not want to make the call. A pudgy coward, he had a poor understanding of how the telephone worked, and I sensed they were very liberal with their Pavlov Boxes out in the backwoods corners of the empire where no one could see.

"Hello?" said my secretary, already terrified. Babies cried and people squawked in the background. The late-night call to his collective flat had caused the precise ruckus I desired.

"Go to the office," I said.

"It's—"

He fumbled loudly, perhaps for his watch, but I barked: "You're finished, if you don't call me back within two hours with the information I need."

I could hear the scritch of pencil on paper as he took down

my request. An hour later he called me, from the office, from the other side of Moscow. The Asset Maximization department of the Ministry of Culture owned two dachas, a mile apart, a day's journey from Elektrograd, for high officials involved in art exchange summits. One of them was already signed out. To Commander Volkov.

I slammed the phone down hard, as if my loyal secretary would feel the blow on his back.

"It doesn't work," Apolek told me, eight days before he vanished.

"What doesn't work?" I asked.

Midnight; homeless clerks snoring over heaps of paper in the Ministry. Hallways smoky from soldiers burning old documents to keep warm.

"Reconditioning. The Pavlov Boxes. The effects . . . they're unstable. After a while, men who've been reconditioned begin to experience severe physical and mental side effects. Muscle spasms, severe insomnia, immune system failure. Suicidal tendencies. Madness."

"How bad can it get?"

"Bad," he said.

"Dead bad?"

Apolek nodded.

I didn't ask how he knew. I never did. From the day we met I believed that Apolek knew absolutely everything.

"Even now, they're building tens of thousands of Boxes, all over the country. Putting boys of all ages into them. Trying millions of different reconditioning regimens. Creating all kinds of monsters. All kinds of terrifying offshoots. Volkov thinks he can fix it with more reconditioning, so whenever it starts to happen to one of his men, he throws them back into a Box for several days. It makes the symptoms go away, but only for a very little while, and then they come back much worse."

"Okay," I said, because I didn't know what to do or think or say. It had never occurred to me to doubt the Boxes, or reconditioning, or the whole grand Soviet plan of human perfectibility.

"I shouldn't have told you this," Apolek said, burrowing deeper into the fur-lined jacket he had stolen.

"So . . . all the men who've been reconditioned . . . they'll . . ."

Apolek nodded. His eyes showed pain, loneliness.

"All of us?" I asked.

"All of us."

"What can we do about it?"

"I don't know, Nikolai."

Which he had never said before.

He clasped my neck with one hand. "I used to think we could put the pieces back together ourselves. Help each other survive this. You know? I used to really believe that."

Dreams of blood woke me up, savage gleeful glorious violence, human bodies shredded like paper.

"They say you can't cry," she said, sitting up and watching the fire. "After you've been reconditioned. Is that true?"

"I don't know," I said, sheepishly shifting my body so the outline of my erection would be invisible beneath the blankets. And that's when I saw that both my arms were sticky with blood, from where I had scratched the skin off.

Zinaida said, "But you haven't. Since."

"No."

"Do you love your work?" she asked. I had no sense of what time it was. Faint light edged the horizon, but it could have been a distant city.

"I guess," I said.

"What do you love about it?"

I shrugged.

"Do you love helping the great Soviet state create a proletarian paradise?" Zinaida asked.

"Sure," I said, and she laughed.

"He is why," she said. "Tell me about him."

"Apolek," I said, and saying the name actually helped. "He's my best friend."

"Why?"

Why. So many questions I could never even ask myself, let alone answer. "I'm missing something," I said. "Apolek was helping me find it."

"What kind of something?"

"I don't know. Something essential."

"But he had it," she said.

"He never knew his father," I said. "I think that's the secret. His mother was impregnated and abandoned. That's why he's such a good man. He said men are beasts by nature, ugly, violent creatures. Women are different."

She snorted, delicately. "He seemed to hold quite a position of power, for someone so young."

"Apolek was a prodigy," I said. "A reconditioning marvel. They started him small. With young children, it either works very well or not at all. Volkov gave him the keys to the kingdom."

"And you? How young did they start you?"

The orphanage. The stink of shit and puke, all the time, everywhere. The men from the Ministry, who chose ten out of a hundred by watching us all fight and picking the most savage. I was twelve and I would have slaughtered every one of those boys for the chance to get out of there.

"It doesn't matter," I said. "I'm not like him. I'm an animal. He's a man."

"Even wolves mourn their dead," she said.

"He's not dead," I said.

"People die."

"But not him."

"Why not him?"

"Why are you here?" I said, spitting out the words. "You hate us. You won't get your painting back. Your stupid husband will still be dead. When we're finished here, you're going back to that camp. So why are you here with me?"

"Because you dragged me along."

"Yeah, well. Go. Leave if you want to."

"I'd be dead in a day," she said, and then touched her hand to the buzz-cut on top of my head. "You are so young."

"Don't touch me," I said. Unconvincingly.

"You never felt manipulated?" she asked, standing up, stretching long lovely arms. "By the men who put you in that Box? By the government? By him?"

I lowered my head. All the sentences in my head involved swearing, and angry as I was I knew that swearing was wrong. It was one of Apolek's simplest rules.

She put a hand on top of my head, then tilted it back until she could see my eyes. "I was a dancer," she said.

I looked away. "So what."

"I'd like to dance for you."

I said, "Do what you want. But if you think you can mess with my mind so much you can steal your stupid painting when we find it, you're wrong."

What did I know or care about dance? Who cared what the body did? But I watched her. She moved like a phantom, dancing. Her body was smoke, the flimsy, ugly dress an extension of the wind. Her body made its own music. My head filled with sad stories and long-buried lullabies.

"That was wonderful," I said, an unaccustomed lump in my throat. Dimly, dumbly, it occurred to me to wonder, really wonder, why she was doing any of this. I felt like I had a lot of weeping to do, and I did not know how to start.

An eight-hour walk, from the station to the dacha. Scorched skeletal trees on both sides of us. The cold here was crueler, cutting through even the thick clothes I commandeered from the town's tiny army depot. We found Volkov's dacha and crept up close. He lay asleep on a couch, camouflaged by empty bottles. All of the tracks in the snow seemed to come from one pair of boots.

He was alone, except for the Broken soldiers who slept obediently in his truck.

"The other dacha, then," she said, and started in that direction. I followed, frightened by her zeal. If Apolek was out here, so close to Volkov, were they working together? My old hate for the commander flared up again, brighter now, from jealousy. Ice cracked under our feet. We were not stealthy.

Night came on us fast, while we walked. Many times we were sure we heard someone following us, but sound moved strangely through the trees. We could see the dacha, a dark spot at the end of the road, but the closer we got, the more it faded into the spreading night. No lights were on inside.

"You asked why I came," Zinaida said, stopping as we climbed the walkway to the front door. "Do you still want to know the answer?"

"No," I said, pulling her inside by the hand, and kissing her hard, even as I nudged the front door with my foot and found it unlocked, too excited about what we would find inside to care about anything else.

Zinaida lit a candle. We watched our breath cloud out into the frigid darkness of the dacha. I looked for a lamp, and found three. I laughed out loud, when they were all lit, at the sheer size and splendor of the place. So much empty space we were wasting.

His rucksack lay abandoned beside the door, spilling out books like entrails.

"You look upstairs," she said.

He wasn't in the first of the three bedrooms. A window was open. A curtain flapped. As if the whole place was waiting. As if the murdered count who lived there would come through the door in the morning and bring summer with him.

The light from my lamp found Apolek in the second bedroom, in a wine-colored velvet chair, with the painting in his lap.

"Apolek!" I said, and rushed forward, but he did not move.

"What is a painting in the dark?" he said. On a table beside him stood a glass of ice.

"What happened?" I asked. "Why did you leave?"

His coldness kept me from coming closer. And asking: why are you sitting here in the freezing dark? I wondered if Apolek was a ghost.

"I spent so long in darkness," he said. "I looked at the paintings, but I didn't see them."

"What did Volkov say to you?" I asked.

Apolek made a perplexed face, but it passed quickly. He was still transfixed by the painting. I imagined him frozen there for days, wasting away and shivering himself to nothing while he stared at it. My Soviet Narcissus.

He said, "Volkov didn't say anything to me. I left that night, straight from the Spasskaya mansion, without speaking with him."

"He doesn't know about the painting?"

"Not from me," Apolek said.

"You haven't spoken with him since?" I asked.

"How would I do that?"

"Christ, Apolek, he's followed you. You didn't know?"

Apolek looked up at me for the first time. "He's here?"

"He's at the dacha at the end of the lane," I said, still wanting to rush over to him, still not daring to.

"He's keeping an eye on me," Apolek said, standing up, resigned. He didn't say anything for a long time.

"Come back," I said. "We can work this out."

"Not after this," he said. I thought he meant his own foolish flight from Moscow, but he was staring at the painting.

"I need you," I said, at last. "I'm not finished . . . becoming. I'm stuck halfway between man and beast."

"So shall you always be," he said. Apolek reached out his arm and touched a candle to mine, lighting up a gaunt face shadowed by a surprisingly thick growth of beard. "So are we all."

From outside, I heard the rumble of a truck approaching.

"Why did you do it?" I asked. "You know what they'll do to you. To throw it all away—"

He handed me the painting.

I looked at it.

This time, I could see. I saw. I hadn't before. For four, maybe five full seconds, I understood.

Two bodies, male and female, mostly naked, grappling. Was it love? Was it violence? Where did they fit into the larger composition, now lost, severed by the bayonet of a brutal long-ago soldier?

But the story did not matter. What mattered were the bodies. The twist and reach of the limbs. The glow of the flesh. The flush of the cheeks; the wideness of the mouth. Nothing mattered more than what the body wanted. And the body did not just want sex. It wanted friendship. It wanted beauty.

Looking at the painting, I understood everything. It was like what I felt when Zinaida danced, but turned up ten thousand-fold. I would have risked what Apolek risked. Life on earth as a human made sense. We are beasts, and we will never understand what we need, what we want, and why, but we will always obey.

My head spun so fast I almost fell over. Zinaida had come up the stairs; stood beside me. One hand on my shoulder. As mesmerized as I was by the painting.

"You brought her here?" Apolek asked, pulling away the painting. I felt her stiffen, when it was gone.

"Yeah," I said. "I took her. From the camp. She would have died in there. And I needed—"

"Why did you bring her here?"

I had never heard fear in Apolek's voice before. My head spun worse.

"Because I—"

Zinaida stepped forward. Her sadness fell away, a wedding veil no longer needed. In that moment, for the first time, grief was not stronger than rage. And I smelled what I should have smelled the whole time, except that it was hidden behind her sadness and my own blind failure to understand who she was and what she wanted. I smelled an all-consuming violence, a blood-lust strong enough to make all other concerns insignificant.

"You," I said to Apolek. "You're the one who killed her husband—"

But he wouldn't move. And I couldn't. Only Zinaida moved, and she moved like a phantom dancing. She darted in, ducked low to snag the dagger from my belt, spun fast around him. One lightning-swift swing of the arm was enough. Blood gurgled out of Apolek's open throat.

I crumpled to the floor with him. I held his hand. I stared into his eyes. I waited for something, some wise final words or a sudden rush of complete understanding as his spirit left his body and entered mine. I got nothing. I don't know how long I knelt there. Until Volkov came through the door, with four Broken soldiers close behind him.

"No," he said, and then said it again and again, faster and faster.

Volkov pointed at Zinaida, standing there with the bloody blade, and the Broken stepped forward. The stink of his rage made me gag. "Rip her to shreds," he said, and although I screamed for them to stop, that's exactly what they did. At least they did not smell of rage. The Broken kill dispassionately.

I wondered if my offshoot would survive. If—after Volkov took me back to Moscow and locked me in a Box until my spirit shattered, and I emerged as one of the Broken—my sense of smell would still be with me. I hoped it wouldn't. I hoped nothing would.

My head stopped hurting. I looked at my hands, and knew—my reconditioning was gone. The painting had wiped it away, cleanly and swiftly, and leaving no fatal time bomb inside me.

That's why Apolek left with it. He looked at it, and felt the burden of his reconditioning break. He wouldn't have known how, or what magnificent artist had created such a thing. All he knew was what it did, and what could be done with it. Was he going to sell it to our enemies? Move like a phantom from our western border east, showing it to every soldier along the way, defusing all those ticking bombs inside us?

I wouldn't die. I wouldn't break down like a faulty machine, like every other soldier spat out of a Pavlov Box.

Volkov crossed the carnage, to kneel beside Apolek. His rage was gone. He held the boy's head in both hands. I still had my superhuman sense of smell, somehow stronger than ever. I had never been able to smell grief before.

"I thought you hated him," I said.

"He hated me," the commander said, his hair and eyes as black as mine. "He's always hated me. I tried to make him into something he's not."

I swallowed, several times. "You're his father."

"Yes."

"He knew?" I asked.

"He did not."

Dagger and painting were filthy with blood. I picked them both up. I handled the painting like Medusa's head, turning it away from my line of sight, and Volkov's too. I wondered what the Broken would see if they saw it. I felt certain it could bring them back to life. It could save us all, the tens and hundreds of thousands of fine young men who would otherwise break down and die under the weight of their botched reconditioning.

"Is there a special Box?" I asked. "A special process, to turn a man into one of the Broken?"

Volkov looked at me, his red face comprehending nothing.

I did not dare to look at the painting again. If I did, I'd lose my nerve. With the dagger, I cut a long slit from top to bottom of the painting, then squatted to remove the glass flute from the lamp and hold the canvas square face down atop the flame.

"I'm ready," I said.

"Ready for what?"

"To be Broken."

Promise me you'll make it quick, I wanted to say, but I didn't say it. I didn't deserve quick. I had unwittingly, idiotically helped destroy my best friend, and I deserved to suffer. But I hoped he'd do it soon. I wanted to stop feeling what I felt.

I stood. He stood. We were so close. Flames from the burning painting singed the hair from my hand, and still I held on to it. I held on until the burning was too much to bear. Now that it was gone, definitively destroyed, I realized what I had done—that without the painting the Pavlov Boxes would quickly cripple the state, bring it to its knees as its best young men died in droves—but that wasn't why I did it. I destroyed the painting because it killed Apolek.

"Oh, Nikolai, no," he said. His face shattered, crumpled. "You're all that's left of him."

Volkov fell forward, his arms tightening around me and his hairy face wet against my neck. He heaved with sobs. My body remembered, and I felt unaccustomed water spilling from my eyes. I had forgotten how hot tears were. We stood like that, dumb and broken, two beasts grieving.

viii.

"I can take people's stories," he says. "Any time I make skin-to-skin contact, I can reach in and take something—a memory, a tale."

This man's eyes are wild and laughing in the dark. I wait for the punchline. There isn't one.

CALVED

My son's eyes were broken. Emptied out. Frozen over. None of the joy or gladness were there. None of the tears. Normally I'd return from a job and his face would split down the middle with happiness, seeing me for the first time in three months. Now it stayed flat as ice. His eyes leapt away the instant they met mine. His shoulders were broader and his arms more sturdy, and lone hairs now stood on his upper lip, but his eyes were all I saw.

"Thede," I said, grabbing him.

He let himself be hugged. His arms hung limply at his sides. My lungs could not fill. My chest tightened from the force of all the never-let-me-go bear hugs he had given me over the course of the past fifteen years, and would never give again.

"You know how he gets when you're away," his mother had said, on the phone, the night before, preparing me. "He's a teenager now. Hating your parents is a normal part of it."

I hadn't listened, then. My hands and thighs still ached from months of straddling an ice saw; my hearing was worse with every trip; a slip had cost me five days' work and five days' pay and five days' worth of infirmary bills; I had returned to a sweat-smelling bunk in an illegal room I shared with seven other iceboat workers—and none of it mattered because in the morning I would see my son.

"Hey," he murmured emotionlessly. "Dad."

I stepped back, turned away until the red ebbed out of my face. Spring had come and the city had lowered its photoshade. It felt good, even in the cold wind.

"You guys have fun," Lajla said, pressing money discretely into my palm. I watched her go with a rising sense of panic. *Bring back my son*, I wanted to shout, *the one who loves me. Where is he? What have you done with him? Who is this surly creature?* Below us, through the ubiquitous steel grid that held up Qaanaaq's two million lives, black Greenland water sloshed against the locks of our floating city.

Breathe, Dom, I told myself, and eventually I could. *You knew this was coming. You knew one day he would cease to be a kid.*

"How's school?" I asked.

Thede shrugged. "Fine."

"Math still your favorite subject?"

"Math was never my favorite subject."

I was pretty sure that it had been, but I didn't want to argue.

"What's your favorite subject?"

Another shrug. We had met at the sea lion rookery, but I could see at once that Thede no longer cared about sea lions. He stalked through the crowd with me, his face a frozen mask of anger.

I couldn't blame him for how easy he had it. So what if he didn't live in the Brooklyn foster-care barracks, or work all day at the solar-cell plant school? He still had to live in a city that hated him for his dark skin and ice-grunt father.

"Your mom says you got into the Institute," I said, unsure even of what that was. A management school, I imagined. A big deal for Thede. But he only nodded.

At the fry stand, Thede grimaced at my clunky Swedish. The counter girl shifted to a flawless English, but I would not be cheated of the little bit of the language that I knew. "French fries and coffee for me and my son," I said, or thought I did, because she looked confused and then Thede muttered something and she nodded and went away.

And then I knew why it hurt so much, the look on his face. It wasn't that he wasn't a kid anymore. I could handle him growing up. What hurt was how he looked at me: like the rest of them look at me, these Swedes and grid city natives for whom I would forever be a stupid New York refugee, even if I did get out five years before the Fall.

Gulls fought over food thrown to the lions. "How's your mom?"

"She's good. Full manager now. We're moving to Arm Three, next year."

His mother and I hadn't been meant to be. She was born here, her parents Black Canadians employed by one of the big Swedish construction firms that built Qaanaaq back when the Greenland Melt began to open up the interior for resource extraction and grid cities starting sprouting all along the coast. They'd kept her in public school, saying it would be good for a future manager to be able to relate to the immigrants and workers she'd one day command, and they were right. She even fell for one of them, a fresh-off-the-boat North American taking tech classes, but wised up pretty soon after she saw how hard it was to raise a kid on an ice worker's pay. I had never been mad at her. Lajla was right to leave me, right to focus on her job. Right to build the life for Thede I couldn't.

"Why don't you learn Swedish?" he asked a French fry, unable to look at me.

"I'm trying," I said. "I need to take a class. But they cost money, and anyway I don't have—"

"Don't have time. I know. Han's father says people make time for the things that are important for them." Here his eyes *did* meet mine, and held, sparkling with anger and abandonment.

"Han one of your friends?"

Thede nodded, eyes escaping.

Han's father would be Chinese, and not one of the laborers who helped build this city—all of them went home to hardship-job rewards. He'd be an engineer or manager for one of the extraction firms. He would live in a nice house and work in an office. He would be able to make choices about how he spent his time.

"I have something for you," I said, in desperation.

I hadn't brought it for him. I carried it around with me, always. Because it was comforting to have it with me, and because I couldn't trust that the men I bunked with wouldn't steal it.

Heart slipping, I handed over the NEW YORK F CKING CITY T-shirt that was my most—my only—prized possession. Thin as paper, soft as baby bunnies. My mom had made me scratch the letter U off it before I could wear the thing to school. And Little Thede had loved it. We made a big ceremony of putting it on only once a year, on his birthday, and noting how much he had grown by how much it had shrunk on him. Sometimes if I stuck my nose in it and breathed deeply enough, I could still find a trace of the laundromat in the basement of my mother's building. Or the brake-screech stink of the subway. What little was left of New York City was inside that shirt. Parting with it meant something, something huge and irrevocable.

But my son was slipping through my fingers. And he mattered more than the lost city where whatever else I was—starving, broke, an urchin, a criminal—I belonged.

"Dad," Thede whispered, taking it. And here, at last, his eyes came back. The eyes of a boy who loved his father. Who didn't care that his father was a thick-skulled, obstinate immigrant grunt. Who believed his father could do anything. "Dad. You love this shirt."

But I love you more, I did not say. *Than anything*. Instead: "It'll fit you just fine now." And then: "Enough sea lions. Beam fights?"

Thede shrugged. I wondered if they had fallen out of fashion while I was away. So much did, every time I left. The ice ships were the only work I could get, capturing calved glacier chunks and breaking them down into drinking water to be sold to the wide, new swaths of desert that ringed the globe, and the work was hard and dangerous and kept me forever in limbo.

Only two fighters in the first fight, both lithe and swift and thin, their styles an amalgam of Chinese martial arts. Not like the big bruising New York boxers who had been the rage when I arrived, illegally, at fifteen years old, having paid two drunks to vouch for my age. Back before the Fail-Proof Trillion Dollar NYC Flood-Surge Locks had failed, and 80 percent of the city sunk, and the grid cities banned all new East Coast arrivals. Now the North Americans in Arm Eight were just one of many overcrowded, underskilled labor forces for the city's corporations to exploit.

They leapt from beam to beam, fighting mostly in kicks, grappling briefly when both met on the same beam. I watched Thede. Thin, fragile Thede, with the wide eyes and nostrils that seemed to take in all the world's ugliness, all its stink. He wasn't having a good time. When he was twelve he had begged me to bring him. I had pretended to like it, back then for his sake. Now he pretended for mine. We were both acting out what we thought the other wanted, and that thought should have troubled me. But that's how it had been with my dad. That's what I thought being a man meant. I put my hand on his shoulder and he did not shake it off. We watched men harm each other high above us.

Thede's eyes burned with wonder, staring up at the fretted sweep of the windscreen as we rose to meet it. We were deep in a days-long twilight; soon, the sun would set for weeks.

"This is *not* happening," he said, and stepped closer to me. His voice shook with joy.

The elevator ride to the top of the city was obscenely expensive. We'd never been able to take it before. His mother had bought our tickets. Even for her, it hurt. I wondered why she hadn't taken him herself.

"He's getting bullied a lot in school," she told me, on the phone. Behind her was the solid comfortable silence of a respectable home. My background noise was four men building toward a fight over a card game. "Also, I think he might be in love."

But of course I couldn't ask him about either of those things. The first was my fault; the second was something no boy wanted to discuss with his dad.

I pushed a piece of trough meat loose from between my teeth. Savored how close it came to the real thing. Only with Thede, with his mother's money, did I get to buy the classy stuff. Normally it was barrel-bottom for me, greasy chunks that dissolved in my mouth two chews in, homebrew meat moonshine made in melt-scrap-furnace-heated metal troughs. Some grid cities were rumored to still have cows, but that was the kind of lie people tell themselves to make life a little less ugly. Cows were extinct, and real beef was a joy no one would ever experience again.

The windscreen was an engineering marvel, and absolutely gorgeous. It shifted in response to headwinds; in severe storms the city would raise its auxiliary windscreens to protect its entire circumference. The tiny panes of plastiglass were common enough—a thriving underground market sold the fallen ones as good luck charms—but to see them knitted together was to tremble in the face of staggering genius. Complex patterns of crenelated reliefs, efficiently diverting windshear no matter what angle it struck from. Bots swept past us on the metal gridlines, replacing panes that had fallen or cracked.

Once, hand gripping mine tightly, somewhere down in the city beneath me, six-year-old Thede had asked me how the windscreen worked. He asked me a lot of things then, about the locks that held the city up, and how they could rise in response to tides and ocean-level increases; about the big boats with strange words and symbols on the side, and where they went, and what they brought back. "What's in that boat?" he'd ask about each one, and I would make up ridiculous stories. "That's a giraffe boat. That one brings back machine guns that shoot strawberries. That one is for naughty children." In truth I only ever recognized ice boats, immediately-recognizable for the multitude of pincers atop cranes along the side.

My son stood up straighter, sixty stories above his city. Some rough weight had fallen from his shoulders. He'd be strong, I saw. He'd be handsome. If he made it. If this horrible city didn't break him inside in some irreparable way. If marauding whiteboys didn't bash him for his dark skin. If the firms didn't pass him over for the lack of family connections on his stuttering immigrant father's side. I wondered who was bullying him, and why, and I imagined taking them two at a time and slamming their heads together so hard they popped like bubbles full of blood. Of course I couldn't do that. I also imagined hugging him, grabbing him for no reason and maybe never letting go, but I couldn't do that either. He would wonder why.

"I called last night and you weren't in," I said. "Doing anything fun?"

"We went to the cityoke arcade," he said.

I nodded like I knew what that meant. Later on I'd have to ask the men in my room. I couldn't keep up with this city, with its endlessly-shifting fashions and slang and the new immigrant clusters that cropped up each time I blinked. Twenty years after arriving, I was still a stranger. I wasn't just fresh off the boat, I was constantly getting back on the boat and then getting off again. That morning I'd gone to the job center for the fifth day in a row, and been relieved to find no boat postings. Only twelve-month gigs, and I wasn't that hungry yet. Booking a year-long job meant admitting you were old, desperate, unmoored, willing to accept payment only marginally more than nothing, for the privilege of a hammock and three bowls of trough slop a day. But captains picked their own crews for the shorter runs, and I worried that the lack of postings meant that with fewer boats going out the competition had become too fierce for me. Every day a couple hundred new workers arrived from sunken cities in India or Middle Europe, or from any of a hundred Water-War-torn nations. Men and women stronger than me, more determined.

With effort, I brought my mind back to the here and now. Twenty other people stood in the arc pod with us. Happy, wealthy people. I wondered if they knew I wasn't one of them. I wondered if Thede was.

They smiled down at their city. They thought it was so stable. I'd watched ice sheets calve off the glacier that were five times the size of Qaanaaq. When one of those came drifting in our direction, the windscreen wouldn't help us. The question was when, not if. I knew a truth they did not: how easy it is to lose something—everything—forever.

A Maoist Nepalese foreman, on one of my first ice-ship runs, said white North Americans were the worst for adapting to the post-Arctic world, because we'd lived for centuries in a bubble of believing the world was way better than it actually was. Shielded by willful blindness and complex interlocking institutions of privilege, we mistook our uniqueness for universality.

I'd hated him for it. It took me fifteen years to see that he was right.

"What do you think of those two?" I asked, pointing with my chin at a pair of girls his age.

For a while he didn't answer. Then he said "I know you can't help that you grew up in a backward macho culture, but can't you just keep that on the inside?"

My own father would have cuffed me if I talked to him like that, but I was too afraid of rupturing the tiny bit of affectionate credit I'd fought so hard to earn back.

His stance softened, then. He took a tiny step closer—the only apology I could hope for.

The pod began its descent. Halfway down he unzipped his jacket, smiling in the warmth of the heated pod while below-zero winds buffeted us. His T-shirt said *The Last Calf,* and showed the gangly, sad-eyed hero of that depressing, miserable movie all the kids adored.

"Where is it?" I asked. He'd proudly sported the NEW YORK F CKING CITY shirt on each of the five times I'd seen him since giving it to him.

His face darkened so fast I was frightened. His eyes welled up. He said "Dad, I," but his voice had the tremor that meant he could barely keep from crying. Shame was what I saw.

I couldn't breathe, again, just like when I came home two

weeks ago and he wasn't happy to see me. Except seeing my son so unhappy hurt worse than fearing he hated me.

"Did somebody take it from you?" I asked, leaning in so no one else could hear me. "Someone at school? A bully?"

He looked up, startled. He shook his head. Then, he nodded.

"Tell me who did this?"

He shook his head again. "Just some guys, Dad," he said. "Please. I don't want to talk about it."

"Guys. How many?"

He said nothing. I understood about snitching. I knew he'd never tell me who.

"It doesn't matter," I said. "Okay? It's just a shirt. I don't care about it. I care about you. I care that you're okay. Are you okay?"

Thede nodded. And smiled. And I knew he was telling the truth, even if I wasn't, even if inside I was grieving the shirt, and the little boy who I once wrapped up inside it.

When I wasn't with Thede, I walked. For two weeks I'd gone out walking every day. Up and down Arm Eight, and sometimes into other Arms. Through shantytowns large and small, huddled miserable agglomerations of recent arrivals and folks who even after a couple generations in Qaanaaq had not been able to scrape their way up from the fish-stinking, ice-slippery bottom.

I looked for sex, sometimes. It had been so long. Relationships were tough in my line of work, and I'd never been interested in paying for it. Throughout my twenties I could usually find a woman for something brief and fun and free of commitment, but that stage of my life seemed to have ended.

I wondered why I hadn't tried harder to make it work with

Lajla. I think a small but vocal and terrible part of me had been glad to see her leave. Fatherhood was hard work. So was being married. Paying rent on a tiny, shitty apartment way out on Arm Seven, where we smelled like scorched cooking oil and diaper lotion all the time. Selfishly, I had been glad to be alone. And only now, getting to know this stranger who was once my son, did I see what sweet and fitting punishments the universe had up its sleeve for selfishness.

My time with Thede was wonderful, and horrible. We could talk at length about movies and music, and he actually seemed halfway interested in my stories about old New York, but whenever I tried to talk about life or school or girls or his future he reverted to grunts and monosyllables. Something huge and heavy stood between me and him, a moon eclipsing the sun of me. I knew him, top to bottom and body and soul, but he still had no idea who I really was. How I felt about him. I had no way to show him. No way to open his eyes, make him see how much I loved him, and how I was really a good guy who'd gotten a bad deal in life.

Cityoke, it turned out, was like karaoke, except instead of singing a song you visited a city. XHD footage projection onto all four walls; temperature control; short storylines that responded to your verbal decisions—even actual smells uncorked by machines from secret stashes of Beijing taxi-seat leather or Ho Chi Minh City incense or Portland coffee-shop sawdust. I went there often, hoping maybe to see him. To watch him, with his friends. See what he was when I wasn't around. But cityoke was expensive, and I could never have afforded to actually go in. Once, standing around outside the New York booth when a crew walked out, I caught a whiff of the acrid, ugly, beautiful stink of the Port Authority Bus Terminal.

And then, eventually, I walked without any reason at all.

Because pretty soon I wouldn't be able to. Because I had done it. I had booked a twelve-month job. I was out of money and couldn't afford to rent my bed for another month. Thede's mom could have given it to me. But what if she told him about it? He'd think of me as more of a useless moocher deadbeat dad than he already did. I couldn't take that chance.

Three days before my ship was set to load up and launch, I went back to the cityoke arcades. Men lurked in doorways and between shacks. Soakers, mostly. Looking for marks; men to mug and drunks to tip into the sea. Late at night; too late for Thede to come carousing through. I'd called him earlier, but Lajla said he was stuck inside for the night, studying for a test in a class where he wasn't doing well. I had hoped maybe he'd sneak out, meet some friends, head for the arcade.

And that's when I saw it. The shirt: NEW YORK F CKING CITY, absolutely unique and unmistakable. Worn by a stranger, a muscular young man sitting on the stoop of a skiff moor. I didn't get a good glimpse of his face, as I hurried past with my head turned away from him.

I waited, two buildings down. My heart was alive and racing in my chest. I drew in deep gulps of cold air and tried to keep from shouting from joy. Here was my chance. Here was how I could show Thede what I really was.

I stuck my head out, risked a glance. He sat there, waiting for who knows what. In profile I could see that the man was Asian. Almost certainly Chinese, in Qaanaaq—most other Asian nations had their own grid cities—although perhaps he was descended from Asian-diaspora nationals of some other country. I could see his smile, hungry and cold.

At first I planned to confront him, ask how he came to be wearing my shirt, demand justice, beat him up and take it back. But that would be stupid. Unless I planned to kill him—and I didn't—it was too easy to imagine him gunning for Thede if he knew he'd been attacked for the shirt. I'd have to jump him, rob and strip and soak him. I rooted through a trash bin, but found nothing. Three trash bins later I found a short metal pipe with Hindi graffiti scribbled along its length. The man was still there when I went back. He was waiting for something. I could wait longer. I pulled my hood up, yanked the drawstring to tighten it around my face.

Forty-five minutes passed that way. He hugged his knees to his chest, made himself small, tried to conserve body heat. His teeth chattered. Why was he wearing so little? But I was happy he was so stupid. Had he had a sweater or jacket on I'd never have seen the shirt. I'd never have had this chance.

Finally, he stood. Looked around sadly. Brushed off the seat of his pants. Turned to go. Stepped into the swing of my metal pipe, which struck him in the chest and knocked him back a step.

The shame came later. Then, there was just joy. The satisfaction of how the pipe struck flesh. Broke bone. I'd spent twenty years getting shitted on by this city, by this system, by the cold wind and the everywhere-ice, by the other workers who were smarter or stronger or spoke the language. For the first time since Thede was a baby, I felt like I was in control of something. Only when my victim finally passed out, and rolled over onto his back and the blue methane streetlamp showed me how young he was under the blood, could I stop myself.

I took the shirt. I took his pants. I rolled him into the water. I called the med-team for him from a coinphone a block away. He was still breathing. He was young, he was healthy. He'd be fine. The pants I would burn in a scrap furnace. The shirt I would give back to my son. I took the money from his wallet and dropped it into the sea, then threw the money in later. *I wasn't a thief. I was a good father.* I said those sentences over and over, all the way home.

Thede couldn't see me the next day. Lajla didn't know where he was. So I got to spend the whole day imagining imminent arrest, the arrival of Swedish or Chinese police, footage of me on the telescrolls, my cleverness foiled by tech I didn't know existed because I couldn't read the newspapers. I packed my one bag glumly, put the rest of my things back in the storage cube and walked it to the facility. Every five seconds I looked over my shoulder and found only the same grit and filthy slush. Every time I looked at my watch, I winced at how little time I had left.

My fear of punishment was balanced out by how happy I was. I wrapped the shirt in three layers of wrapping paper and put it in a watertight shipping bag and tried to imagine his face. That shirt would change everything. His father would cease to be a savage jerk from an uncivilized land. This city would no longer be a cold and barren place where boys could beat him up and steal what mattered most to him with impunity. All the ways I had failed him would matter a little less.

Twelve months. I had tried to get out of the gig, now that I had the shirt and a new era of good relations with my son was upon me. But canceling would have cost me my accreditation with that work center, which would make finding another job almost impossible. A year away from Thede. I would tell him when I saw him. He'd be upset, but the shirt would make it easier.

Finally, I called and he answered.

"I want to see you," I said, when we had made our way through the pleasantries.

"Sunday?" Did his voice brighten, or was that just blind, stupid hope? Some trick of the noisy synthcoffee shop where I sat?

"No, Thede," I said, measuring my words carefully. "I can't. Can you do today?"

A suspicious pause. "Why can't you do Sunday?"

"Something's come up," I said. "Please? Today?"

"Fine."

The sea lion rookery. The smell of guano and the screak of gulls; the crying of children dragged away as the place shut down. The long night was almost upon us. Two male sea lions barked at each other, bouncing their chests together. Thede came a half hour late, and I had arrived a half hour early. Watching him come, my head swam at how tall he stood and how gracefully he walked. I had done something good in this world, at least. I made him. I had that, no matter how he felt about me.

Something had shifted, now, in his face. Something was harder, older, stronger.

"Hey," I said, bear-hugging him, and eventually he submitted. He hugged me back hesitantly, like a man might, and then hard, like a little boy.

"What's happening?" I asked. "What were you up to, last night?"

Thede shrugged. "Stuff. With friends."

I asked him questions. Again the sullen, bitter silence; again the terse and angry answers. Again the eyes darting around, constantly watching for whatever the next attack would be. Again the hating me, for coming here, for making him.

"I'm going away," I said. "A job."

"I figured," he said.

"I wish I didn't have to."

"I'll see you soon."

I nodded. I couldn't tell him it was a twelve-month gig. Not now.

"Here," I said, finally, pulling the package out from inside of my jacket. "I got you something."

"Thanks." He grabbed it in both hands, began to tear it open.

"Wait," I said, thinking fast. "Okay? Open it after I leave."

Open it when the news that I'm leaving has set in, when you're mad at me, for abandoning you. When you think I care only about my job.

"We'll have a little time," he said. "When you get back. Before I go away. I leave in eight months. The program is four years long."

"Sure," I said, shivering inside.

"Mom says she'll pay for me to come home every year for the holiday, but she knows we can't afford that."

"What do you mean?" I asked. "'Come home.' I thought you were going to the Institute."

"I am," he said, sighing. "Do you even know what that means? The Institute's design program is in Shanghai."

"Oh," I said. "Design. What kind of design?"

My son's eyes rolled. "You're missing the point, Dad."

I was. I always was.

A shout, from a pub across the Arm. A man's shout, full of pain and anger. Thede flinched. His hands made fists.

"What?" I asked, thinking, here, at last, was something.

"Nothing."

"You can tell me. What's going on?"

Thede frowned, then punched the metal railing so hard he yelped. He held up his hand to show me the blood.

"Hey, Thede—"

"Han," he said. "My . . . my friend. He got jumped two nights ago. Soaked."

"This city is horrible," I whispered.

He made a baffled face. "What do you mean?"

"I mean . . . you know. This city. Everyone's so full of anger and cruelty . . ."

"It's not the city, Dad. What does that even mean? Some sick person did this. Han was waiting for me, and mom wouldn't let me out, and he got jumped. They took off all his clothes, before they rolled him into the water. That's some extra cruel shit right there. He could have died. He almost did."

I nodded, silently, a siren of panic rising inside. "You really care about this guy, don't you?"

He looked at me. My son's eyes were whole, intact, defiant, adult. Thede nodded.

He's been getting bullied, his mother had told me. *He's in love.*

I turned away from him, before he could see the knowledge blossom in my eyes.

The shirt hadn't been stolen. He'd given it away. To the boy he loved. I saw them holding hands, saw them tug at each other's clothing in the same fumbling adolescent puppy-love moments I had shared with his mother, moments that were my only happy memories from being his age. And I saw his fear, of how his backward father might react—a refugee from a fallen, hate-filled people—if he knew what kind of man he was. I gagged on the unfairness of his assumptions about me, but how could he have known differently? What had I ever done, to show him the truth of how I felt about him? And hadn't I proved him right? Hadn't I acted exactly like the monster he believed me to be? I had never succeeded in proving to him what I was, or how I felt.

I had battered and broken his beloved. There was nothing I could say. A smarter man would have asked for the present back, taken it away and locked it up. Burned it, maybe. But I couldn't. I had spent his whole life trying to give him something worthy of how I felt about him, and here was the perfect gift at last.

"I love you, Thede," I said, and hugged him.

"Daaaaad . . ." he said, eventually.

But I didn't let go. Because when I did, he would leave. He would walk home through the cramped and frigid alleys of his home city, to the gift of knowing what his father truly was.

ix.

"*Bullshit, man,*" *I say, laughing.*

"*I took one of yours,*" *he says. "Your mom. The time you ran away from home. She took drugs, trying to track you down . . .*"

He keeps talking. Tells me the whole thing. Even though I already know it.

WHEN YOUR CHILD STRAYS FROM GOD

EVERYONE SAYS IT but no one believes it: attitude makes all the difference. People parrot the words but the words don't penetrate, not really, not down to the core. That's why Carolina Bugtuttle has all those lines on her face, always scowling when I reach for that third or fourth cookie after Sunday worship, always emailing me LOW FAT RECIPES and MIRACLE DIETS peppered with those godforsaken, soulless smiley-face things. That's why she's always stressed out about six hundred things that don't have a smidge to do with her. Because she has a bad attitude. She needs to worry less about my weight and more about that degenerate son of hers, if you ask me, but you didn't, so.

My smile isn't just on the surface. That's why I knew, Wednesday morning, when I woke up and Timmy still hadn't come home, when I checked my phone and he still hadn't replied to my texts and voicemails, why I knew I had the strength to go find him—wherever he was. And bring him home. And get started on a new installment of *The Deacon's Wife* for the church e-bulletin. Write it raw, rough, naked, curses and gossip intact, more a letter to my sweet, wise husband Pastor Jerome than anything else, so he can go through it with scissors and a scalpel before sending it out to the four-thousand-strong flock of the Grace Abounding Evangelical Church.

WHAT TO DO WHEN YOUR CHILD STRAYS FROM GOD.

Timmy's rebellion had spent a long time percolating. By the time Timmy vanished I had seen the signs—seen him in Facebook photos with That Whore Susan; seen him sketching the Spiderman logo that webheads were so fond of—and had armed myself with knowledge, courtesy of the Internet. I knew more about spiderwebbing than any God-fearing mother has any business knowing. I had logged enough hours on websites and wikis and forums to bring me to the attention of a couple dozen law enforcement agencies, places Carolina Bugtuttle would never in hell have spent a single second. Not even if it meant the difference between saving her son's soul and losing him forever.

I climbed the steps slowly, aware of the sin I was about to commit. I paused at the door to his room.

Let me tell you something about the bedrooms of teenage boys. They are sovereign nations, islands of liberty hedged in on all sides by brutal tyranny. To cross the threshold uninvited is an act of war. To intrude and search is a crime meriting full-scale thermonuclear response: neutron-bomb silence, mutually-assured temper tantrums.

So I did not enter Timmy's room lightly, and panic seized me in the instant that I did. Fear stopped me in my tracks, threatened to turn me around. The smell of stale laundry made my head swim—the bodily odors that meant my little boy had become a man. I summoned him up as the smiling boy he had been before puberty caused him to declare independence, defy us as righteously and violently as America spurned its colonial overlords.

I searched swiftly, joylessly. Praying, somehow, that I'd get caught. Desperate for him to come home, no matter what the cost to me might be.

And that's when I realized I was in over my head. I missed him, my boy, my son, the obedient, wide-eyed one who loved his father and loved me—as opposed to the cruel and sullen thing with a heart full of hate he'd become. I'd built walls around the Bad Timmy, moats and turrets to protect my heart. Against Good Timmy I had no defense.

I found plenty. Sperm-stiffened socks; eerily-empty browser history. A CD that looked Satanic. None of it was what I wanted.

Permit me a digression here, fellow congregant, beloved pastor.

You probably know none of this, because you're a good churchgoing Christian who'd never dream of Googling illegal substances. Nor have you ever had need to learn about the complex moral codes of conduct common to drug dealers and other criminals.

Thanks to the *60 Minutes* and the *Dateline* and the nightly national news, you already know that spiderwebbing is a hallucinogen—but you don't know what a weird one it is. The basic legend of its manufacture goes like this: in top secret farms run by the Taliban or the Chinese government or some other Existential Threat, Amazon psychovenom spiders chimerically combined with God Knows What get dusted with US mind-meld pharmaceuticals, then fed a GMO protein ooze that makes their web-producing glands go into overdrive, producing webs that get sprayed with wonky unstable Soviet-era hallucinogens intended to induce extreme suggestibility, then the spray crystallizes, the crystallized web is broken down into a dust and put into solution, which, after various alchemical adulterations, is dripped into the user's eye with a dropper. All of this is speculation, of course, since the origins of the drug are so shrouded in mystery. For all I know they just dissolve LSD in liquid Ativan and sprinkle it with fairy dust and boom.

Two or more users who drop from the same web will experience a shared hallucination. If one of them sees the ground open up and an angel with a centipede face fly out, they all do. No matter how far apart they go, as long as the drug lasts they're in synch. Like, they're in each other's minds. Psychically linked. No one knows why this is. No one knows much about anything when it comes to spiderwebbing. We made that stuff so illegal in the early days of the crisis that no lab in the country can legally possess a shred of it. Wise Pastor Jerome says you can be damn sure the government's doing research on how to use it against traditional-minded Americans, but it's his job to scare people about What The Government Is Up To.

So. Invading someone's webbing experience is a potentially fatal act of aggression. You can imagine how much damage an evil person could do, with unfettered access to your psyche. Drug dealers used to sell webs to someone, then sell webbing off the same branch to their enemies, who would send in some psychically-skilled mind assassin to Break Their Brain. Plunge them into a black midnight sea full of squid-shark monsters that slowly dismember them—leaving them permanently paralyzed—or change their cognitive processes so that for the rest of their life whenever they look at another person's face they see only a pulsing ravenous mouth full of jagged, slobbery teeth.

What I'm saying is, I was taking a big risk.

Finally, I found it. Three eye droppers, wrapped in Kleenex, hidden inside a Dr. Seuss book. Full of thick liquid dyed Spiderman's-tights-blue. I took them to the Winnie-the-Pooh mirror on the wall, which badly wanted Windexing. Now I just had to hope they came from the same branch as the one Timmy was on, and hope that getting inside his hallucination would help me find the boy himself. And that I wouldn't break us both.

You can do this, I thought. *You watched enough tutorials on YouTube.*

I tilted my head back, held my hair, dropped one tiny drop into my left eye, and then, in the eternity it took the drop to fall into my right eye, experienced a long, slow moment of absurd, utter panic in which I would have given anything to take it back, go downstairs, sit quietly by the phone, wait for my son to come home or my husband to arrive and fix everything, which is what my mother would have done, which is what she trained me to do Always, in Every Situation, which is what I'd been doing all my life.

"Morning, Beth," my next-door neighbor said, when I stepped outside.

"Morning, Marge," I called—

When I turned to look at her, Marge had a pug face. Actually, she was all pug. A five-foot bipedal pug kneeling in her garden, with a frilly, ridiculous Elizabethan collar around her neck.

Don't freak out, I told myself, feeling a laughing fit coming.

Laughing was safe. Screaming was a problem. A bad trip could trigger a spiderburst, making thousands of spiders literally erupt from the ceilings and floorboards around you, holes opening up in walls and the bodies of your loved ones, vomiting up arachnids ranging in size from penny to medium-sized dog. On *60 Minutes* they showed an eighteen-year-old girl who got caught in a spiderburst, strapped down to a psych ward bed for the rest of her life, twitching and jerking away from nothing—as far as we could see—although the voice-over breathlessly described what she saw, the swarm that never ceased to flow over her, how she tried hard not to scream, and then screamed, and then gagged as dozens of fat, black furry spiders poured down her throat.

And if I triggered a spiderburst, anyone else in the webworld would get caught up in it too.

Which is why I was the only one who could do this. Which is why Carolina Bugtuttle would break her own brain and her son's to boot if she ever had the guts to try something like this, which she didn't. But I—I have a good attitude. All the time, about everything. No matter what I went through. No matter what hurts I carried around in my heart.

"Bye, Marge," I said, and started up the car.

A dinosaur sat buckled into the backseat, passenger side, where Timmy always sat. Preening glorious blue-and-red feathers in the unkempt backyard. Ceratosaurus, I remembered. The favorite dinosaur of Timmy's childhood best friend Brent. Brent, son of Colby.

A tether of warmth tugged at me from the west. From Route 29. Was it my son? Or someone else? I knew only one person who lived in that direction.

"Colby's house," I said without meaning to. The ground trembled beneath my SUV with the sound of a train passing far underground, although of course there are no subways in rural Scaghticoke.

I pushed the tether aside and resolved to visit That Whore Susan.

I kept my hands on the wheel and watched a flock of crows shift shapes as they flew: now butterflies, now jellyfish, now a swarm of black letters spelling out words I spent my whole life trying not to say.

Driving while spiderwebbing is not the kind of activity I'd encourage you to ever engage in. You might not have to contend with packs of roving velociraptors herding gallimimuses across County Route 6 the way I did, or pterodactyls picking off baby mammoths, but it won't be an easy drive all the same.

Spiderbursts were the least of my concerns. My Timmy was so full of anger that I was scared of him in the real world, where all he had the power to do was hurt my feelings . . . and here I was opening my mind up to him as much as his mind was open to me. If he was drug-addled and out of balance and I caught him off guard, he might be able to lock me up inside my worst memory for all eternity, or show me parts of myself I'd never recover from, or who knew what else.

Understand: Timmy was not a bad boy. There was a sweet, curious, creative little nugget inside that lanky, angular body he'd metamorphosed into. Love and kindness, buried under all the hate and anger. He acted like everyone in the world hated him, and preemptively acted to hate them harder. Every single day, it seemed, he made my husband so mad he spit nails.

This, of course, was my fault. Everything a child does is his mother's fault.

We venture now into territory that could potentially be the subject of another e-bulletin: CONFRONTING THE WHORE YOUR SON IS DATING. I have lots to say on the subject, not all of it germane to the subject at hand, although my husband Pastor Jerome would say that's never stopped me before, since *The Deacon's Wife* routinely goes On and On about Unnecessary Details No One Cares About, but I say what the heck. That's what the internet is for.

A brachiosaurus raced me most of the way to Susan's house, every heavy footfall shaking my teeth, some of them an arm's length from my soccer-mom SUV, and I wondered what would happen if one of them came down squarely on top of it.

Webslingers have a lot of theories about the things they see in the webworld, none of it backed up by science but all of it rooted strongly in This Happened to a Friend of a Friend of Mine. Some visions were real things, transformed, like how

Marge became Pug-Marge. The brachiosaurus could have been a tractor, or a bug. Some visions were total figments of the imagination—though whose imagination exactly, and what they meant, was the subject of endless webhead debate. Some slingers said the visions couldn't hurt you—*So-and-So got stabbed like a dozen times by Bettie Crocker and that teapot from Beauty and the Beast one time and she bled until she passed out and when she woke up she was stone cold sober and unharmed*—and some said webworld wounds would follow you, Freddie-Kruger-style, into the real world. Drugs are maddeningly resistant to methodical study, or even rational scrutiny.

To be honest, though, all the dinosaurs were a good sign. Timmy used to love dinosaurs. When he was little. The fact that his webworld was packed full of them meant maybe he was in a peaceful, happy, childlike state of mind.

I passed a skate park. Teenagers moved through the little hills and curves, on rollerblades and skateboards, enjoying the sudden snap of early-spring warmth. What did it mean, I wondered, that every one of them had a horse head? That they were dumb animals, or that they were strong and noble? Being on drugs was a lot of work. I'd only been under for a half hour and already I was *exhausted.*

You may imagine, fellow congregant, that risking death or imprisonment by venturing out into the world Under the Influence was the most frightening part of my ordeal. Not so! For I realized, as the horses watched me pass with hostile looks on their faces, that the law and bodily harm were the least of my worries. The real terror came from two warring forces that threatened to crack me open. The first was love: that tether that tied me down, a choking, liquid swamp I floundered in, thick and warm as phlegm, floodwaters that had started rising the second I took a hit of webbing, the only thing I couldn't vanquish with a Good Attitude. Love for Timmy, helpless maternal love that overpowered my anger at everything he'd put us through.

The second was fear.

Every webworld has a boogeyman. That's because pretty much every person has a boogeyman. A monster, a nemesis, a person or thing they fear most. I felt mine, as I drove. I had no idea what it was. I had no phobias, no enemies, except maybe for Carolina Bugtuttle, but she doesn't count, for anything, ever. But something was there, and it had always been there, just below the surface, and now it was threatening to burst through.

A Barbie doll answered Susan's door, oversized headphones yoking her neck, looking for all the world like a chicken disturbed while doing something it shouldn't be.

"Ummm . . . hi?"

"Morning, Susan!" I said, suddenly inexplicably frightened by the emptiness of her porcelain-rubber stare.

"Um . . . my mom's not . . . here?"

"Not here to see your mom, Susan. I'm here to see you."

"Oh. Come in?" A slight bow, church manners intact, so maybe her mother didn't raise her quite as badly as I'd thought she had. "You, uhh . . . want a soda?"

"No, Susan, thanks so much."

She sat. I sat. The couch sagged. They'd needed to buy a new one when Susan was six and her mother worked at Wal-Mart, and now she's sixteen and her mom's still there and the couch is still here.

"Nice . . . weather we've been having?"

"It is."

We watched each other. I wasn't sure how to start, though surely I wasn't the first mother in history to plant her feet in the living room of her son's Whore Girlfriend. Probably not even the first one who used to babysit said son's Whore Girlfriend.

But I figured awkward silence benefited me more than her, threw her off balance, so I'd let it ride for as long as I could.

"You're looking for Tim," she said.

"You know where he is?"

"Nope."

"I wonder if I believe you."

Barbie-Susan shrugged, hardening, and I saw that I'd miscalculated—she'd found her footing, gotten over the awkwardness, she was seizing the reins, danger, abort. "He said you were a meek, obedient housewife," she said. "That doesn't seem . . . accurate."

"My son thinks he knows me," I said. "But he's wrong."

No one knows me, I thought, but was that true? I didn't. My husband didn't. Did Tim? There it was again—the tug, the pull from Route 29. I shut my eyes, tried to seize hold of it and snap it, but it stuck to my hands like flypaper and tied me tighter.

Susan said, "Because here you are, with a very faint but very definite gray tint to the white of your eyes. You're webbed, Mrs. Wilde. Don't worry. It's nothing anyone would spot if they didn't know what they were looking for."

"And you?" I asked. "Are you? Is he? Are you both here—"

"Ugh, no," she said. "I hate that stuff. Do you even know what you're doing? Let me guess—you Googled it? Christ, an old woman Googling is more dangerous than a drunk, blind bus driver asleep at the wheel."

"Did you just call me old?"

"Ummm . . . no?"

"I don't believe you," I said. "You know where he is. You two—"

"Your son might not know you, but you clearly don't know him either." We watched clouds, out the thin, dusty windows. I wondered what she saw when she looked at them. For me they were cheese, vast walls of cold supermarket cheese. "What did you want to be when you grew up?" she asked.

"My favorite subject was biology," I said, willing to tolerate any digression that might eventually lead me where I wanted to go. "Followed closely by chemistry. Isn't that the most ridiculous thing you ever heard?"

"Why is that ridiculous?" she asked. "You never dreamed of doing something with that?"

"I wanted to get married," I said, the words coming easy from lots of practice. "I met someone wonderful, and I wanted to be his wife and support his dreams and have his kids. Speaking of whom. Where is Timmy?"

Her voice, now, was weirdly gentle. "Tim and I broke up six months ago, Mrs. Wilde. If we were ever really a thing."

Spiders rattled against the glass of her boxy old television. I listened while the sound got louder.

Whore Susan scooched closer. "Tim told me that you never defend him, when his father is screaming at him. When your husband hits him."

"That is most certainly not true," I said, quick enough to keep from wondering whether it was true and what it meant.

I longed to curse her out. Hiss *That boy has shattered our domestic harmony, my husband is trying his make his son a good man the best way he knows how, shut your filthy mouth you Skank Whore Bitch.* But this is why people with bad attitudes make a mess of everything. Because this wasn't about me. It was about Timmy. My own hurt feelings at her attempt to wound me would have to wait.

"I'm trying to help here," she said, unhelpfully. "Tim said he'll be damned if he ends up like you."

A word, perhaps, would be useful, here, about my son Timmy.

My fellow congregants may remember him as the charming

rapscallion seven-year-old who delighted in shredding hymnals. Or perhaps you recall the smiling scallywag twelve-year-old who got on the PA system and made farting noises after Sunday worship on more than one occasion. You probably remember very little after that, because he decided then that he Hated Church and God and Religion and Pastor Jerome and decided to settle for merely making our home lives miserable. Before you—my beloved husband, my wise Pastor Jerome—decided to stop ignoring Timmy's harmless aggressions and engage him as an enemy combatant, matching each new hostility with one of your own, an arms race that never abated, and of course anyone who's ever sat through one of Pastor Jerome's sermons when he's in a foul mood knows well enough how deep his dagger-tongue can stab. Pretty soon the Bible stayed on the dinner table, and every night brought a new lecture on the evil of rock and roll or idolatry or rap music or vegetarianism or socialism or feminism, and Timmy never, *never* failed to argue back, until the shouting became superlatively unkind on both sides. And the favorite subject of Timmy's screaming was his parents' marriage, the sham he believed it to be.

So I didn't doubt that he told her vicious things, spectacularly ridiculous, absurd lies, preposterous suggestions no sane churchgoing Christian could have spent a half-second taking seriously. But who knew what this unbeliever believed. "God bless you," I said, smiling to beat the devil, and fled that kitty-litter stinking house.

A twelve-year-old boy sat on the bumper of my car. My son, but not. Identical to how Tim had looked, at that age, but something in his face told me at once that he was someone else. And that he was terrified.

"Hi, mom," he said, and got up to give me a hug. His arms clasped me below my breasts.

"Hi, Matt," I said, because I knew who this was, this perfect little boy I'd met inside my son's mind. At twelve, Timmy wanted a twin brother more than anything else in the world. He'd had one for an imaginary friend, named him and given him all sorts of attributes (favorite color: blue, to Timmy's red; favorite food: spaghetti, while Timmy's was hamburgers), and now here he was, in the flesh, in the wonderful, terrible world of my son's head.

"Where's your brother?" I whispered, squatting to stroke the cheek of this marvelous creature, this fly stuck in amber, this last vestige of a beautiful, happy boy I'd lost a long time ago—but why was he so pale, why did his lip tremble so? He was an emissary, this poor wretch, sent to me by my son's subconscious, a harkening-back to the last safe place he'd known. Even before Matt answered my question, I knew what he was going to say.

Colby's house. The last place on the planet I wanted to go.

The place the tether of warmth had been tugging me all along.

"Do you want to come with me?" I asked.

"No," Matt said. "I can't."

"Why not?"

His face reddened, my little boy, my son who never was, precisely like my real son in the quick, uncontrollable rush of his emotions. "Timmy doesn't need me anymore."

"Okay," I said, and sadness cut through something essential, one of the cords that kept the hot air balloon that is my soul anchored to the good and the positive. The world began to wobble. I kissed his forehead, grabbed both shoulders and shook, in that way that Timmy had liked, but did not like anymore.

Matt grinned, a puppy after a belly rub, and then shivered, and looked away.

Figment of my son's imagination or not, I felt sorry for the little tyke.

Matt was a cry for help. A demand to be rescued. Rescued from a monster. A vicious, cruel captor, determined to mold him into a man my son had no interest in becoming. Timmy's boogeyman.

And here, fellow congregant, I don't mind saying, is where I started getting worried. Maybe it was the parked police cruiser I passed. Or the heavily-populated part of town where I was heading. But mostly it was this: the boogeyman was real. I knew who he was. Before my eyes the double-yellow line in the middle of the road stretched and bulged, a seam that barely held back a tidal surge of spiders.

The sky darkened. I drove faster. Shut my eyes. But with my eyes shut I could hear them, scritching away, three fat, gray, furred spiders stuck under the sun visor. The warmth got warmer, the tether pulled tighter, and it was him, my son, my Timmy, the boy I abandoned, the boy whose heart I broke by siding with his father, his boogeyman.

When I arrived, her car wasn't there. That was one blessing. Carolina Bugtuttle was out, of course, working hard, neglecting her son and husband, keeping the books and preparing the pamphlets down at Christ the Healer, so focused on God's reward for her in heaven she failed to see the one he gave her on earth, because God is merciful, God is kind even to the unkindest, lavishing largesse on selfish, gossipy wenches.

"Beth," he said, opening the door.

"Hi, Colby," I said, to Brent's dad, Carolina Bugtuttle's husband.

Colby, Pastor Jerome had said, the night they met, the night I'd been trying to prevent in the six months since we got married. *What the hell kind of a man is named after a cheese?* Then he gave me that chin-twitch that says Laugh At My Joke, which is what you sign up for when you say Till Death Do Us, so I laughed, but maybe not as much as I normally did, because then he gave the subtle head tilt that says You Have Disappointed Me—but to be honest I knew Colby before I ever heard of such a cheese, and to this day when I taste it I think of him, and hold it in my mouth until it is gone.

In the webworld, Colby Goldfarb stood before me precisely as he was when we were eighteen, in the parking lot outside Crossgates Mall, lit up by arc-sodium lights that turned him amber in that pelting rainstorm, right after I said the sentence I'd spent all week working up to, the one that broke his heart, and mine to boot, but mine didn't matter, and he stood outside the car, looking in, at me, for so long. Thin, young, wide-eyed, all hipbones and elbows and nose and thick black hair. He was even soaking wet, here, now, although his skin was dry and warm as summer when he stuck out his hand and I shook it.

"You're looking for your son," he said.

"Is he here?"

"I am under strict orders not to answer that question."

He grinned, and my mighty, unbendable momma-bear knees buckled.

"What the hell, Colby," I said, pushing past him, hand hot on his shoulder. "I would have called you, if Brent was hiding out at my place."

"That's because you're a better person than me."

I wasn't, and I wondered if I really would have called him. I had no idea what I'd do to keep my son's trust, because I hadn't had it in a long time. Because I didn't deserve it. Because I'd left him to fight his boogeyman alone. I had failed him so utterly. The magnitude of it sent twitches down my arms, started spiders leaking from the door hinges.

Colby's smile made my head hurt, ushering me in, the smile of a man who loved his son, who didn't believe they were mortal enemies and his mission in life was to crush the child's spirit.

"Sit," Colby said, gesturing to the kitchen table, turning to the Keurig machine to make me a coffee. Spiders swam in the thing's water tank. At any moment now the burst would shatter my brain and my son's.

"Where is he?"

"In the basement."

"With Brent?"

"Do you have any secrets from your husband?" Colby asked, and his freckled face was so earnest and sad I knew he wasn't talking about him and me. The fridge shook, rumbled, packed with spiders to the point it could not keep closed.

"Of course not," I said, because no other answer could be admitted, let alone uttered aloud.

"Could you keep one? A big one?"

Stuck to the fridge was a gorgeous drawing, in colored pencils, of a blue-and-red feathered ceratosaur. Colby's son was an incredible artist. "Brent's favorite dinosaur," I whispered. "I saw one of those this morning. It led me here."

Colby raised an eyebrow, leaned in, scanned the white of my eyes. Laughed out loud, the magnificent heaven's-trumpet sound I'd given up on ever hearing again. "Bethesda Wilde, are you webslinging?"

"Shut up," I said.

He laughed harder. "Is it fun? I confess there's a part of me that's always—"

"I'm not doing this for fun," I said, standing up, getting angry on purpose because anger was safe, anger was armor, against the spiders, against what Colby was doing to my gut; anger was the weapon my husband used whenever he didn't know what to do, and there had to be something other than my son that I had to show for all the time I'd spent with Pastor Jerome. I headed for the basement.

"No no no," Colby said, genuinely afraid, actually running, but I had a head start and for all my size I can move fast when I need to, and I got to the basement and wrenched open the door and slammed it behind me and locked it, and stomped down into the laundry-and-mildew smell of Carolina Bugtuttle's underground nest.

"Beth, stop," he said, pounding on the door. "Listen to me. You can't. Okay? Respect their privacy. You'll only—"

A cocoon, I guess, is the best I can do when it comes to describing what I found in the basement. A globe of densely-wrapped spiderwebs the size of a small car, lit up slightly from within, and I felt him in there, smelled him, my son, and I put my hands against it, felt its heat, felt the warm, safe world it contained, and slowly seized fists full of spiderweb and *ripped,* tore it open, watched thickened water slosh out in a rush that reminded me of giving birth. Upstairs, I heard Colby unscrewing the lock to take off the doorknob.

"Timmy!" I screamed.

Two shapes churned out of the web cocoon—dolphins, I thought, but then not, because fast as blinking they were boys, young men, drenched, hands clasped.

"Mom?" my son said, and let go of Brent's hand like it had suddenly caught fire. "What the hell, Mom!"

"Where were you?" I asked. "What's in there?"

"In . . . there?" Timmy said, and turned to take in the ruined cocoon. "Wait—you can see this? You're here? You're in the web with us?"

"Now, look," I said, stammering for the explanation I'd practiced, back when this all seemed like a good idea.

Timmy laughed out loud. "Look, Brent! A ceratosaurus. We've been trying for months to make one."

The dinosaur stood between me and Colby, who had just arrived, disemboweled doorknob in hand. Father and son exchanged a glance that said *let's keep quiet, let's let them say what they need to say,* and I ached for that, for the kind of trust that lets parents communicate wordlessly with their kids.

"I want you to come home with me, Timmy. We'll get you help. One of your father's friends runs a Christian rehabilitation clinic—"

"You think I'm a drug addict, mom?" He started laughing again. "I told you guys my parents work so hard to not see the truth that they don't know how to stop."

Brent started to say something, then decided against it. They watched me put the pieces together. These boys, these men, my teenage son, my teenage lover, his teenage son who was my teenage son's lover; they dripped with blue-green amniotic fluid and watched the truth widen my eyes, watched me fight it all the way.

They watched me grasp the magnitude of my son's sin. The unthinkable, unimaginable crime he had committed. Where did it come from? How did he learn it? How did he fly in the face of my husband's efforts and my own, our lifetime of accumulated craven cowardice? How did he find the courage to commit the sin of choosing love, the bravery of going for what your heart wants instead of the path a parent chose for you?

People fear spiderwebbing for all the wrong reasons. Going mad, having a breakdown, seeing inside your own soul—none of those should scare you. The most frightening side effect is also the one people crave it for: empathy. To truly feel what someone else is feeling, to see the other as yourself, to watch your ego obliterated in the face of universality—that's a trauma you may never recover from.

"Tim," I said, but could say no more. Not yet. He had never turned into something else. He was what he always was. His father couldn't handle that—hell, I wasn't sure *I* could handle it. But I had done him wrong, had sided with his father, because it was easier. And what irony: I took the drug to bring my son back to me, and instead the drug brought me back to my son.

Colby came closer, put one hand on my shoulder. "Beth," he whispered, "I think you and Tim should talk."

"Okay," I said, at last, furious, miserable, delirious, hurt at how little I knew my son, frightened by what he was, how much I had to atone for, how long it might take for him to forgive me, how long it might take me to forgive him, sad at all the paths I hadn't chosen, but ready, for whatever would come, and I said *Okay* again, letting it encompass so much more than the sentence he'd said, letting it settle like an unfurled bedsheet onto the hard, new decisions I finally felt strong enough to make. Like choosing my son over my husband.

This, then, all of this, is part of that *okay*. Print this blog post if you dare, Jerome, but since I know you won't I'll let it stand as a message from me to you. The Story of Where Things Stand. The hard-earned, blood-soaked, spiderweb-wrapped shreds of insight I earned by descending into the underworld for the sake of love. My gift to you. My one scrap of true wisdom. What to do when your child strays from God.

So. When your child strays from God you should praise Him, for putting a mirror in your hand so you can hold it up to yourself—if you have the stomach for it. When your child strays from God you should thank Him, for giving us the freedom to make our own mistakes, and the strength to maybe one day find our way back.

x.

I want to scream. Want to run. Can't do either. At first I think he's done something to me, but no. This panic, this fear, it's all me. All animal. Deer in headlights; possum playing dead. No magic to it.

"What are you?" I say, eventually, with great difficulty.

"Just a person," he says. "Just like you."

"No. Not like me. You're a—"

"I can give you one," he says, his smile demonically convincing. "If you want it, boy." He extends two fingers, still slick from the inside of my mouth. Touches them to my forehead.

One knee wobbles. So maybe I can move again. Maybe I could run. I don't. Who knows why.

THINGS WITH BEARDS

MacReady has made it back to McDonald's. He holds his coffee with both hands, breathing in the heat of it, still not 100 percent sure he isn't actually asleep and dreaming in the snow-drifted rubble of an Antarctic research station. The summer of 1983 is a mild one, but to MacReady it feels tropical, with 125th Street a bright, beautiful sunlit oasis. He loosens the cord that ties his cowboy hat to his head. Here, he has no need of a disguise. People press past the glass, a surging crowd going into and out of the subway, rushing to catch the bus, doing deals, making out, cursing each other, and the suspicion he might be dreaming gets deeper. Spend enough time in the ice hell of Antarctica and your body starts to believe that frigid lifelessness is the true natural state of the universe. Which, when you think of the cold vastness of space, is probably correct.

"Heard you died, man," comes a sweet, rough voice, and MacReady stands up to submit to the fierce hug that never fails to make him almost cry from how safe it makes him feel. But when he steps back to look Hugh in the eye, something is different. Something has changed. While he was away, Hugh became someone else.

"You don't look so hot yourself," he says, and they sit, and Hugh takes the coffee that has been waiting for him.

"Past few weeks I haven't felt well," Hugh says, which seems an understatement. Even after MacReady's many months in Antarctica, how could so many lines have sprung up in his friend's black skin? When had his hair and beard become so heavily peppered with salt? "It's nothing. It's going around."

Their hands clasp under the table.

"You're still fine as hell," MacReady whispers.

"You stop," Hugh says. "I know you had a piece down there."

MacReady remembers Childs, the mechanic's strong hands still greasy from the Ski-dozer, leaving prints on his back and hips. His teeth on the back of MacReady's neck.

"Course I did," MacReady says. "But that's over now."

"You still wearing that damn fool cowboy hat," Hugh says, scoldingly. "Had those stupid centerfolds hung up all over your room I bet."

MacReady releases his hands. "So? We all pretend to be what we need to be."

"Not true. Not everybody has the luxury of passing." One finger traces a circle on the black skin of his forearm.

They sip coffee. McDonald's coffee is not good but it is real. Honest.

Childs and him; him and Childs. He remembers almost nothing about the final days at McMurdo. He remembers taking the helicopter up, with a storm coming, something about a dog . . . and then nothing. Waking up on board a U.S. supply and survey ship, staring at two baffled crewmen. Shredded clothing all around them. A metal desk bent almost in half and pushed halfway across the room. Broken glass and burned paper and none of them had even the faintest memory of what had just happened. Later, reviewing case files, he learned how the supply run that came in springtime found the whole camp burned down, mostly everyone dead and blown to bizarre bits, except for two handsome corpses frozen untouched at the edge of camp; how the corpses were brought back, identified, the condolence letters sent home, the bodies, probably by accident, thawed . . . but that couldn't be real. That frozen corpse couldn't have been him.

"Your people still need me?" MacReady asks.

"More than ever. Cops been wilding out on folks left and right. Past six months, eight people got killed by police. Not a single officer indicted. You still up for it?"

"Course I am."

"Meeting in two weeks. Not afraid to mess with the Man? Because what we've got planned . . . they ain't gonna like it. And they're gonna hit back, hard."

MacReady nods. He smiles. He is home; he is needed. He is a rebel. "Let's go back to your place."

When MacReady is not MacReady, or when MacReady is simply not, he never remembers it after. The gaps in his memory are not mistakes, not accidents. The thing that wears his clothes, his body, his cowboy hat, it doesn't want him to know it is there. So the moment when the supply ship crewman walked in and found formerly-frozen MacReady sitting up—and watched Mac-Ready's face split down the middle, saw a writhing nest of spaghetti tentacles explode in his direction, screamed as they enveloped him and swiftly started digesting—all of that is gone from MacReady's mind.

But when it is being MacReady, it is MacReady. Every opinion and memory and passion is intact.

"The fuck just happened?" Hugh asks, after, holding up a shredded sheet.

"That good, I guess," MacReady says, laughing, naked.

"I honestly have no memory of us tearing this place up like that."

"Me either."

There is no blood, no tissue of any kind. Not-MacReady sucks all that up. Absorbs it, transforms it. As it transformed the meat that used to be Hugh, as soon as they were alone in his room and it perceived no threat, knew it was safe to come out. The struggle was short. In nineteen minutes the transformation was complete, and MacReady and Hugh were themselves again, as far as they knew, and they fell into each other's arms, into the ravaged bed, out of their clothes.

"What's that," MacReady says, two worried fingers tracing down Hugh's side. Purple blotches mar his lovely torso.

"Comes with this weird new pneumonia thing that's going around," he says. "This year's junky flu."

"But you're not a junky."

"I've fucked a couple, lately."

MacReady laughs. "You have a thing for lost causes."

"The cause I'm fighting for isn't lost," Hugh says, frowning.

"Course not. I didn't mean that—"

But Hugh has gone silent, vanishing into the ancient trauma MacReady has always known was there, and tried to ignore, ever since Hugh took him under his wing at the age of nineteen. Impossible to deny it, now, with their bare legs twined together, his skin corpse-pale beside Hugh's rich dark brown. How different their lives had been, by virtue of the bodies they wore. How wide the gulf that lay between them, that love was powerless to bridge.

So many of the men down there wore beards. Winter, he thought, at first—for keeping our faces warm in Antarctica's forever winter. But warmth at the station was rarely an issue. Their warren of rectangular huts was kept at a balmy seventy-eight degrees. Massive stockpiles of gasoline specifically for that purpose. Aside from the occasional trip outside for research—and MacReady never had more than a hazy understanding of what, exactly, those scientists were sciencing down there, but they seemed to do precious little of it—the men of his station stayed the hell inside.

So. Not warmth.

Beards were camouflage. A costume. Only Blair and Garry lacked one, both being too old to need to appear as anything other than what they were, and Childs, who never wanted to.

He shivered. Remembering. The tough-guy act, the cowboy he became in uncertain situations. Same way in juvie; in lockup. Same way in Vietnam. Hard, mean, masculine. Hard drinking; woman hating. Queer? Psssh. He hid so many things, buried them deep, because if men knew what he really was, he'd be in danger. When they learned he wasn't one of them, they would want to destroy him.

They all had their reasons, for choosing Antarctica. For choosing a life where there were no women. Supper time MacReady would look from face to bearded face and wonder how many were like him, under the all-man exterior they projected, but too afraid, like him, to let their true self show.

Childs hadn't been afraid. And Childs had seen what he was.

MacReady shut his eyes against the Antarctic memories, bit his lip. Anything to keep from thinking about what went down, down there. Because how was it possible that he had absolutely no memory of any of it? Soviet attack, was the best theory he could come up with. Psychoactive gas leaked into the ventilation system by a double agent (Nauls, definitely), which caused catastrophic freak-outs and homicidal arson rage, leaving only him and Childs unscathed, whereupon they promptly sat down in the snow to die . . . and this, of course, only made him more afraid, because if this insanity was the only narrative he could construct that made any sense at all, he whose imagination had never been his strong suit, then the real narrative was probably equally, differently, insane.

Not-MacReady has an exceptional knack for assessing external threats. It stays hidden when MacReady is alone, and when he is in a crowd, and even when he is alone but still potentially vulnerable. Once, past four in the morning, when a drunken MacReady had the 145th Street bus all to himself, alone with the small woman behind the wheel, Not-MacReady could easily have emerged. Claimed her. But it knew, somehow, gauging who knew what quirk of pheromones or optic nerve signals, the risk of exposure, the chance someone might see through the tinted windows, or the driver's foot, in the spasms of dying, might slam down hard on the brake and bring the bus crashing into something.

If confronted, if threatened, it might risk emerging. But no one is there to confront it. No one suspects it is there. Not even MacReady, who has nothing but the barest, most irrational anxieties. Protean fragments; nightmare glitch glimpses and snatches of horrific sound. Feedback, bleedthrough from the thing that hides inside him.

"Fifth building burned down this week," says the Black man with the Spanish accent. MacReady sees his hands, sees how hard he's working to keep them from shaking. His anger is intoxicating. "Twenty families, out on the street. Cops don't care. They know it was the landlord. It's always the landlord. Insurance company might kick up a stink, but worst thing that happens is dude catches a civil suit. Pays a fine. That shit is terrorism, and they oughta give those motherfuckers the chair."

Everyone agrees. Eleven people in the circle; all of them Black except for MacReady and an older white lady. All of them men except for her, and a stout Black woman with an Afro of astonishing proportions.

"It's not terrorism when they do it to us," she says. "It's just the way things are supposed to be."

The meeting is over. Coffee is sipped; cigarettes are lit. No one is in a hurry to go back outside. An affinity group, mostly Black Panthers who somehow survived a couple decades of attempts by the FBI to exterminate every last one of them, but older folks too, trade unionists, commies, a minister who came up from the South back when it looked like the Movement was going to spread everywhere, change everything.

MacReady wonders how many of them are cops. Three, he guesses, though not because any of them make him suspicious. Just because he knows what they're up against, what staggering resources the government has invested in destroying this work over the past forty years. Infiltrators tended to be isolated, immersed in the lie they were living, reporting only to one person, whom they might never meet.

Hugh comes over, hands him two cookies.

"You sure this is such a good idea?" MacReady says. "They'll hit back hard, for this. Things will get a whole lot worse."

"Help us or don't," Hugh says, frowning. "That's your decision. But you don't set the agenda here. We know what we're up against, way better than you do. We know the consequences."

MacReady eats one cookie, and holds the other up for inspection. Oreo knock-offs, though he'd never have guessed from the taste. The pattern is different, the seal on the chocolate exterior distinctly stamped.

"I understand if you're scared," Hugh says, gentler now.

"Shit yes I'm scared," MacReady says, and laughs. "Anybody who's not scared of what we're about to do is probably... ... well, I don't know, crazy or stupid or a fucking pod person."

Hugh laughs. His laugh becomes a cough. His cough goes on for a long time.

Would he or she know it, if one of the undercovers made eye contact with another? Would they look across the circle and see something, recognize some deeply-hidden kinship? And if they were all cops, all deep undercover, each one simply impersonating an activist so as to target actual activists, what would happen then? Would they be able to see that, and set the ruse aside, step into the light, reveal what they really were? Or would they persist in the imitation game, awaiting instructions from above? Undercovers didn't make decisions, MacReady knew; they didn't even do things. They fed information upstairs, and upstairs did with it what they would. So if a whole bunch of undercovers were operating on their own, how would they ever know when to stop?

⌣

MacReady knows that something is wrong. He keeps seeing it out of the corner of his mind's eye, hearing its echoes in the distance. Lost time, random wreckage.

MacReady suspects he is criminally, monstrously insane. That during his black-outs he carries out horrific crimes, and then hides all the evidence. This would explain what went down in Antarctica. In a terrifying way, the explanation is appealing. He could deal with knowing that he murdered all his friends and then blew up the building. It would frighten him less than the yawning gulf of empty time, the barely-remembered slither and scuttle of something inhuman, the flashes of blood and screaming that leak into his daylight hours now.

MacReady rents a cabin. Upstate: uninsulated and inexpensive. Ten miles from the nearest neighbor. The hard-faced old woman who he rents from picks him up at the train station. Her truck is full of grocery bags, all the things he requested.

"No car out here," she says, driving through town. "Not even a bicycle. No phone, either. You get yourself into trouble and there'll be no way of getting out of here in a hurry."

He wonders what they use it for, the people she normally rents to, and decides he doesn't want to know.

"Let me out up here," he says, when they approach the edge of town.

"You crazy?" she asks. "It'd take you two hours to walk the rest of the way. Maybe more."

"I said pull over," he says, hardening his voice, because if she goes much further, out of sight of prying protective eyes, around the next bend, maybe, or even before that, the thing inside him may emerge. It knows these things, somehow.

"Have fun carrying those two big bags of groceries all that way," she says, when he gets out. "Asshole."

"Meet me here in a week," he says. "Same time."

"You must be a Jehovah's Witness or something," she says, and he is relieved when she is gone.

The first two days pass in a pleasant enough blur. He reads books, engages in desultory masturbation to a cheaply-printed paperback of gay erotic stories Hugh had lent him. Only one symptom: hunger. Low and rumbling, and not sated no matter how much he eats.

And then: lost time. He comes to on his knees, in the cool midnight dirt behind a bar.

"Thanks, man," says the sturdy, bearded trucker type standing over him, pulling back on a shirt. Puzzled by how it suddenly sports a spray of holes, each fringed with what look like chemical burns. "I needed that."

He strides off. MacReady settles back into a squat. Leans against the building.

What did I do to him? He seems unharmed. But I've done something. Something terrible.

He wonders how he got into town. Walked? Hitchhiked? And how the hell he'll get back.

The phone rings, his first night back. He'd been sitting on his fire escape, looking down at the city, debating jumping, though not particularly seriously. Hugh's words echoing in his head. *Help us or don't.* He is still not sure which one he'll choose.

He picks up the phone.

"Mac," says the voice, rich and deep and unmistakable.

"Childs."

"Been trying to call you." Cars honk, through the wire. Childs is from Detroit, he dimly remembers, or maybe Minneapolis.

"I was away. Had to get out of town, clear my head."

"You too, huh?"

MacReady lets out his breath, once he realizes he's been holding it. "You?"

"Yup."

"What the hell, man? What the fuck is going on?"

Childs chuckles. "Was hoping you'd have all the answers. Don't know why. I already knew what a dumbass you are."

A lump of longing forms in MacReady's throat. But his body fits him wrong, suddenly. Whatever crazy mental illness he was imagining he had, Childs sharing it was inconceivable. Something else is wrong, something his mind rejects but his body already knows. "Have you been to a doctor?"

"Tried," Childs says. "I remember driving halfway there, and the next thing I knew I was home again." A siren rises then slowly fades, in Detroit or Minneapolis.

MacReady inspects his own reflection in the window, where the lights of his bedroom bounce back against the darkness. "What are we?" he whispers.

"Hellbound," Childs says, "but we knew that already."

The duffel bag says *Astoria Little League*. Two crossed baseball bats emblazoned on the outside. Dirty bright-blue blazer sleeves reaching out. A flawless facsimile of something harmless, wholesome. No one would see it and suspect. The explosives are well-hidden, small, sewn into a pair of sweat pants, the timer already ticking down to some unknown hour, some unforeseeable fallout.

"Jimmy," his father says, hugging him, hard. His beard brushes MacReady's neck, abrasive and unyielding as his love.

The man is immense, dwarfing the cluttered kitchen table. Uncles lurk in the background. Cigars and scotch sour the air. Where are the aunts and wives? MacReady has always wondered, these manly Sundays.

"They told me this fucker died," his father says to someone.

"Can't kill one of ours that easy," someone says. Eleven men in the little house, which has never failed to feel massive.

Here his father pauses. Frowns. No one but MacReady sees. No one here but MacReady knows the man well enough to suspect that the frown means he knows something new on the subject of MacReady mortality. Something that frightens him. Something he feels he has to shelter his family from.

"Fucking madness, going down there," his father says, snapping back with the unstoppable positivity MacReady lacks, and envies. "I'd lose my mind inside of five minutes out in Alaska."

"Antarctica," he chuckles.

"That too!"

Here, home, safe, among friends, the immigrant in his father emerges. Born here to brand-new arrivals from Ireland, never saw the place but it's branded on his speech, the slight Gaelic curling of his consonants he keeps hidden when he's driving the subway car but lets rip on weekends. His father's father is who MacReady hears now, the big, glorious drunk they brought over as soon as they got themselves settled, the immense shadow over MacReady's own early years, and who, when he died, took some crucial piece of his son away with him. MacReady wonders how his own father has marked him, how much of him he carries around, and what kind of new, terrible creature he will be when his father dies.

An uncle is in another room, complaining about an impending

Congressional hearing into police brutality against Blacks; the flood of reporters bothering his beat cops. The uncle uses ugly words to describe the people he polices out in Brooklyn; the whole room laughs. His father laughs. MacReady slips upstairs unnoticed. Laments, in silence, the horror of human hatred—how such marvelous people, whom he loves so dearly, contain such monstrosity inside of them.

In the bathroom, standing before the toilet where he first learned to pee, MacReady sees smooth purple lesions across his stomach.

Midnight, and MacReady stands at the center of the George Washington Bridge. The monstrous creature groans and whines with the wind, with the heavy traffic that never stops. New York City's most popular suicide spot. He can't remember where he heard that, but he's grateful that he did. Astride the safety railing, looking down at deep, black water, he stops to breathe.

Once, MacReady was angry. He is not angry anymore. This disturbs him. The things that angered him are still true, are still out there; are, in most cases, even worse.

His childhood best friend, shot by cops at fourteen for "matching a description" of someone Black. His mother's hands, at the end of a fourteen-hour laundry shift. Hugh, and Childs, and every other man he's loved, and the burning glorious joy he had to smother and hide and keep secret. He presses against these memories, traces along his torso where they've marked him, much like the cutaneous lesions along Hugh's sides. And yet, like those purple blotches, they cause no pain. Not anymore.

A train's whistle blows, far beneath him. Wind stings his eyes when he tries to look. He can see the warm, dim lights of the passenger cars; imagines the seats where late-night travelers doze or read or stare up in awe at the lights of the bridge. At him.

Something is missing, inside of MacReady. He can't figure out what. He wonders when it started. Antarctica? Maybe. But probably not. Something drew him to Antarctica, after all. The money, but not just the money. He wanted to flee from the human world. He was tired of fighting it and wanted to take himself out. Whatever was in him, changing, already, Antarctica fed it.

He tries to put his finger on it, the thing that is gone, and the best he can do is a feeling he once felt, often, and feels no longer. Trying to recall the last time he felt it he fails, though he can remember plenty of times before that. Leaving his first concert; gulping down cold November night air and knowing every star overhead belonged to him. Bus rides back from away baseball games, back when the Majors still felt possible. The first time he followed a boy onto the West Side Piers. A feeling at once frenzied and calm, energetic yet restive. Like he had saddled himself, however briefly, onto something impossibly powerful, and primal, sacred, almost, connected to the flow of things, moving along the path meant only for him. They had always been rare, those moments—life worked so hard to come between him and his path—but lately they did not happen at all.

He is a monster. He knows this now. So is Childs. So are countless others, people like Hugh who he did something terrible to, however unintentionally it was. He doesn't know the details, what he is or how it works, or why, but he knows it.

Maybe he'd have been strong enough, before. Maybe that other MacReady would have been brave enough to jump. But that MacReady had no reason to. This MacReady climbs back to the safe side of the guardrail, and walks back to solid ground.

MacReady strides up the precinct steps, trying not to cry. Smiling, wide-eyed, white and harmless.

When Hugh handed off the duffel bag, something was clearly wrong. He'd lost fifty pounds, looked like. All his hair. Half of the light in his eyes. By then MacReady'd been hearing the rumors, seeing the stories. Gay cancer, said the *Times*. Dudes dropping like mayflies.

And that morning: the call. Hugh in Harlem Hospital. From Hugh's mother, whose remembered Christmas ham had no equal on this earth. When she said everything was going to be fine, MacReady knew she was lying. Not to spare his feelings, but to protect her own. To keep from having a conversation she couldn't have.

He pauses, one hand on the precinct door. Panic rises.

Blair built a space ship.

The image comes back to him suddenly, complete with the smell of burning petrol. Something he saw, in real life? Or a photo he was shown, from the wreckage? A cavern dug into the snow and ice under their Antarctic station. Scavenged pieces of the helicopter and the snowmobiles and the Ski-dozer assembled into . . . a space ship. How did he know that's what it was? Because it was round, yes, and nothing any human knew how to make, but there's more information here, something he's missing, something he knew once but doesn't know now. But where did it come from, this memory?

Panic. Being threatened, trapped. Having no way out. It triggers something inside of him. Like it did in Blair, which is how an assistant biologist could assemble a spacefaring vessel. Suddenly MacReady can tap into so much more. He sees things. Stars, streaking past him, somehow. Shapes he can take. Things he can be. Repulsive, fascinating. Beings without immune systems to attack; creatures whose core body temperatures are so low any virus or other invading organism would die.

A cuttlefish contains so many colors, even when it isn't wearing them.

His hands and neck feel tight. Like they're trying to break free from the rest of him. Had someone been able to see under his clothes, just then, they'd have seen mouths opening and closing all up and down his torso.

"Help you?" a policewoman asks, opening the door for him, and this is bad, super bad, because he—like all the other smiling, white, harmless allies who are at this exact moment sauntering into every one of the NYPD's one hundred and fifty precincts and command centers—is supposed to not be noticed.

"Thank you," he says, smiling the Fearless Man Smile, powering through the panic. She smiles back, reassured by what she sees, but what she sees isn't what he is. He doffs the cowboy hat and steps inside.

He can't do anything about what he is. All he can do is try to minimize the harm, and do his best to counterbalance it.

What's the endgame here, he wonders, waiting at the desk. What next? A brilliant assault, assuming all goes well—simultaneous attacks on every NYPD precinct, chaos without bloodshed, but what victory scenario are his handlers aiming for? What is the plan? Is there a plan? Does someone, upstairs, at Black Liberation Secret Headquarters, have it all mapped out? There will be a backlash, and it will be bloody, for all the effort they put into a casualty-free military strike. They will continue to make progress, person by person, heart by heart and mind by mind, but what then? How will they know they have reached the end of their work? Changing minds means nothing if those changed minds don't then change actual things. It's not enough for everyone to carry justice inside their hearts like a secret. Justice must be spoken. Must be embodied.

"Sound permit for a block party?" he asks the clerk, who slides him a form without even looking up. All over the city, sound permits for block parties that will never come to pass are being slid across ancient, well-worn, soon-to-be-incinerated desks.

Walking out, he hears the precinct phone ring. Knows it's The Call. The same one every other precinct is getting. Encouraging everyone to evacuate in the next five minutes if they'd rather not die screaming; flagging that the bomb is set to detonate immediately if tampered with, or moved (this is a bluff, but one the organizers felt fairly certain hardly anyone would feel like calling, and, in fact, no one does).

And that night, in a city at war, he stands on the subway platform. Drunk, exhilarated, frightened. A train pulls in. He stands too close to the door, steps forward as it swings open, walks right into a woman getting off. Her eyes go wide and she makes a terrified sound. "Sorry," he mumbles, cupping his beard and feeling bad for looking like the kind of man who frightens women, but she is already sprinting away. He frowns, and then sits, and then smiles. A smile of shame, at frightening someone, but also of something else, of a hard-earned, impossible-to-communicate knowledge. MacReady knows, in that moment, that maturity means making peace with how we are monsters.

xi.

Now I've come unfrozen. My legs can move. Now my terror is animal, agitated. I step back, stagger, stumble. Fall to the ground. Hear water slosh.

"What the hell, man?" I cry, my voice startlingly loud in the wet dark. "What the fuck was that? Is that real? Are there shape-shifting aliens all around us? Have they—are they—am I—"

He laughs. Holds out his hand. Pulls me to my feet. Puts his arms around me, hugs tight. Whispers soothing noises, which somehow actually soothe me.

GHOSTS OF HOME

THE BANK DIDN'T PAY for the oranges. They should have—offerings were clearly listed as a reimbursable expense—but the turnaround time and degree of nudging needed when Agnes submitted receipts made the whole process prohibitive. If she bugged Trask too much around the wrong things she might lose the job, and with it the gas card, which was worth a lot more money than the oranges. Sucking up the expense was an investment in staving off unemployment.

Plus, she liked the feeling that since they came out of her pocket, it was she that was stockpiling favor with the spirits, instead of the bank. What did JPMorgan Chase need with the gratitude of a piddling household spirit in one of the hundreds of thousands of falling-down buildings that dotted its asset spreadsheets? All her boss cared about was keeping the spirits happy enough that roofs would not collapse or bloodstains spread on whitewashed walls when it came time to show the place—or a hearth god or brownie cause a slip or tumble that would lead to a lawsuit. The offerings came from her, and with each gift she could feel their gratitude. Interaction with household spirits was strictly forbidden, but she enjoyed knowing they were grateful. As now, entering the tiny red house at 5775 Route 9, just past the Tomahawk Diner. She breathed deep the dry wood-and-mothballs smell. She struck a match, lit the incense stick, made a small slit in the orange peel with her fingernail. Spirits were easy to please. What they wanted was simple. Not like people.

Wind shifted in the attic above her, and she caught the scent of potpourri. A sachet left in a closet upstairs, perhaps, or the scented breath of the spirit of the place. Agnes knew nothing about this one, or any of the foreclosed houses on her route. Who had lived there. Where they went. All she knew was the bank evicted them. A month ago or back in 2008 when the bubble first began to burst. Six months on the job and she still loved to investigate, but her roster of properties was too long to let her spend much time in each. And the longer she stayed, the harder it was to avoid interacting.

When she turned to go, he was standing by the door.

"Hello," he said, a young man, bearded and stocky and be-spectacled, his voice disarmingly cheerful. She thought he was a squatter. That's the only reason she spoke back.

"Hi," she said, carefully. Squatters weren't her job. Trask had someone else to handle unlawful inhabitants. Most of the ones she'd met on her rounds were harmless, down on their luck and hiding from the rain. But anybody could get ugly, when they thought their home was threatened. Agnes held up an orange. "I'm just here for the offerings," she said. "I won't report that you're sleeping here. But they do checks, so you should be prepared to move on."

He tilted his head, regarded her like a dog might. "Move . . . on?"

"Yeah," she said, and bit her tongue to keep from warning him. *The guy Trask uses, he's a lunatic. He'll burn the place down just to punish you.* She knew she should have been sympathetic to all the people overcrowded or underhoused because the banks would rather keep buildings empty than lower the prices. But nobody knew better than Agnes that when you broke the law, you had to be ready for the consequences.

"Oh!" he said, at last. "Oh, you think I'm a human!"

She stared. "You're . . . not?"

"No, no," he said, and laughed. A resounding, human, manly laugh. It reverberated in her belly. "No . . . let's just say I *can't* move on. This is my house."

"I'm so sorry." Agnes bowed her head, panic swelling in her stomach at her accidental disobedience. If Trask knew they spoke, she could get fired. "I meant no disrespect."

"I know," he said. Spirits could see that much, or so the stories went. Beyond that it was tough to tell. Some were all-knowing and some were dumb as boxes of rocks. What else did this one know about her?

Agnes had given up long ago trying to figure out why household spirits manifested differently. Sometimes it made sense, like the Shinto-tinged ancestor embodiment in the house where a Japanese family had lived, or the feisty boar-faced domovoi in a rooming house they had seized from a Russian lady. Others resisted explanation—who knew why an ekwu common to the Igbo people kept a vigil in a McMansion six thousand miles from Nigeria that had never been occupied by anyone, of African descent or otherwise . . . or why a supposedly timeless spirit would manifest as a scruffy, hot man with a sleeve of tattoos like a current-day skateboarder? Weird, but no weirder than the average manifestation.

"Thank you for the orange," he said, and crossed the room to take it out of her hand. She could smell him: He smelled like any other man. She could feel his heat. His hair was brown red.

His glasses magnified his eyes slightly, making him look a little like a cartoon character.

"You like oranges? It's usually a safe bet. Some houses like some pretty wacky shit, though. I don't kill cats for anybody." She realized she was doing that thing. The thing where she talked too much. Because she wanted somebody—a man—to like her. For an instant she did that other thing, where she immediately hated herself for this, and then realized none of it mattered. This wasn't a man. It could never leave. It knew nothing of the world but what it found between these walls. And she had to go. Now.

He peeled the orange. She half-expected his hand to pass right through it, but that was silly. She knew spirits could affect the physical world in ways far more varied and impressive than any human. Once she watched a building burst into sudden, all-encompassing flames, reducing itself to ash and windblown smoke in four minutes.

"I like oranges," he said. "Also whiskey. Could you bring me some of that, next time?"

"Bourbon, rye, scotch—single-malt, blended . . ." She recited the names like a list of lovers, men who had done her wrong, men who she still loved and would take back in an instant. She had no intention of bringing him booze. But saying the names made her blood thicken and her mouth dry.

"Bring me your favorite," he said.

"That's maybe not such a good idea," she semi-whispered.

He shrugged. "Whatever you like."

She wondered if she could trust the sadness in his voice. If spirits really were all that different from men. If, at bottom, they wanted something, and once they had it they were through with you.

"Why don't you stay?" he said, his eyes wide and throbbing with loneliness.

"I've got two dozen houses left to visit today," she said. "And then I've got to turn the keys in. Otherwise, the other maintenance workers won't be able to get in."

"After, then. Come back here. You're nice. I can see it."

"I wish I could," she said. "But there's people expecting me."

He nodded, and handed her half the orange.

A door slammed, upstairs, in the long seconds that came next. The spirit's head whipped to the side, his lips curling into a snarl, and for an instant Agnes saw the face of something savage and canine.

"The wind," she said.

"Sorry," he whispered, human again, pale and embarrassed. "I've been very on edge lately. I don't know why."

"I'm Agnes," she said, telling herself she had imagined the momentary monster-face. The next house was 12 Burnt Hills Road, and she hated that one. The spirit manifested as the house itself, floorboards opening like mouths and bricks shifting as she walked through.

"Call me Micah."

He wiped one juice-wet hand on the hem of his flannel shirt, then extended it. They shook. She bowed her head again, and he laughed protestingly. Then she left.

It was a lie, of course. No one was expecting her. No one cared where she was.

Her mother gave her a stiff-armed hug, her hands slick with tuna fish and mayonnaise.

"Wouldn't have been smoking if I knew you were coming over," she said, stubbing out a Virginia Slim she'd just lit off the stove burner.

"It's fine, really," Agnes said, sitting down at the kitchen table. The tiny trailer never failed to make her feel immense. "Can I help?"

"Boil me some water."

Two days later, and Agnes couldn't stop thinking about the man—the spirit—in the tiny red ranch. Even though her job was keeping spirits happy, she had only cared about them insofar as it might help her keep her job, and maybe one day get a better one.

Her mother tore plastic wrap roughly off the roll. "You never come by without a reason."

Agnes almost said she simply missed her mother, but the woman was too sharp for lies. "I wanted to ask. About our house."

Her mother snorted cruelly. Pear-shaped, crookedly ponytailed, smelling of church-basement bingo, her mother's mind still terrified Agnes. The woman probably knew lots about household spirits and how they worked, from all those endless Sunday services and prayer groups. All Agnes remembered from church was that God was the prime spirit, present in all things and tying it all together, and Jesus was his emanation. Just like Micah was the emanation of 5775. Anyway Agnes should have known they couldn't have a civil conversation. Her mother had spent six months waiting for an apology, and Agnes didn't believe she had anything to apologize for.

"I wanted to ask about the spirit."

"Ganesha."

"It wasn't actually Ganesha, Mom. It just took that form."

"Took that name, too."

"Fine. But you never wondered why it took that form, and not another? Considering we're not Hindu?"

"You could have called," her mother said. "If you just wanted to ask me stupid questions."

"I'm sorry to bother you," Agnes said, and stood up. "I actually thought you might be happy to see me."

"You on something?" She looked at Agnes for the first time since she'd arrived.

"No, Mom." She looked around, debated asking about the trailer and *its* spirit, but the subject was a sore one.

She wondered if her mother knew. Where she slept at night.

"Better not be," her mother said. "You don't want to lose that job." She stirred a third spoonful of powdered milk into her instant coffee. Her face was hard as winter pavement. "Considering what you had to do to get it."

"There *is* a crisis," Trask said, clicking through pictures on his computer. Graffiti someone spray-painted onto the back of the bank—*bloodsuckers, vampires, profiting from crisis.* "A crisis of accountability! These people did it to themselves. They signed mortgages they didn't understand . . ."

Agnes discretely texted herself the word *accountability.* She had lost the thread of what he was saying, as often happened during their supervisory meetings. Trask didn't mind when she texted, when they talked. He did it himself, incessantly. *Work is more important than etiquette,* he said.

"How's everything out on Route 9?"

"Same old," she said.

"No signs of dissatisfaction?"

"I heard singing in a couple. That could mean—"

His hand flapped impatiently. "It's in the reports?"

Agnes nodded.

"Good."

Around her, the bank bustled. Trask watched the two television screens mounted on his wall. A new stack of spiral-bound printed reports sat on his desk.

"What're these?" she asked.

"The central bank has a big analysis division, and they've been looking at trends on underoccupied homes. These reports are . . . actionable."

He was doing that thing, the thing people had done to her all through school. Trying to make her feel stupid. She didn't mind it, coming from him. Trask trusted her.

Once, at a party, someone found out she worked for the bank and started yelling at her about how they had been thrown out when her husband got hurt on the job and couldn't work. Agnes had kept her mouth shut because the girl was a friend of a friend, but she agreed with Trask: *These people did it to themselves.* The world didn't owe you a house. The world is a swamp of shit and suffering and you have to bust your ass to keep your head above water and sometimes you still drown. Sometimes you drown slow. Like Agnes.

"You were late today," he said.

"I know. I didn't remember what day it was until it was almost too late."

"You need to start using a calendar app."

"I know," she said.

"I've showed you how like ten times," he said, swiveling his monitor to show her the calendar in his browser window, synched to his phone.

A map of the county hung below the televisions. Hundreds of pushpins peppered it, showing homes the bank owned. Lines divided the county into five transects, each of which had its own spirit maintenance worker. Hers was Transect 4, the westernmost one, the space least densely settled, the one that required the most driving. She scanned the map idly, avoiding even looking at Transect 1, and the pin that stabbed through the heart of the house where she grew up. The house her mother lost. The house that got her this job.

Agnes picked up a crude jade frog from his desk, weighed it in her hand, felt the tiny spirit inside. Could it see her? Know her heart? Every object had a spirit, and while stories said that long ago the trees talked and mountains moved to hurt or help humans, only homes still spoke. For the thousandth time, she thought of Micah.

His snarl, his momentary monstrousness, did not make him less appealing. It made him more so. Being with so many bad men had hardwired fear into desire.

"Lunch meeting," Trask said, rising. "File the hard copies?"

Alone in his office, she wrenched open the bottom drawer of his filing cabinet. She flipped through folders, added incident reports and travel logs. Rooting around in the filing cabinet made her feel frightened, like a trespasser. Every time, she had to fight the urge to browse through things that had nothing to do with her. To learn more. To understand. Trask would not tolerate that kind of intrusion. One more way she could lose her job.

But then—*there.* 5775 Route 9. The house where Micah lived. Was *lived* even the right word? Micah's house. But that wasn't right either. The house didn't belong to him. It *was* him.

Cheeks burning, she pulled the folder from the cabinet. Deeds, contracts, mortgages, spreadsheets—all the secrets and stories of the house, encoded in impenetrable hieroglyphics. Resolve settled in her stomach, bitter and hard. Like when, ages ago, in another life, another Agnes had decided for the thousandth time to return to whatever bar or trailer park would best get her whatever illegal substance her body was enslaved to then.

She looked around, wondered if anyone else could see the

guilt on her face. Trask's computer screen was still on, logged in to the property management system. Because he trusted her.

Did banks have household spirits? Places where no human had ever lived? Lots of people spent more time at work than at home, but work was different. What difference would that difference make? Once, she'd slept in a hotel. Its spirit had been flimsy, insubstantial, shifting shapes in an abrupt and revolting fashion. Even her car had a spirit. It never spoke or showed itself, but sometimes its weird, jagged dreams rubbed up against her own while she slept.

Agnes shut her eyes and listened. Felt. Called out to the dark of the echoey old space around her.

And something answered. Something impossibly big and distant, like a whale passing far beneath a lone swimmer. Something dark and sharp and cruel and cold. She opened her eyes with a gasp and saw she was shivering.

Smiling and confident on the outside, screaming on the inside from joy and terror, seeing in her mind's eye exactly how this course of action might cost her everything, Agnes took the folder to Trask's Xerox machine and began to make herself copies.

He was waiting for her on the porch of 5775. He hugged his knees to his chest like some people held on to hope. When he saw her, his face split into a smile so glorious her own face followed suit.

"Hi," he said, rising, T-shirted, eyes all golden fire from the last of the evening sun.

"Hello," she said, and held up a bag full of fast food. "Hungry?"

He clapped his hands, his face all joy. "You're here early," he said. "You usually only come through here every couple of weeks."

"You've been watching me for a while now," she said, handing him the bag.

"I don't know. Something wouldn't let me stay silent." He opened the bag, stuck his face in, breathed deep. Happiness made him laugh. Agnes wondered when she had last heard someone laugh from happiness.

She had made the mistake of visiting 12 Burnt Hills Road right before. It had spoken to her, its voice like bricks dragged across marble. It said *I want to show you something,* over and over. She did not let it.

The file on 5775 had told her nothing. The house was fifty years old, had been owned by a perfectly banal couple who left it to their son and his wife, who sold it to a woman who couldn't keep up with her mortgage when she got laid off when the school districts consolidated, and had been evicted four years prior. No Micahs anywhere.

He ran down the hall, and came back with a bed sheet. This he spread on the living room floor, and sat upon. "Instant picnic!" Micah said, his enthusiasm so expansive she barely felt the pain in her knees when she squatted beside him. Sleeping in the fetal position night after night was beginning to take a toll.

While he took the food from the bag and began to set it up, she watched his arms. Pixelated characters from the video games of her youth adorned his arms, along with more conventional tattoo fodder—a castle; a lighthouse. "How long have you looked like this?" she asked.

"I don't know." He ate a French fry, then four. "Forever? A couple months?"

"The band on your T-shirt didn't exist when this house was built," she said. "Or do you have a whole ghost wardrobe upstairs somewhere?"

He shrugged. "No. I don't know why they're the clothes they are."

"Did you ever look like something else?"

He laughed. *Micah* laughed. "Sometimes I think so. Did you?"

"Not that I know of. So there's not a household spirit Book of Rules?"

"Not that I know of."

They ate burgers, drank sodas. She had so many questions, but what happened inside her chest while she watched him eat answered the only real one. He bit off giant, greedy, childish bites, and barely chewed.

It made sense that after being empty for a long time, a household spirit might become something different. And lose track of everything it had been before. She asked, "Do you remember the people who used to live here?"

He nodded, eyes on her, lips on his soda straw. "Well. Sort of. I feel them. I can't really remember them, but they're there. Like . . ." *Like a dream you've woken up from,* she thought, but didn't say out loud.

"I'm not supposed to interact with you," she said. "I could lose my job."

"What's your job?" he asked, all earnestness.

"I make offerings at houses where nobody lives."

He nodded. The last drops of soda slurped noisily up his straw. "They must pay you well for that."

"They don't."

"But what you do is so important!"

"I'm an independent contractor—basically a janitor," she said, and thought back to the old maintenance man at her high school, muttering prayers and burning incense beneath a defaced wall once he'd washed away the graffiti. "My mother says we're all doomed," Agnes continued. "She says these empty houses are going to add up to a whole lot of angry spirits. She says all the oranges and incense in the world won't make a difference. When people move back in, the spirits will have turned feral."

Micah wiped grease from his lips with his sleeve. "There's a lot of empty houses?"

Agnes nodded. Obviously Micah didn't watch the news or read the papers. She had been imagining that he knew all sorts of things, through spirit osmosis or who-knows-how. "Chase owns hundreds, in this county alone. Bank of America—"

"That's sad," he whispered. His face actually reddened. He was like her. He felt his emotions so hard he couldn't hide them. The air in the room thickened, grew taut. The hairs of her arms stood on end. His didn't. *At any moment he could start flinging lightning bolts,* she thought, *or burn us both to ash.* She put her hand on his arm, and the crackling, invisible fury ebbed away.

"What's it like? When there's no one here?" She was thinking of him, but also thinking of Ganesha. Alone in her old house. The rambunctious thing that had been her only friend for so long, who played strange, complex storytelling games with her and gave her spirit candy when she made a wise decision. She could taste the anise of it, still, feel it stuck between her teeth like taffy, although even if she ate it all day it would never give her cavities or make her fat. She had spent years trying not to think of Ganesha.

"It's horrible," Micah answered.

Agnes scooted closer. He wasn't human. He could kill her just by thinking it. He was a monster, and she adored him. She took his face in both hands, moved them down so the roughness of his stubble felt smooth, and kissed him.

"I need to go," she said, hours later, when she woke with her head on his bare, strong chest and her body gloriously sore from the weight of him.

"No you don't," Micah said, his hand warm and strong on her leg. Somehow, he knew. That she had no home, that she slept in her car. He sat up. His eyes were wet and panicky. He kissed her shoulder. "Please don't go," he said. "Why do you want to leave?"

Because Trask sends late-night goons to check for squatters sometimes.

Because I might lose my job if I stay.

Because this is not my home—I didn't earn it, didn't pay for it, can't afford it.

Because I don't deserve a home.

Because love makes me do dumb things.

"You're like me," Micah whispered, and his whispers vibrated in her ears even once she was back in the Walmart parking lot in the cramped backseat of her car under a blanket: "You're on your own. We're what each other needs."

Trask said routine was the key to success, which is why every morning Agnes woke and went to Dunkin' Donuts for coffee and an unbuttered bagel and a rest room wash-up and tooth-brushing. Which is what she did the morning after making love to Micah. This time, though, when she emerged from the rest room and a woman was waiting for it, she didn't think to herself: *Oh no, what if she guesses what I was doing in there and immediately knows I'm homeless and pathetic,* but rather: *What if she's doing the same thing as me—for the same reason as me?*

Which is maybe why, this time, she broke the routine slightly and instead of heading straight to the bank for her day's assignments Agnes drove east into Transect 1, feeling her chest tighten, struggling to breathe deeply against the weight that could not possibly be guilt, because she had done nothing to feel guilty about, because she had done the right thing—Trask said so—

And found the deep, raw crater, lined in red clay like a wound in the belly of the universe, where the house she grew up in used to be.

"Agnes?" Trask said, looking confused. "Everything okay?"

"Hi," she said, stopping herself from apologizing for disturbing him. An unscheduled visit was an unprecedented breach of propriety. They texted, or they talked in supervisory meetings. She had never just *shown up* before. "What's happening to the houses in Transect 1?"

"We're demolishing them, Agnes." His voice now was like when teachers wanted to shame her into silence.

"Why?"

"I told you. Actionable recommendations from the central analysis division. Even with emanation placation measures in place, we've been noticing some disturbing patterns."

My mother was right, she thought. *They've gone feral.* His computer made soft pinging noises as the day's pitches arrived. Every bank routinely made offers for every other bank's underoccuppied property, usually for ridiculously low amounts, knowing they'd be rejected. Fishing for hunger. Trying to "assemble development portfolios" and other concepts she had not initially understood.

"But people could be living there," she told Trask, knowing, as soon as she said it, that the argument had no financial weight and was therefore worthless.

"What do you mean, you can't step onto the lawn?"

"I just can't," Micah said, grinning, face glistening with French fry grease and her kisses. He leaned over the porch railing; reached out his arm to her.

"But it's part of the property," she said, stepping just out of his reach.

Micah shrugged. *"Property* is a legal fiction," he said. "Words on paper don't change anything. A house is a house."

"A legal fiction," she said, and texted the phrase to herself. "I thought you didn't know The Rules."

"Some things I just know," he said. "I don't know why I look like this, but I know what I can't do. And I know that when you're here, it feels right."

"But this is crazy, isn't it? You and me. A spirit and a person? I've never heard of that."

"Me either," he said. "So?"

"We can't . . . be together."

"We're together now."

"This isn't my house."

"Why not?" His eyes were wide, sincere, incredulous. She wanted to eat them. She wanted to have them inside her forever.

"Because it costs money to buy a house. I don't have money."

Micah nodded, but she knew he did not understand.

Back in the car, she stared at the wooden block studded with keys. Her roster for the day: three dozen homes, defenseless.

Agnes had made mistakes before. She'd shattered friendships. She'd had a drink when she knew the whole long list of horrible things that would come next. One thing was always true, though: She knew they were mistakes before she made them. She decided to make a mistake and that's what she did. The hard part was figuring out the right mistake to make.

"Twice in two weeks," her mother said, stubbing out her Virginia Slim. "You hard up for a place to take a shower?"

"Happy to see you, too, Mom."

Her mom sat back in her chair and sighed, a long aching sound. Her eyes did not seem able to open all the way. Walmart had demoted her from the cash register to the shoe section. They talked in terse, fraught sentences until the water boiled and the instant coffee was prepared.

"I'm sorry, Mom."

"Sorry for what?" her mother muttered.

"Sorry for what I did. To you."

Her mother's mug clinked against the counter. Now her eyes were wide. "What did you do?"

"You know what I did. We both do. You even said so, the last time I was here."

"Tell me."

Agnes nodded. She owed her mother this much—to spell it out, to look her in the eyes. "I told the bank you were still living there, in the house, after you'd stopped paying the mortgage. After you'd been evicted. I got you kicked out."

Her mother's eyes were harsh, unblinking. Agnes took a sip: The coffee was so strong it hurt to swallow. "Do you know? What they did to it?"

Her mother nodded. "I drive by there, sometimes."

"I didn't think I did anything wrong," Agnes said. Her voice felt so small. "I thought you were in the wrong, to keep on living there when you couldn't pay."

"What changed?"

Agnes shrugged, opened her mouth, shut it again.

Her mother took her mug, added hot water, handed it back. "Last time you were here, you asked why the spirit took on the shape of Ganesha. I said I didn't know, and I don't. But I have a theory. When I was a little girl, our next-door neighbors were Indian. They had a Ganesha statue on their porch. They had a girl my age, we used to play together. She always made me rub the statue's stomach for good luck. I think when a house finds its perfect owner, it takes on the shape that owner needs to see."

Agnes sipped. Diluted to human strength, the coffee wasn't bad.

12 Burnt Hills Road again. She lingered, left an extra orange. The house frightened her, but sometimes being frightened wasn't bad. Sometimes fear brought you where you needed to be.

Agnes, it said, when she turned to go. This time the squeal of glass and wood, grinding together: All four windows in the front room trembled, spoke as one.

"You know my name?"

We all know your name.

"We?"

The empty ones. I want to show you something. Will you let me show you?

"Yes."

Press your hands to the brick, the voice said, and she did. *Shut your eyes,* it said, and she did.

Laughter. A little girl ran into a swathe of sunlight. Herself, age five.

"No," she whispered.

Watch.

Agnes at ten, Agnes at twelve. The house. Her house. Each

room, each smell. Christmas cooking and make-up and wet paint. Her mother's smile growing slimmer and the rest of her less so as time sped by. Ganesha, scrambling from room to room with one long, undiminishing, mischievous giggle.

Joy, then. Ganesha's joy. The bliss of wholeness. The ecstasy of love, of family. Home meant love, meant wholeness. Shrinking, suddenly, when Agnes stormed out at age sixteen. After that a bereft, endless wondering. *Where did she go? Why was she so upset? How have I failed her?*

Her mother standing alone at the top of the stairs. Cigarettes. Burned TV dinners.

"Please," Agnes said, too loudly, knowing what was next.

The house, empty. Ganesha stumbling. Shrinking. And then weeping, as pain began to break him apart. Hands growing twisted, pudgy child-fingers becoming cat-sharp claws. Pieces of trunk sloughing off. The transect maintenance worker brought oranges, but they did not stop what was happening to her friend. They merely channeled off his anger, his rage, his ability to lash out. When the wrecking ball came it was almost a relief. Ganesha went gladly, already mostly gone. Something bigger was there, though. A bigger, deeper something that was Ganesha but wasn't. It shrieked. She wept, hearing it wail.

The windows went still.

"I thought you were all . . . on your own. Separate. Micah didn't know what was happening to any of the other houses."

A rippling shifted through the walls, and when the voice came again it came from a crude and jagged mouth that opened in the bricks above the fireplace. *Autochthonous sentient structural emanations are complex. The spirit that takes on physical form, the thing that humans interact with, is only one piece. There is another piece. One that grows out of the earth the house is built on. One that springs from a common source with all the other autochthonous emanations in the area. These pieces are rarely aware of each other. Until they need to be. Do you understand?*

"Sure," and Agnes was startled to see that she did. She thought of how her mother understood God. She thought of the thing she had sensed, for an instant, in the bank. Something bigger and colder and crueler and more terrifying than a human mind could ever comprehend.

We saw you, Agnes. We saw what was inside of you. We knew that you were the one who could help us.

Trask was stressed out about something. His forehead had extra lines in it; his eyebrows were arrows aiming at each other. He was immersed in his phone. When she logged the block of house keys back in, he left the key in the cabinet lock. Like he always did.

"Are you going to demolish all of them?"

He looked up from his phone, his face contorted briefly. By what? Hate, she thought at first, but that wasn't right, whatever it was had no such intensity. Apathy, maybe, but that was only half the story. Trask took two reports from the top of the stack and flung them at her. "Read it yourself if you're so nosy."

He doesn't care about you, she realized. *He never has.*

He thinks you're stupid.

Agnes filled paperwork with scribbles until Trask left the office to take a call, and then she opened the cabinet and pocketed the key to Micah's house. She dumped the rest of the keys from Transect 4 into her backpack, and put the block back in the cabinet, and locked it.

After thirty awful seconds, Agnes unlocked the cabinet again and took the keys to the rest of the Transects.

Trask's screen was still on. She stared at it. Her plan was a terrible one. She could destroy the keys, but how much time would that buy them? Trask would learn what had happened soon enough, and he didn't need a key to knock a building down. She'd be out of a job and those spirits would still get destroyed.

Agnes sat down at his desk. He didn't leave her alone with so much power at her fingertips because he trusted her. He did it because he didn't think she was smart enough to do anything about it. He gave her the job not because he liked her or saw potential, but because she showed him how desperate she was. How hungry. Hungry enough to betray her own mother for a shit job with no health insurance.

She clicked over to the window where the day's offers had piled up. One by one she clicked yes, selling off a couple dozen buildings with Trask's credentials. And then she made a series of offers on the Bank of America properties scattered throughout the county, offering ten million dollars for each of them when most were barely worth ten thousand.

Then she opened his calendar and typed in an appointment for him, tomorrow at twilight, at 12 Burnt Hills Road, with the plumbing maintenance foreman.

Trask might wonder what that was, how it had gotten there; he might even call the plumber to confirm. But most likely he would not. He was a man who trusted his calendar.

Would it kill him? she wondered. The thought of being a party to Trask's murder did not disturb her as much as it should have. What she'd mistaken for officious mentorship had been contempt, combined with a love of feeling smarter than someone. More importantly, she'd do anything to keep Micah from going through what her home had gone through.

Chase would dispute the sales she had approved as Trask,

and the offers he'd made, but Bank of America would take them to court to get them to honor these entirely legal contracts.

Later she buried the backpack full of keys in the red, raw clay where her house had been.

"That's the last of it?" Micah asked, when she set the milk crate down on the porch.

"Such as it is."

"You were living *there?*" he asked, wrinkling his nose in the direction of her car.

"Who really *lives,* anyway," she asked, squatting to kiss his mouth. He handed her a glass of iced tea.

She took a sip, then drained the glass. "This is seriously the best iced tea I have ever had in my life."

"I know," he said. "And it has the added benefit of not having any calories."

He put his arm around her. Night was coming and so was November. His heat was so strong and clear she didn't believe it wasn't real.

That morning, she had visited 12 Burnt Hills Road. Trask had been missing for two days. She expected blood and carnage, but the inside of the house was as it had always been. Wind wailed, weakly, somewhere.

The police came, said the stones above the mantel.

"They would have seen the address in his calendar," she said. "I'm sorry, but there was no way for me to erase it after he saw it . . ."

He is well hidden. As is his vehicle. They found nothing, and departed. Touch the stones, if you want to see.

She didn't, but she did. And saw him get out of his fancy

truck, call out for the plumber, pat his pockets for the keys he knew he had not brought because the plumbers had their own set. Saw the front door creak open. Saw Trask step inside. Saw stones and wood and brick crawl together. Saw windows shatter into long cruel talons at the end of stumpy fingers. Saw the seat of Trask's trousers darken.

"This is temporary," she said, thinking of the cold, cruel, immense entity she had glimpsed at work. With Trask missing and the police involved, the court battle would drag on for a while. But not forever. "Eventually, the bank will move forward with a way to do what it wants."

Yes, the house said. *And so will we.*

She didn't ask *What about Micah? His shape, his personality—is he part of you? Did you use him to manipulate me?* As long as she didn't know the answer, she could pretend it didn't matter.

Micah startled her back to the here-and-now, carrying a radio on an extension cord. They danced to the Rolling Stones on the porch of the house that was hers, but not. Later, they lay in a bed so big she could not believe her stupidity—to think that this had been here all along, empty and waiting, while she slept in a car in the Walmart parking lot. Because of Trask, inside her head, and the bank and the school and everyone else in this world who said you only deserved what you could pay for. When she wept, he woke up. They spooned together.

Agnes fought sleep, not wanting to be anywhere else. She counted questions instead of sheep.

When we fight, will he accidentally incinerate me? When he is angry or sad, will blood drip from ceilings and swarms of hornets spell out hateful words on the wall?

She wondered if she would still have her job, without Trask. Probably she would. For now. Both banks would want to maintain the properties while they fought over them in court. She could fix the place up, get real human food, buy Micah the punk rock records he liked. She could lay low, but eventually there would be a confrontation. Ownership would be settled. Someone would come, looking to knock it down or clear it out. But wasn't that part of what it meant, to have a home? The knowing that it could always be taken away from you? That's what she never grasped, those long nights in her old house aching to be anywhere else. She had taken "home" for granted, something unbreakable and allotted to each of us, because that's the way the world should be. And once it was gone she believed everyone deserved the same pain she and her mother went through. Ganesha was dead because of the lies she believed, and her mother's heart was broken.

But now that she knew something could be taken away, she also knew she could fight for it.

"I love you," she whispered, to him, to her home, and fell asleep marveling at how easy both things were to claim once you let yourself.

xii.

"Tell me it isn't real," I whisper.

"I see so many things," he says. "Allosauruses in rural barns. King Kong falling from the sky. All I can say for sure is, they believe it's true. Some of it might be nightmare, or mental illness, but some of it—maybe most of it—is real."

I'm so scared I'm sobbing. He shushes, gives me a maternal peck on the forehead. Whispers:

"Turns out, the world is way weirder and more full of monsters than any of us ever suspect, boy."

THE HEAT OF US:
NOTES TOWARD AN ORAL HISTORY

Craig Perry, university administration employee.

JUDY GARLAND, DEAD. That's where it started. Dead five days before, in London, "an incautious overdosage" of barbiturates, according to the coroner, and her body had just come back to New York for burial. Twenty thousand people lined up to pay their respects. Every gay man in Manhattan must have gone, but I couldn't do it. I couldn't go see her in that coffin and disturb the delicate Dorothy Gale I had in my head. I don't know, I needed to move, to walk, to run. To do something. So I headed for the Hudson River Piers.

My sadness buoyed me up, made me feel like I was looking down on the entire city. I watched the sky go blue and orange and red and purple and indigo as the sun set, then watched the lights come on across the river in Jersey City. June, 1969: The wet Manhattan air was like sick breath coming out of our collective throat.

I felt it in me, then. A spark. I didn't see it for what it really was, but I felt it.

That's why I went to the Stonewall.

Sadness is a better spark than rage. I remember thinking, *Revolutions are born on nights like this.* So many people would be mourning Judy. We'd all be miserable together. What couldn't we do, if we were all on the same page like that? Now it sounds like I'm trying to be portentous, given what ultimately went down that night, but I really did have that feeling.

Ben Lazzarra, NYPD beat cop.

I checked with the sarge that afternoon. I always did, when I was off-duty and felt the urge and knew I couldn't fight it, knew I'd have to find a place to dance it out of me. I was lucky I was a cop and could check to make sure I wouldn't get swept up in a raid. Nothing was on the list for the Stonewall that night. That's how I know for a fact that what went down that night was not your standard gay club raid. Someone upstairs was pulling strings.

I spent the whole week agonizing over whether or not to go. That's how it always went. I'd wrestle with my fear and shame, and win, and go, and then feel so miserable and ashamed afterwards that I leapt back into the closet for another few weeks. I needed some action, some booze, and some sweat and some sex with a stranger. Quentin and I had gone to the gym together, that afternoon, and I knew he had to work that night. He didn't ask where I was going, when I went out. Even twins are allowed to have little secrets. But he was the reason I stayed in the closet, and was always so careful to not get dragnetted. Seeing my name in the paper in a story on a gay bar raid—that would kill Quentin quicker and deader than any bullet.

The world changed in two huge ways that night.

In the first place, the world changed because the gays fought back. The police and the press were equally dumbfounded by the idea that a bar full of fairies would refuse to submit to one of the raids that were standard—if monstrously unjust—operating procedure. The Stonewall itself had been raided less than a week before. The night of June 28, 1969, should have been no different.

Secondly, the Stonewall Uprising was the first public demonstration of the supernatural phenomenon that would later be called by names as diverse as collective pyrokinesis, group magic, communal energy, polykinesis, multipsionics, liberation flame, and hellfire.

None of the eleven different city, state, and federal government agencies that investigated the events of that night have ever confirmed or even acknowledged the overwhelming number of witness testimonies describing the events that caused the police to so catastrophically lose control of a routine operation. The facts, however, do not seem to be in doubt. Ten police officers were vaporized that night, vanishing so utterly that the NYPD still considers them missing persons. Three more were cooked alive, charred to the point where dental records were needed to identify the bodies. No incendiary or flammable substances were found at the scene. Five paddy wagons full of arrestees were stopped when their engines spontaneously overheated, and the metal doors of the wagons were melted away to free the people inside—yet no blowtorches or welding equipment were found at the scene.

Since testimonials are all that's left to those of us frustrated with the Official Version, the oral history format seems to be our best bet. I know that many of the most outspoken voices of the Stonewall Uprising have reacted with anger and hostility at the

news that I, of all journalists, was planning to compile such a history, and are urging their comrades not to speak with me. I understand their objections, and have precious little to show by way of proof that I've changed. I simply cannot not tell this story.
—Jenny Trent, Editor (formerly of The New York Times)

Craig Perry, university administration employee.

I know it's dumb, but I felt like I had failed. Rage hadn't gotten me anywhere. Being Black, being gay, I'd been raising hell my whole life. Screaming nonstop, at the top of my lungs, at the bullies and the cops and the priests and the rest of the hateful sons of bitches, trying to get my brothers and sisters to stand up together, and for what? The world was still so rotten that beautiful creatures like Judy Garland couldn't wait to get out of it. Sadness felt like the only rational response to a world like that.

Walking wasn't enough, so I went to the gym to get my mind off things. It didn't work. The twins were there, but not even the sight of *them* could cheer me up. One bearded and one mustachioed, both of their bodies the same impossible lumberjack-rugby-player shape, wide-necked and wide-thighed, who did not seem to have aged a day in the seven years I'd been going to that gym. Sadness kept swallowing me back up, distracting me from the spectacle of them, happy and secure in their bubble of hetero-bro-confidence. By the time I walked out of there, I was feeling incurably alone.

All I kept thinking was, *Tonight, more than any other night, I need to dance. I need to be among my people.*

Ben Lazzarra, NYPD beat cop.

Stonewall was fucking depressing. People paint it as this great place where you could be who you really were. If that's who you really were, you were really fucked. Run by the mob, painted all black inside, stinking of mold and charred wood because it had been boarded shut for twenty years after a big fire. I mean, every gay bar was a piece of shit—what did you expect when you couldn't operate legally? The State Liquor Authority wouldn't issue licenses to gay bars, and nobody runs illegal business-es but the mob. They didn't even have running water, just a big plastic trough behind the bar, where they'd dunk the used glasses and then use them again. Not even any soap. The sum-mer it opened there was a hepatitis outbreak.

But you went, because where else were you going to go? How else could you escape from the crushing weight of your waking life, and be among your own sick, twisted, beautiful kind?

Chief Abraham Asher, NYPD—6th Precinct.

We knew it was a full moon. Basic rule of policing: Don't do crowd-control-type stuff on full moon nights. I don't know why—people just lose their minds a little easier. This one had some pressure from upstairs, though, and was kind of a last-minute decision. But I can tell you this for goddamn sure: If I'da known Judy Garland had just died, we'd never have gone any-where near the damn place.

That night essentially ruined my life. I got demoted. Every article painted me as a colossal idiot, and that's taken a huge toll on my family. But I got no cause to complain, because a lot of my men didn't come back from that night.

I used to think that faggots were poor creatures who couldn't help their perversion. I've changed my mind about that. Now I know for a fact they're born of hellfire and bent on burning us all up. And that we ought to put them all on a big boat, put it out to sea, and torpedo the son of a bitch.

Shelly Bronsky, bookstore owner.

I was a waitress then, at the Stonewall, although "waitress" is a stretch. We picked up glasses and gave them to the bartenders, and we kept the cigar boxes full of money—no cash register, ever, or the cops would take it away during a raid as evidence that we were selling liquor without a license, as opposed to holding a private party, which is what the mob lawyers would argue to get the case against the building owner thrown out. We mopped up the toilets when they overflowed, which was always. At the end of every night, we'd go through the garbage of the neighboring bars and steal empty bottles of top-shelf liquor, so the next night when the mob guys came through, they could fill them up with their own shitty, diluted bootleg stuff.

Abraham Asher, NYPD—6th Precinct.

I hated the raids. We had to do them, because you can't just let filth and sickness fester in your city, but going into those places made my officers really lose their shit.

By midnight, we were in position around the corner, thirty cops, waiting for the signal from the undercovers we'd sent inside. That was standard for a raid—undercovers went in early, always women, to finger the people who worked there, because those were more serious charges. The Stonewall had a big, heavy door with wooden reinforcements, so every time we raided the place, it would take us six or seven minutes to break it down and get inside, and in that time the workers would drop everything and blend in with the crowd. Once we were in, it'd be like no one worked there.

But that night, it was weird. We kept waiting and our girls inside did not come out, and I tried to radio headquarters and couldn't get through. So we got pretty antsy pretty fast.

Tricksie Barron, unemployed.

You got to talk to somebody else for that. I was there, but I was so drunk that night that we might have called up a bunch of flying monkeys to burn it down. All I remember is, I met the man of my dreams that night. I meet him most nights, but this one was extra special. Complimented my dress and everything. While we were dancing, he grabbed me by the ass, pulled me close, and said, "I like a girl who's packing more heat than me."

Craig Perry, university administration employee.

It was a rough night for the older queens. Men wept like babies for Judy. I stood in their midst, baffled. What was wrong with them, these fools, these people, my people, dancing like all was well in the world? I wanted to grab them, shake them, fill them up with the rage that choked me.

A lot of them were men I'd been seeing there for the longest. Many had lost everything over the years, for being who they were, for living in the world they lived in. But they were too beaten down to ever fight back. Less than a month before, when I tried to organize a campaign against *The New York Times* for its policy of publishing the names of men arrested in vice raids—lists that invariably got everyone on them fired or divorced or sometimes institutionalized and lobotomized against their will—not a one of them wanted to do a damn thing.

Judy Garland got played again and again, sparking fresh tears and howls each time a song started. A bunch of women I had never seen before, who looked like they wandered into the wrong bar by mistake, joined in on a sing-along to the fifth straight time someone played "Somewhere Over the Rainbow." Now I know they must have been the undercovers, but then I just thought they were confused tourists.

I watched them dance, the poorest of our poor, the kids who got beaten and thrown out and sometimes way worse. Smokey Robinson said *Take a gooood look at my face* and they all sang along, even the boy with the scar across his face shaped like the iron his mother burned him with.

Again I thought about the twins at the gym, men of steel or stone, their bodies as perfect as the bond between them. I had never known any bond remotely like that. I was forty that summer, and I had come to believe that loneliness was an essential and ineluctable aspect of gay identity, or at least my own.

Diana Ross came on the radio. We danced, and we sang *I hear a symphonyyyyyy*, and we *were* the symphony, for as long as the song lasted.

Annabelle Kowalski, stenographer.

Judy who? Child, please. Don't you let the gay boys hoodwink you. Sure, some old queens were crying in their beer to "Over the Rainbow" that night, but divas die every day and nobody bursts into flames. That shit happened because we *made* it happen.

The raid itself came at one in the morning. I was in bed already. I lived a block and a half away. I heard the screams and shouts. I went to the window and saw two young Black men, laughing, running. I hollered down, asked what was happening.

"Riot at the Stonewall!" they shouted. "Us faggots is fighting back!"

And I don't know how, but I knew this was my story. My chance. I pulled a jacket on over my bedclothes, and ran.

—Jenny Trent, Editor (formerly of The New York Times)

Ben Lazzarra, NYPD beat cop.

What you need to know is that I was *always* scared, when I did stuff like that. Meeting men in darkness under the West Side Highway, accepting hurried blowjobs on late-night subway platforms, entering the Stonewall, I always expected the worst. It's ridiculous, but I wished Quentin could have been there. I never felt whole or safe without him. But of course he couldn't be.

We were dancing, all of us, packed together in that shitty room, hot and sweaty and happy. And for once, I wasn't scared.

For once, I felt good and happy about who and where I was. We were safe there, from the cops and the mob and all the other bad men, safe in the heat our bodies made together.

I don't know what was different. I never liked dancing before. For me, like for a lot of the Stonewall boys, dancing was what you did to figure out who you were going home with. But what I felt that night was a lot like what I had always felt at the gym, the same sense of power and energy, except without the constant shame and terror that I always felt around Quentin. The fear that he'd see me staring at some boy's backside, or spot some infinitesimal fraction of an erection, and Know Everything.

What I felt that night was joy. There is no other word for it.

This, I kept thinking. *This is sacred. This is joy.*

My twin brother and I added up to something, together. Quentin made me feel love, power, and safety, but never joy. We were locked into each other, a closed loop that gave us much but took away more.

People have told me that maybe if I had been honest with him, things would have gone down differently. I'd still have him. They're right, of course, every time. And every time, I want to punch them in the face until my fist comes out the other side.

Craig Perry, university administration employee.

The frenzy was on me by then, and I was dancing like I might die when I stopped.

I danced up on a short, built, sparkplug of a man with his back to me. The shape of his ass assured me he'd be a prime catch.

That's when the house lights came up, blindingly bright and white, flickering like a theater warning us intermission was ending. I'd been caught up in a raid before. Taken to the precinct along with twenty other guys, and one of them got so scared because his name would be in the paper and his parents would find out and disown him, he jumped out the second-story window—and got impaled on the points of a wrought-iron fence. Took them six hours to get him off of there, with blowtorches and everything, and when they brought him to St. Vincent's, he still had spikes of iron in him. He survived, but he wished he hadn't.

So a lot of us knew what to expect when the Stonewall gave the signal. A lot of us screamed, high, theatrical, exaggerated wails, and laughed, and faked swooning, and to be honest I heard myself laugh. Kind of a crazy laugh, though, because I could finally feel the sadness start to ebb out of my rage. I didn't want to run. I wanted to fucking kill somebody.

The sparkplug, on the other hand, wasn't laughing.

"Fuck," he said, looking around in a panic, looking for another way out. Of course there wasn't one, because the fucking Stonewall was a death trap with no fire exit. He turned around. I saw his face.

"Hi," I said, absurdly, cheerfully, finding room in my rage for more laughter, because it was the bearded one of the twins from the gym.

Ben Lazzarra, NYPD beat cop.

Nobody told me that the flashing white lights meant a raid. I thought there was a fire, or somebody won a raffle I didn't know about. It took me a while to pick up what was happening from what people were saying around me.

"What do we do?" I said, to Craig, except he wasn't Craig then, he was just the weirdly friendly Black dude standing behind me.

"We wait, and keep our fingers crossed they don't take anybody in."

But I knew they'd be taking us in. An unscheduled raid, less than a week after the last one, meant this was more than just the shake-up each precinct was obliged to give from time to time. And for a minute I was fine. Relieved, even. When the worst thing you can possibly imagine happens, you're free from the fear of it for the rest of your life.

But sometimes the worst thing you can imagine isn't the worst thing that can happen.

"Everybody up against the walls," said a loud, scary cop voice, and then repeated it, and the second time I knew who was speaking.

Quentin led the brigade into the back room, two rows of cops, each with a dozen sets of handcuffs at the ready. The dance floor emptied out, but I couldn't move. He stopped, five feet from me, snarling with rage at having to repeat himself, because someone had not immediately obeyed. And then he saw who it was.

"Benjy?" he said. His face, that perfect cop blank slate, cracked under the weight of what he was seeing. His twin brother, the man whose side he'd hardly ever left, the man with whom he'd joined the police force and struggled valiantly to fight the forces of evil, who now stood before him in a sweaty, tight T-shirt in a den of iniquity, had been keeping from him a secret so terrifying that it threatened to strip the flesh from both our bones. The man who he knew better than anyone, he had not known at all.

Some lady with a gruff voice beside me hissed "Oh, *Hell* no."

Quentin said my name again, no question mark now, and that was the last word he ever said.

Shelly Bronsky, bookstore owner.

Those gay boys parted like the Red Sea for the boys in blue. The cops marched in and men fell over themselves, running for the walls. One guy didn't, and that's what gave me the courage to pry myself free from the crowd and step forward. The scary-mustache cop who led the brigade stopped short, not five feet from me, and I saw something like fear come over his face.

"Oh, *Hell* no," I hissed.

Someone behind me yelled, "Yeah!"

Some Black gay protest queen, who I'd been seeing around since forever, stepped forward to join the two of us. "Hell no!"

The shouts spread. *Oh no honey, no you won't,* and *Ain't you got no real criminals to arrest.* I thought of the beautiful boy I knew from school, whose father pressed his face to the burner on the stove to make the men leave him alone, and the cigarette burns on my own upper arm where my mother tried to burn the lez out of me. We'd been swallowing fire for so long, fire and violence and hate, and in that moment of panic and fear and anger everything fell into place to feed the fire back.

And that's what we did.

Abraham Asher, NYPD—6th Precinct.

I was born and bred in the Bronx, but I went to fight in Europe during World War Two. As a Jew, I felt I had to play my part in ridding the world of the fascist menace. Later on I'd join the police force for the same reason, because I felt it was my duty to make my city safe.

In the war I saw some rough things, went on some scary missions. And I've never in my life been more frightened than I was in that fag bar.

I'll tell you what I've told everyone else: It was too dark and too full of screaming and the smell of cooked flesh for me to say one way or another whether a wave of devil fire really shot out of nowhere to murder my men. If some of our boys who survived said that's what happened, I'm not going to call them liars.

Accounts of the uprising have been unsurprisingly whitewashed. All the major news outlets have blocked any mention of multipsionics—or whatever you want to call it. My own articles have been rejected by dozens of papers and magazines because I've refused to take out what they call "supernatural elements." Time, for example, is the least biased of the bunch, and their most enlightened pronouncement on the subject of sexual difference is that "homosexuality is a serious and sometimes crippling maladjustment."

Responsible parties have conducted exhaustive experiments. They won't talk about them publicly, but through my connections to the Stonewall veterans, I know that almost everyone who has gone on record about that night has subsequently been approached to participate in studies by the U.S. government, foreign governments, defense contractors, pharmaceutical companies, and leading organized crime families.

While the phenomenon has since been observed in hundreds of minor and major incidents, it simply refuses to submit to science. Studying individuals or groups, with or without duress, in labs or on the street or in the still-smoldering remains of the Stonewall itself, no one has been able to replicate those events, not

so much as the lighting of a lone candle on a birthday cake.
   —*Jenny Trent, Editor (formerly of* The New York Times*)*

Ben Lazzarra, NYPD beat cop.

Fire sparked in the air all around us. It hung there like the burning of invisible torches, and then it spread, like fire does. It moved, writhed, twisted into a ring, surrounded the three cops that had led the battalion into the back room. Three that included my brother Quentin. The flames rushed in, fast as floodwater when a levee breaks, and incinerated them.

The rest of those cops ran. Fifteen of them, but the door from the back to the front rooms only let them out one at a time, and the anger of my fellow queers was quicker and smarter. Somehow, so swiftly, they had learned to control the flames. Without saying a word, the crowd turned its full rage on them—and the fire lashed out with such white-hot hunger that ten men simply vanished from this planet. Flame broke them down into the atoms they were made from, and carved a huge hole in the stone wall between the front and back rooms, too.

Everyone was screaming and yelling by then, rushing out into the street after the rest of the cops. Streaks of fire zinged and whooshed through the air around them. They left me alone with the charred heap of my brother.

Tyrell James, security specialist.

I was there. I felt it. I know what we did. And I've been going all over the world, training people who've been pushed too far for too long, telling them how to fight back when the moment comes when their backs are up against the wall. And one day very soon, the people who like to push other people around are going to wake up and find out everything's changed.

Abraham Asher, NYPD—6ᵗʰ Precinct.

I find it offensive, what those people are saying. They expect you to believe all you've got to do is get a bunch of people together who are mad and scared and then fire will rain down on the evildoers? So, the Jews who went to the gas chambers weren't scared enough? The slaves weren't mad? It's a bunch of manure, if you ask me.

I'll tell you this much. Cops are a pretty cynical bunch, and we don't buy ghost stories. But there isn't a man or woman of the twenty thousand on the force that doesn't know in our guts that something really real and really scary happened that night. Finding a couple fairies in a park and ticketing them for disorderly conduct used to be an easy count toward your quota, but to this day most officers will think twice before they do it. And we don't ever raid gay bars.

Craig Perry, university administration employee.

It's not that no one in the whole history of human oppression was as pissed-off and fucked-over as we were that night—I think it's happened lots of times, except we're reading history the wrong way. We read it the way The Man wrote it, and when he was writing it, I bet he didn't know what to do with multipsionics. But I've studied this shit. The Warsaw Ghetto Uprising happened on Passover, after all, and the Haitian Revolution began with a spontaneous uprising at a Vodoun religious ceremony. When people come together to celebrate, that's when they're unstoppable.

Ben Lazzarra, NYPD beat cop.

People say the world changed for us that night, but I'm not sure I buy it. The world is the same, only more so. People still hate and fear us, they just hate and fear us *more*. People still bash and kill and lobotomize us, they just do it more. And we still know in our hearts, under the shame and self-loathing and all the other shit society has heaped on us, that we were born blessed by God with an incredible gift.

I've steered clear of all the scientists and scholars and reporters trying to turn that night into a research paper, but there's one thing I do know. It was *us*. The heat of us, of all those bodies full of joy and sadness and anger and lust, and the combination of the three of us: Me and Craig and that dyke. I can't explain it, that's just what I felt in that moment. We were the match and the sandpaper, coming together. All I know is it was *us*.

Craig Perry, university administration employee.

We all went a little mad that night. Nobody knew what the hell had happened, but we knew nothing would be the same again.

People danced and whooped and hollered and laughed. Three men skipped into the distance with their arms locked, singing *We're off to see the wizard.*

I don't know why I didn't want to be with my people, then. I felt empty. Like I'd put my whole self into wanting something, and now I had it. I'd licked envelopes and organized protests and screamed at the top of my lungs for a decade or several, and the revolution had finally come . . . but answered prayers are always terrifying. What are you, when you get the thing you've built your life around trying to get?

My rage had burnt itself out. So instead of joining the jubilant crowds, I went to the Day-O Diner, where the Meatpacking District meets the Hudson River, where the coffee is strong and cheap and nobody goes there but bloody meatmen ending their shifts, or clean meatmen beginning theirs.

The twin sat by himself. His back was to the door but after what had just gone down I would have known that rugby-wide neck anywhere. I strolled past, pretending to be selecting a bar stool, to confirm that he wasn't sobbing. His face was blank, staring into scalding black coffee for answers we both knew were not there.

"I'm sorry about your brother," I said, cautiously.

He looked up. "I know you from the gym," he said.

"He didn't know," I said, "did he? About . . ."

He shook his head.

"I'm sorry. I can't imagine. I just wanted to say—but you must want to be alone—"

"Don't go," he said. "Being alone is what I'm worst at."

He began to weep then, with his whole body. I sat and ordered refill after refill of black coffee, for both of us, until the sun came up.

I've interviewed Craig Perry a dozen times since Stonewall, and I don't think he's ever recognized me, ever made the connection. But he had come to see me, two weeks before the fire. He visited me at the office of The New York Times. He came to demand we stop printing the names of gay people caught up in vice raids and decency arrests. I think he thought I was merely the secretary, which is why my face didn't stay in his mind, but I was not. I was the one who wrote those articles. I had been writing them for eight years by then. Later on I went through all my old clippings and did the math: thirteen hundred names, thirteen hundred people whose deepest darkest secret I spilled. If I put in the time, I could probably track down how many of them killed themselves, how many got fired or dishonorably discharged or institutionalized, but that wouldn't help anything but my own guilty need to suffer. Telling the story, the real story, is a much better way to pay off the crippling karma-debt I built up in the years before I knew better.

Craig before Stonewall was a different person. His rage was enormous, overwhelming, cutting him off from the rest of the human race. He wanted the revolution, right away, wanted it to come with fire and brimstone and the blood of every heterosexist son /daughter of a bitch to be spilled in the streets. I don't want to speculate on what changed, what he had after that he didn't have before, what aspect of what went down inside the Stonewall broke down his old anger. I don't know him like that. Journalists tend to write about people like they know what makes them tick, why they do the things they do, and at the end of the day it's the stories people tell about themselves that matter.

—Jenny Trent, Editor (formerly of The New York Times*)*

Ben Lazzarra, NYPD beat cop.

No matter how many hours I spent at the gym after that, it was never the same. My muscle tone was never as sharp, my stamina flagged faster. Two months after Quentin died, I noticed wrinkles in my forehead for the first time. Whatever we were, together, the weird magic of us against the world, was broken.

Craig and I slept together for a while, but that wasn't meant to be. We wanted different things in bed—plus what we both needed then was not a boyfriend. I had never had a best friend before. I loved Quentin with my whole heart, more than I loved myself, but until he was taken away I never had to think about how much happiness I had sacrificed by living my whole adult life with the paralyzing fear that he'd find out what I was.

Every year, on my birthday, Craig brings over two cakes and we blow out the candles with our minds. And every year he wonders why stopping fires is so much easier than starting them. For us, anyway. I don't tell him my theory, because he'd just laugh at it, but I believe joy is the only thing stronger than sadness.

xiii.

"Why," I say, wiping snot from my face. "Why show me all of that?"

He spins me around slowly, spoons me from behind. His arms are so tight, so strong. We watch the black horizon.

"Same reason you went out looking for somebody to blow tonight, boy," he whispers. Lips warm in my ear, in the curve of my neck. "Same reason people tell stories. I'm fucking lonely. I'm desperate to connect with someone. To feel less like the only creature like me in this whole dark, cold cosmic multiverse."

ANGEL, MONSTER, MAN

1. ANGEL
Jakob

Tom wasn't fiction. He was not a lie. He was a higher truth, something we invented to encapsulate a reality too horrific to communicate to anyone outside our plague-devastated circle. Maybe myth, but definitely not fiction. Myth helps us make sense of facts too messy to comprehend, and that's what Tom Minniq was supposed to be. A fable to ponder, and then forget.

We birthed Tom at one of Derrick's Sunday coffee kvetches, salons of bitchery and wit that had once seen dozens of men gather every week, punctual like they never were for the club or the party or dinner before the opera; photographers handsome as the models, models as wise and cruel as the writers, writers as numerous and delicious as the omelets churned out in unflinching succession by the small army of fey fledgling chefs in Derrick's kitchen. Fourteen-year-old runaways and sixty-something *Times* critics, homeless dancers and trust fund filmmakers fresh-returned from failing to win the Academy Award for

Documentary, but really it was an honor just to be nominated, and next year, certainly, next year.

But this was 1987. None of us could count on next year. Most of us no longer belonged to this one. Wind tugged at our bare forearms. Early yellow leaves lapped like waves at our feet. Hate made it hard to breathe, filling the air like the stink of burning plastic. Adulterous toad-priests and clean-cut closet-case politicians croaked endless joy at God's vengeance upon the sodomites, and cawed opposition to any effort to fund care or find a cure. Since New Year's, the population of Derrick's patio had plummeted with every successive week.

This week, there were only three of us: Derrick himself, the forty-something literary agent who had seemed old before the plague and now seemed ancient; Pablo, the photographer whose art had been eclipsed by rage, who now turned all his creative energy into direct actions and angry letters and random fights picked with assholes overheard on street corners; and me, Jakob, a minimally-published writer of only modest talent and looks, already leaving behind the age bracket where youth earned you credit in both categories.

An empty chair, left askew, brought a tidal rush of water to my eyes. Donuts had replaced the omelets. Only the coffee was the same, strong and hot and bitter. We swallowed it greedily, desperately. Blood for vampires.

We were friends, we three. In a way it felt like cruel, just fate— that all the bright inessential boys had been burned away, leaving only us, who loved each other with the fierce hate-tinged love of brothers.

Pablo was telling us about the third memorial service he'd attended that week, for a photographer friend. "Afterward, his brother just handed me his entire photo archive. I told him Joe was just beginning to make a name for himself, and he should shop them around to dealers, find an agent for them, carry on Joe's artistic legacy. Man looked at me like I was crazy. Said he looked at a couple pictures and that was enough for him. I think he saw one fisting shot and was finished. And now I've got all this incredible art, languishing in a drawer. I can't even make a name for *myself* as a photographer, so how am I supposed to do it for someone else?"

Derrick sighed, his face pained at the unfairness of it all. "At least his brother had the decency to recognize his limitations, hand the art over to someone who might know what to do with it. You'd be amazed how many writers die without a will, and their families snatch up things or throw them away or worse. I've spoken to lovers who had to smuggle manuscripts out in shoeboxes, or who watched fathers set drawers full of documents on fire."

"Me, too," I said. "When Whit died last February, his mother gave me a laundry bag full of his writing to 'see what I could do with it.' I said yes, because what else can you say to a grieving mother? When I got it home, I found the work of two other writers in that sack along with his own—guys who had died, and who had left their work to him to 'see what he could do with it.'"

Again the waters rose, with the thought: and me? When I die, in six months or one, or ten years if the gods are good, will someone end up with a laundry sack containing my work—and Whit's—and the two who died before him?

"Fuck Hemingway," Pablo said sourly. "We're the real lost generation."

"Except we don't have a Hemingway," I said.

"Who the hell wants a Hemingway?"

"A Hemingway has its advantages," I said. "As is evidenced by the fact that we know his name twenty years after he died, and all our friends are forgotten as soon as they hit the earth."

Pablo hadn't heard, wasn't listening. His mind was on our enemies, as it so often was. "Did you guys hear that the federal government sent inspectors to New York, and they expressed concern over the high number of homeless people with AIDS, and the city said not to worry, they were dying so fast there would be no visible increase, certainly nothing to impact tourism?"

"Yeah," I said. We had all heard it—a rumor, possibly hopefully a fiction, but all the worse for that, for the effortless way it encapsulated our world.

"I'm against the death penalty," Pablo said. "But those motherfuckers should be shot."

We sipped coffee, said nothing, our eyes following a swirl of dead leaves and dark thoughts.

I firmly believe the idea entered all three of our brains at the same exact time, like Tom Minniq wasn't so much a figment of our imagination as a wandering soul who got lost on the way to reincarnation and instead of entering a woman's womb ended up in the brains of three grief-broken gay boys.

"No one cares about a pile of dead gay artists," Pablo said, and something in his tone made us all three scooch our chairs closer to the table—something hopeful and inspired, something dangerous and secret. "People can't identify with statistics."

"They need one face," Derrick whispered, the fraught tone leaping from Pablo to him like the wind passing a shudder from one tree to the next.

"One name," I said.

"A composite," Derrick said. "A synthesis of every brilliant artist who died before they could make their mark."

"A collective pseudonym," I said. "For every writer in our lost generation. If we don't have a Hemingway, we'll invent one."

"Tom," Derrick said. "A good, simple, macho name."

"Tom Minniq," Pablo said, and spelled it for us. "Minniq was an Eskimo boy who the Natural History Museum brought to New York City along with his father and ten kinsmen, all of whom but Minniq died from pneumonia almost immediately. Separated from his tribe. Stranded among savages who thought *he* was the subhuman one. I *read*, you two."

Derrick inclined his head.

"Also, he needs to be a little ethnic," Pablo said. "Minniq sounds . . . other. People who aren't white die too, you know."

They came easy: the mechanics of fraud, the logistics of forgery. We spent all day on the patio bouncing ideas around, and went inside when it got dark to fill up pieces of paper. Identifying all the problems likely to pop up. Finding ways around them.

Being a criminal is not so different from being an artist. Both depend on the same degree of audacity. Derrick would handle the business end: submissions and edits, pitches and contracts. I would handle the work itself, the unread stories and unfinished novels gleaned or inherited or rescued or stolen.

Finding a face and body for our Frankenstein proved more difficult. Fifty years earlier, we could have gotten away with a single blurry picture, or said he was a recluse who feared photographs would steal his soul. Our Tom had to be one of us: an urban butterfly, a creature of Saturday night dancing and Fire Island beach parties, and photo-shyness was incompatible with our pride and vanity.

Pablo had the solution. From his bag, he pulled a thick folder of the late Joe Beem's photos and spread them on Derrick's coffee table, sweeping aside the Chinese take-out containers that had blossomed like mushrooms at some point in the preceding hours.

"There," he said, pointing to a black-haired dancing boy with his back to the camera, "and there," another boy, shirtless on the beach, black hair cut the same way, "and this one," and if you looked at them right you could see it, the rough outline of the same man in dozens of different ones. "We find photographs of men who meet this general type—average height, black hair, muscular build, stubble—and that's him. I can work them in the darkroom to blur out the parts that don't fit, or add distinguishing marks. Jug-handle ears, maybe, or a birthmark over his jugular."

"It's perfect," Derrick said. "No author photos, no glossy head shots. Candids, glimpses. A life lived out of the public eye."

Because to succeed as myth, Tom had to be dead. Otherwise the charade became too complicated to maintain. And who would know, in this city where the dying stacked up faster than firewood, that this one particular name in the long litany had never been an actual person? Who could prove that Tom Minniq was any more fictional than the rest of the gay men and women who fled horrific far-off small-town lives and reinvented themselves upon arrival in our city, sometimes changing their names and cutting all family ties and spinning the most ridiculous lies to cover them?

We laughed about it, on our way out. Giggled like schoolboys plotting a prank. The streets of my city felt alive and inviting in a way they hadn't for months.

I was waiting at West Fourth for the train to Hell's Kitchen, strolling the platform with the never-resting eyes of the gay man on the lookout for something fetching. I found nothing— no handsome busker or breakdance boy, no aging sanitation worker with a pleasant smile and an ample bulge—and this popped my good mood like a bubble, made me think *all the beautiful boys and men are dead.*

An express train pulled into the station as I stepped onto my local one. I watched its doors open. My train's doors slid shut. A boy stepped off the express, so gorgeous I pressed my hand to the door in helpless Pavlovian need. Clothes and hair soaking wet. *How funny,* I thought, *No one else is wet.* Now I'm eerily certain he was fresh-birthed from the womb of the earth or had hacked his way out of Cronos' stomach, or whatever creation myth we had tapped into when we called Tom Minniq into being. Because this man looked right at me, all black hair and jug-handle ears and sturdy build, and smiled as my train carried me away.

We had agreed to give each other complete autonomy in our own areas. We could consult over the telephone, or in person, but never put anything into writing; no matter how clever or cryptic we thought we were being.

We planted Tom like a rumor, dropped him into everyday conversation alongside names of notorious friends—*the party? Oh it was grand, especially the part where the Governor's wife caught Tom Minniq getting a blowjob from Edward Albee in the bathroom, and in her shock and embarrassment said "I'm sorry, dear," and shut the door to let them finish.* Derrick used his connected exes to plant Pablo-concocted photographs in the society pages, where our Tom smiled at an opera premiere or museum gala, third from the right, his name in print and therefore incontrovertible. I sent orphaned short pieces to scrappy fledgling literary journals. Piece by piece, we stitched Tom Minniq together.

Tom made me a better person from the day he was born. I went to parties; I went to readings. I had been in hiding, mourning endlessly and aimlessly, focused more on men that had died than ones who still lived. Planting Tom-seeds sent me out into the world, brought me back to a generation I thought I had lost, when in fact I had turned away from it in grief. I think I intuited almost immediately what Tom really was.

For months, maybe years by then, my mantra had been *We could have changed the world*. Queer lit had blossomed like a glorious cancer, poised to kill off all that was patriarchal and oppressive about English-language literature, the transformative force that James Baldwin and Walt Whitman dreamed of. And then came AIDS, like the English language's revenge, a toxic bastard child of imperialism and every other exploitative impulse that let English grow to global lingua franca status. I gave up hope. But once Tom touched down among us, a Biblical messenger bearing scarcely-credible word of the new world about to be birthed, my mantra became *We will change the world*.

Derrick sold a story of Tom's to the *Paris Review*. On the strength of that, he got Tom a book deal. Oprah did a special, "Voices from the Whirlwind," about writers lost to AIDS, with Tom the centerpiece. Pablo and I thought this was a bad idea, knew her producers would do research, which they did—which, to our great shock and mild concern, actually led somewhere: an Oklahoma foster home, where nuns told vague stories and pointed to where *TOM MINNIQ* was graffitied onto a wall.

My job was easy. So many boxes and folders and notebooks of beautiful work had been abandoned upon their author's exit. My rules were few, and simple. Only truly orphaned work could become Tom's—with all the attention he was getting, we couldn't take the chance of someone stumbling upon a story attributed to Tom and remembering it as something a dead lover once read to him in bed. Only work that had no earthly champion, no competent executor or agent or chutzpah-wielding mother to fight for it. And I would never change a word or comma of it.

The most marvelous thing of all? When Tom came in, the tide of despair went out. Now I only imagined strolling out to the center of the George Washington Bridge and leaping off once a week or so, instead of dozens of times a day.

Tom was a polyglot, gleeful master of memoir and essay, poem and fable and smut and polemic. Tom had as many prose styles as the river had fish. Derrick and I stitched together his book, *My Shattered Darlings: An AIDS Memoir*, from dozens of disjointed and distinctive voices, the pieces so incongruous and alien to each other that it somehow came together into a harmonic whole. It opened on a brief glimpse of five men fucking in the Rambles of Central Park, the prose vulgar and plebian, then segued immediately into an E.M.-Forster-worthy memorial service that few could read without weeping. Space opera set on a rocket ship where Earth's last survivor mourns his dead; fifties noir where a private detective helps a concentration camp survivor stalk Nazi killers through New York City sewers. A narrative even emerged, from this chaotic choir: a coherent narrator who was the sum total of all these dying writers, making his way through a devastated world, trying and failing and trying again to find a reason to keep going. A critic, one of our own, wrote in *The Atlantic* that it was "a museum of a holocaust, somehow capturing the swirl of voices—some angry, some elegant, all beautiful—that are being silenced one by one while the men with the power to do something about it do nothing." Speaking in so many voices, it could speak to almost everyone.

It sold insanely well.

"Of course he isn't *dead*," I heard someone say, two tables over at the Chelsea Diner one Sunday brunch. "I talked to him the week before he did it. He said this country made him so sick, he was seriously contemplating faking his own death and fleeing to Canada or something."

"Or staying right here in New York City and living like a ghost."

I did not know these men. I had never seen them before. I

smiled, watching the creamer cloud my coffee, thinking of Tom spreading through men's minds.

Like a virus, I thought, and frowned.

Late that night, my phone rang. "Hello?" I said, quietly, for I had been lying awake, and when the phone rang I knew it was what I had been waiting for. No one said a word. In the background, I heard what might have been wind, running water. I hung up the phone, and lay back into an immediate, blissful, healing sleep.

I sent Derrick stories and poems and songs and rants, and he found a home for all of it. Everyone wanted a piece of Tom. Derrick used some kind of business magic to make the messy problem of money go away, squirreling it through a maze of foundations and other IRS-befuddling tools his expensive accountants advised. As much as possible, we donated it anonymously to the loved ones left behind by the writers whose words became Tom's. Pablo set up a photo exhibit at one of New York's largest galleries, which for years had turned up its nose at requests for benefit shows and retrospectives of lost artists.

The show broke records. Crowds of the left-behind came. Tom smiled and leered and glowered and flirted and cruised from dozens of images, blown up to be bigger than any of these men had been in life. Our boys, our men, our dead lived once more. They looked down on us with pity, and with love.

I watched the faces in the crowd. I wondered how often it happened that someone suspected, or intuited, on a subliminal level, that in gazing up at a photo they believed depicted a stranger they were actually looking into the eyes of someone they had loved and lost.

Outside, a young man wept. I sat down beside him and offered a handkerchief, which he did not want, and a cigarette, which he did.

"Everything okay?" I asked. A Harlem kid, straight and sporty.

"It is," he said. "It actually is. My brother—my older brother? He died. And it's been bad. Like, worse than when my dad kicked him out. And for some reason, tonight, I felt like he didn't die for nothing. I don't know why. It's just how I felt."

"I've felt that too, lately," I said, and he looked at my eyes, and saw no mockery, and nodded.

That's what Tom Minniq is. An angel. I whispered this last word out loud, allowing myself to use it for the first time.

Two weeks later, my doorbell rang.

"Jakob, sweetie, hi," Derrick said when I opened the door, ushering himself in. "I'm sorry to drop in on you unannounced"—and with an artful hand wave he implied *without giving you a chance to clean up the place*—"but I'm just a little, well, *annoyed* with you and I had to come right over."

I turned down the television. On the news someone kept using the phrase "gay terrorists."

"We all agreed how this was going to work, Jakob. We all have our part to play. If you're going to cut me out and start sending stuff directly to producers, you'll make it a lot more difficult for this elaborate fiction to be maintained."

He followed me into the kitchen, and I put on a pot of water.

"Derrick, I'm sorry, but I didn't do any such thing."

"If you wanted to get a screenplay produced in Tom's name, you should have called me. Granted, it's not my area of primary expertise, but I know people who—"

"Derrick! I've never sent anything to anyone but you. *Ever.*"

"Really, Jakob?" He handed me a copy of *Variety*, pointing to a page in the middle.

"I can't read this gibberish," I said, after trying several times and finding the movie-speak as comprehensible as a cross between shorthand and Swahili.

"Orion Pictures announced they've bought a screenplay, by Tom Minniq, for seven figures."

"Oh, come on," I said. "You know I don't have the connections or skill to negotiate that kind of sale."

"If not you, then who?"

Tom did it, was what I wanted to say. What I said instead was "Pablo?"

Derrick shook his head. "Pablo's falling apart. He called me the other night, sobbing, saying he was scared. When I asked him why, he practically had a nervous breakdown trying to explain it. I can't see him doing something like this."

The tea kettle whistled. I let it. "Have you . . . noticed things, Derrick?"

"Things?"

"Weird stories. Rumors. People saying they saw him. Saying they spoke with him."

"Of course," he said. "I think that's part of the point, isn't it? He's real to us. That's what we wanted. Someone who would take on a life of his own."

"But what if . . ." And I simply couldn't say it. *What if he really does have a life of his own? What if we made him real?*

"Someone's taking it too far, now," he said, evidently accepting that I had nothing to do with it. "That's all. We'll get to the bottom of it."

A car waited outside, shining expensively. "That yours?"

"Yes, yes," he said, smiling, his marvelous brain having moved on to other, happier things. His wealth, perhaps. Not that I begrudged him it. He'd taken less than the standard agent's ten percent on all Tom's profits; ensured the rest went to Tom's families. But still—eight percent of tens of millions was not chump change. I thought about asking him for some. He'd have said yes, of course. I needed it. But something inside me panicked, at the thought of taking money from Tom.

I learned why, not long after. Midnight; leaving the club; moving through a Chelsea drizzle, my head and thighs still throbbing from the music and the men and the way I moved with them. I had work in the morning, and I hadn't written anything in weeks, and the world was still a vile cesspool of hate and suffering, but the music had been good and my body fairly hummed with happiness. A payphone rang from down the block, getting louder as I got closer, stopping as soon as I took one step past it. I chuckled at the weirdness of the timing, but kept walking, weaving through a clot of boys coming up the stairs from the C train, charmingly rambunctious things whose nights were just beginning while mine was winding down, and the weight of that realization slowed my step, so that when I passed another ringing payphone I stuck out my arm and answered it purely for the sake of getting my mind off my own mortality.

"Hi, Jakob?" A man's voice, bright and healthy.

"Yes . . ."

"It's Tom," the man said.

"Tom." I said, and knew this was no joke. "Tom Minniq?"

"That's me."

I looked across the street to where one boy groped another up against a wall. Water dripped in the background of wherever Tom was. "What can I do for you, Tom?"

"What you've been doing. Help spread the word. The gospel according to Tom Minniq. I'm just getting started, and I'd hate to have to stop because someone decided to spill the beans."

"Hadn't dreamed of it," I said.

"No, of course not. *You* haven't. But Pablo has. Pablo's not well, Jakob. You need to do something about that."

"Do . . . something?"

"Go see him. Talk to him. Cheer him up. I don't know—you're a smart boy. Figure something out. Because if you don't, I will."

"Tom, wait. I need to ask you—"

A click, then the dial tone. Mocking poor helpless mortal me with its all-knowing, ever-listening song.

Tom's last sentence had chilled me, but it only proved my theory. Tom was an angel. But no winged pale thing in white playing a harp on a cloud: Tom was an Old Testament angel, willing to slay an Assyrian army or rain hellfire and brimstone down on your city if you didn't do what was asked of you.

The next morning, I called Pablo. No answer. Later, I'd hear he had been in Central Booking with thirty of his closest, angriest friends, locked up for some stunt protest in Grand Central. But there and then, listening to the phone ring, imagining him dead in a bathtub or walking out toward the middle of the George Washington Bridge, murdered by Tom Minniq or choosing his own severance package, I felt the tide come back in. That same surging wash of loneliness, of life's utter meaninglessness and the universe's profound indifference to our hurt.

I stared at the story in my hands. "Sam," it was called, by a boy named Leo who I remember arriving in our scene. How marvelous it had been, hearing him read to us, those enigmatic little scraps. When he got sick, he kept it secret; before dying, he demanded there be no memorial.

I stared at the phone, trying to pretend I hadn't already made my decision.

"Sam" was about a street hook-up, the details so spare and matter-of-fact that I could feel the fear and excitement of it, the man who brought him home to a strange apartment, who stripped down to reveal tattoos and endowment of astonishing scope. Watching him shave after. AIDS was nowhere; AIDS was everywhere. Bits of Leo had found their way into *My Shattered*

Darlings, but reading him now, I felt like these rich, enigmatic fragments deserved their own chapbook. They all deserved their own books.

I told myself I'd make it my business to track Pablo down and deliver Tom's warning. I swore I'd keep calling. Maybe visit his house. But every time I reached for the phone, I'd feel that same lunar tug of misery, and pull my hand back, and soon I stopped trying, and then it was too late.

God, it all felt so easy on the page. Sex, life, fearlessness. AIDS and death and aging and my own receding hairline vanished. Is it any wonder I didn't want to stop reading? Leo was alive as long as I read. I could hear his thoughts. I could cling a little longer to the lie that love and literature would let us live forever.

2. MONSTER
Pablo

My throat hurt from screaming. Fifty of us packed the lobby of the governor's New York City office. He'd blocked a bill that would help house the HIV-positive homeless. Occupying his lobby had been one of the tamer options—myself, I'd wanted to burn his fucking house down—but it didn't feel tame now. It felt marvelous.

But still: I was terrified. Two things terrified me. Two men. The first was watching me from across the crowded lobby. Shaggy red hair licked like flames at the air around him. Eyes, somehow brown and blue at once and aimed at me, stirred terrifying wants. I looked at him and my finger tapped at an absent camera shutter, aching to snap his picture. But that was as impossible as sex. I had forbidden myself to ever take another photograph.

Andy did portraits, homeless people dying, faces expressionless over hunger-jutting cheekbones and under grime and KS splotches. "Why expressionless?" I asked, at the gallery, free cheap wine and outrage thickening my pulse, "why not furious at what hate did to them?" Andy couldn't answer me. Andy was already dead.

Redhead chanted with the rest of the crowd, still watching me. *"Hey, Mario, what do you say?/ How many kids did you kill today?"* Slowly, smiling, the first man I was frightened of made his way toward me.

The second man who frightened me was me.

Minh did empty spaces, vacated hospital rooms and clothes bagged for the Salvation Army; late morning beds abandoned by their occupants and unmade, sex stains still visible, sending shivers of loss and absence sharp as paper cuts across the viewer's heart. His own absence was the white border around every shot; the final heartbreaking detail in every composition.

"Hey," Redhead said, arriving at my side. "You chant *loud.*" His smile was somewhere between admiration and desire.

"Thanks," I said.

"I'm Tripp."

"Pablo," I mumbled.

The frenzy was on me. Anger stoked my lust, which fed my anger. I wanted to fuck this man. And I wanted to fucking kill someone. And both wants were so strong and scary that as soon as it was tactful, I abandoned the protest and fled southwest.

Everything was tainted, toxic. Even eye contact felt potentially fatal. Walking home, into twilight, I heard him. Somewhere behind me; walking with stomping confidence that mocked my own fearful hurry. Not the redhead, I knew, without turning around.

That first day, leaving the coffee kvetch, I felt something. A glimmer of terror that started in my groin. It passed quick, but later, walking home from Derrick's, I felt something else. A presence, and an unfriendly one. Something following me. Something that wanted to break me open and spread my guts in the sun. Different, somehow, from the everyday hate in the air. Mere hate strengthened me, fed the righteous rage to fight back. This hate sapped me. Made me smaller. I wouldn't let myself look back. I forgot about it until I felt the same feeling two weeks later, fleeing the redhead and the protest.

I found out that night who—what—was following me. I couldn't sleep, my mind scrambling monkeylike from grief to rage to fear and back. I went to my window, like I often did, to look out at the city, and *not* smoke cigarettes, anymore. Except this time, when I went to my window, someone was there. Crouched on the fire escape of the building behind, staring across the courtyard at me. Just a dark shape, but I could tell he was staring at me. I could feel it. I don't know how. The same way I knew enough to feel physically afraid of him, even though our buildings were so far apart he could never have reached me. A burning red ember kindled as the shape sucked on a cigarette.

That's Tom, I whispered, sweat freezing into frost along my shoulders. *That's Tom Minniq.*

In the morning, there was a cigarette butt squashed into the marble ledge below my window.

Maurice did a series called After/Before, deathbed photos of skeleton boys and girls on the left and on the right a picture of that person in their prime, radiantly healthy on a long-ago beach or rooftop. When he couldn't find a gallery home for it, he printed them up as posters and went out at night to wheat-paste them onto subway doors and store windows, windshields and sidewalks, every morning a fresh harvest of dead men and women smiling tolerantly at their own death-masks and the walking corpses who shuddered as they walked by. Maurice talked about self-immolating in Times Square, but by then he was too weak to strike a match.

In the afternoon, an explosion shook midtown. Tiny ripples shirred the surface of my coffee, at the cubicle where I did data entry for Kaiser Permanente and plotted violent revenges I lacked the courage to carry out.

Word spread fast. The governor's office: vaporized. Two floors of a fifty-story skyscraper gutted. No one killed; a call came in with ample time to evacuate. In the morning the *New York Post* wondered *QUEER COINCIDENCE?* above a photo of the protest, me in focus and screaming and my redhead friend looking lustily at my back, and then, under us: *Governor's office bombed hours after AIDS protest.* "The radical homosexual agenda has finally revealed its true face," crowed a Methodist minister in the article, "unleashing violence on anyone who dares to stand up to them."

Tom, I thought, and shivered, finally seeing the magnitude of my mistake. All the anger I carried inside of me: I had given it flesh.

Cops questioned us. Tails were assigned. But I couldn't stop. I chained myself across Fifth Avenue, blocking traffic in front of St. Patrick's Cathedral when Cardinal O'Connor came for eucharisting. Snuck into the offices of a recalcitrant pharmaceutical company at night to splatter fake blood. In the morning, when the news told of catastrophic fires set simultaneously at offices of that same corporation in seven different cities, I was disturbed without being surprised.

This is out of hand, I thought. *There must be limits, even to rage.*

But Tom is a machine. Something we switched on, somehow. And I can pull the plug.

I called a *New York Times* reporter, a queer dilettante hovering on the fringes of the movement, who we tolerated because we needed coverage, although, generally, his coverage was weak at best. We even protested his apartment one time, part of a "Walk of Shame" tour of the homes of reporters whose coverage of the crisis lacked luster. Still, he came to meetings, hailed us by name when he saw us at our events, clung to us like the lonely kid on the playground who puts up with abusive friends because it's better than none.

"What do you know about Tom Minniq?" I asked him. The clatter of the newsroom was almost comical behind him: another world, one I had glimpsed in movies but never imagined might be real.

"Haven't read him. Supposedly a big deal. My mom bought his book, can you believe that?" He typed speedily, merrily, as he talked.

"I believe anything," I said, and caught sight of myself in the mirror. Was I losing weight? Was it fear? Was it something worse? "But you know how shrouded in mystery his whole life is?"

"Of course. Word is, *60 Minutes* is doing a thing, interviewing his former—"

"*60 Minutes* doesn't have what I'm offering you," I said.

His typing stopped. "What are you offering me?"

"Meet me in the plaza outside the Times Tower in an hour." I turned my head away from my reflection. Whatever was making me lose weight wasn't worse than fear. Nothing was worse than fear.

"I don't know," he said. "I'm under deadline on another story. Give me a tease. So I know you're not bullshitting me."

"I can put you in touch with his parents."

"See you in an hour."

I sprinted north. I had to move fast. I'd back out if I stopped to think about it. If I stopped, I'd worry about the scandal my revelation would cause, how the true story of Tom's origin would hurt Derrick, how it would pop the giant bubble of goodwill that Tom's work had built for our movement. I was close enough to the plaza to hear the plummeting shriek when it happened.

I heard the yelling, the cries for help, the wails of terror. I knew, as I joined the crowd knotting up into a tight circle, what I would find. My reporter, split wide open from the force of impact against the plaza stone.

"Someone's up there!" a woman screamed, pointing to the fifteenth-floor terrace. A man stood (*grinning?*) and then was gone. I looked down and saw blood fringing the hem of her pants.

At home, from fear, I wept beneath blankets on the floor of my closet.

SCRIBE DIVE!—TARGETED REPORTER POSSIBLE SUICIDE, said the *Post*, and ran a picture from our protest outside his apartment building. How had they gotten it? I didn't even remember any cameras that day.

"Gay terrorists" became a buzzword. Politicians who had previously called for the concentration-camping of everyone with AIDS now felt emboldened to demand the internment of gays in general. And while some of the bigger gay groups claimed our escalating bolshevism would alienate straights we needed on our side, our own numbers swelled fast enough to drown out those more decorous voices.

Tom was in our blood. While Tom might have kicked off the "terrorism," plenty of others took part. Senators were kidnapped, ministers murdered. The hot new thing among the dying was to demand cremation, and ask that the ashes be inserted into heavy porcelain balls, and after the memorial the mourners would march to a target of the dead man's choosing—the Mayor's mansion, the summer home of the head of the New York Stock Exchange—and shatter every window with them.

Gay men self-immolated at opening night at the Met, and at the Rockefeller Center Christmas tree lighting. The blaze claimed the entire tree.

Subway conversation suddenly became a lot more exciting. Impassioned debate became de rigueur. Buskers and bankers alike boasted incredibly articulate analyses, but also swallowed conspiracy theories like vitamins.

The CIA made the virus to exterminate Blacks and gays.

The KGB made the virus as a Cold War weapon to cripple our economy.

Every time I hear Jesse Helms' voice I fantasize about slinging a balloon full of AIDS blood right in his face.

I never stopped wanting to take pictures, or have sex. It wasn't just beautiful men that triggered me. A packed protest; a good brunch . . . every day, a dozen sights made my heart fill up with longing, with love for this fallen, foul world. And those moments made Tom angry. When Tom got angry, buildings burned, civil servants died, graffiti ripened on dozens of the doors of our enemies' homes, Tom's words in reds and blacks:

The heat of us

Will burn you down

At coffee kvetches, Jakob had been forever saying *We could have changed the world.* I'd roll my eyes each time, but the sentiment stuck with me. Following hot on the heels of the Civil Rights Movement and the Gay Liberation Front, Stonewall and the Black Panthers, a disease that hit queers and African Americans the hardest felt too . . . precise. Too perfectly calibrated. AIDS was a tactical nuke aimed right at the revolutionary heart of America's oppressed, and nukes don't just happen. I didn't believe the FBI or Glaxo Wellcome cooked it up in a lab, but I did think that the evil at work in the status quo was rooted in something deeper, primal, chthonic, something that worked through people when it could—the Inquisition, slavery—and erupted into raw, virulent horror when it had to (the Black Death, the Great Northern Famine of the Qing Dynasty).

And if *that* was true, maybe there was an opposing force. Not purely good or benevolent, necessarily, just like the demonic power I imagined gave birth to AIDS was not purely evil. They were simply two different forces, two kinds of energy eternally interlocked. And maybe that second power had tapped into us, somehow, Jakob and Derrick and me, and fed on our emotions, used us to access the raw-grief tidal wave that AIDS had unleashed, and fashioned it into Tom. And that made me more scared, not less. A power that big didn't care who got hurt while it tried to get its way. Just ask Joan of Arc. Or Jesus.

At night, we broke into boarded-up buildings. We popped locks and moved people in, leveraged rogue employees of the power company and the waterworks to bring the building back to life. Through it all I could feel Tom's eyes on me, hear his footsteps half a block back. I would have to move fast, to keep him from catching up. I would have to work harder.

We started out housing homeless people with AIDS, but soon that came to seem grossly unjust. Homeless people without AIDS were victims of our vicious system too. The same hate that let people bleed to death blocks from a hospital because they were gay let other people freeze to death on subway grates for being poor. After a while, abandoned buildings proved inadequate, the housing stock damaged and deteriorated. We moved a single mom with four kids out of the shelter and into a midtown suite that belonged to Queen Elizabeth II, which the monarch had occupied for precisely nine days in the past forty years. Queer concierges booked hoboes into hotel rooms for free, charging their room service meals to corporate accounts that they knew went unexamined. Real estate agent comrades helped us find empty apartments in otherwise occupied buildings, many of them second or third homes for corporate CEOs and faraway celebrities. When we put out the call for round-the-clock eviction defense, we were shocked by the size of the response. Tens of thousands of the straights we were supposedly alienating came to surround the buildings and stop any cops or landlords from stepping foot inside.

Tom was the spark, but we were the fire. And we were burning out of control. And I was terrified. Every protest put me in a place where it would be so easy to slip. To do something fatal. To bash a cop's head in, or find some beautiful boy to fuck up against a wall.

Pablo was a fashion photographer. He shot everyone. Every magazine; every cover. His style was edgy, editorial, high-contrast and grainy, urban, often black and white, think Weegee-meets-Avedon. He was also a bit of a dog. He loved his man but some force of willful evil or childish selfishness would not let him resist the smiles and winks of boys on subway platforms and photo shoots. He refused to get tested, even when Allen withered before his eyes. Only afterward, at the graveside, did he vow to change his ways. By then, it was more about self-punishment than self-improvement.

Pablo was a monster. That's why he would die, and why he would die alone.

Reagan canceled a trip to New York City, citing security concerns. Sources said he didn't fancy getting splattered with fake—or real—blood. Embarrassed, the city started cracking down on activism even harder. People in poor neighborhoods were targeted for random stops and searches, Gestapo-style. At night I dreamed of blood and sperm, sex and murder, the monsters coming for me from the Outer Dark.

The Piers. Sick malnourished arms reaching out over the

Hudson; vestigial organs of the City's vanished industrial glory. Once the pride of shipping magnates, long since abandoned to the homeless and the homosexuals. I entered an old warehouse with every window broken. Wind whistled erotically through high, bare eaves. I told myself I was there to hand out flyers. I knew I was lying.

Darkness. A smell of urine so old, it had ceased to be unpleasant. There was something almost sacred in the smell, pure as linen vestments. Incense in the church of desperation. Someone grunted with the accelerated rhythm of approaching orgasm. I looked back once, to the skyline's haughty crown of lights, and then strolled deeper into the gloom. Past pairings and groupings, and lone watchers with eyes even hungrier than mine.

"Hello, Pablo," said a sex-nightmare voice, as I arrived at the back of the warehouse. I heard the slop and slosh of the Hudson River underneath me.

"Hi, Tom," I said. I had known this conversation would come, but conversation was the wrong word. Sentence. My sentence was being carried out.

"You made me," he said, and his voice was so manly and mellow that goosebumps of desire emblazoned my forearms, even as I looked about on the floor for a potential weapon. "Why would you try to unmake me?"

"Because you're out of control. Because you're hurting people."

"Isn't that what you wanted? Isn't that what you were thinking, when you summoned me? I heard what was in your heart. *Someone to do what the rest of us are too scared to do. No man can do it. We need a monster.*" Here, speaking my thoughts, his voice was mine.

"But you've gone too far," I said.

"Have I? I don't think I've gone far enough. I don't think *you've* gone far enough."

"I left paperwork," I stammer-said. "I wrote it all down—the truth about who you are. I left it with someone. If—"

Tom laughed. Laughing, his voice was not sexy. It was the sound a jackal might make, in the night. "That's a lie. I told you—I can hear what's in your heart, Pablo. It's where I came from."

He came closer. I could see the outlines of him now, in the gloom, broad shoulders and bushy eyebrows, his tight jeans and the way he filled them out. The composite features of hundreds of men. And in a shaft of rogue amber light from an arc-sodium light miraculously left unbroken at the edge of the pier, I saw the singular curve of his lips. No generic substitutions there: in every Tom-photo I conjured up through darkroom necromancy, I always used the same pair of lips. Allen's lips.

"It's not me you fear," Tom said, those lips inches from my ear. "It's yourself. You fear your emotions will lead you into a terrible mistake."

"Yes." A whisper; a squeak.

"You crave violence and destruction, yet you fear those things."

"Yes."

"Why?" He moved to stand behind me, put his hands on my hips. I could feel his heat. It surprised me.

"I don't know."

"I do."

Tom scooped one arm around my belly from behind, wrapped the other around my neck. My eyes shut in irresistible ecstasy. His hips ground against me. I could feel him then, the whole of him, the thing behind or inside of Tom. We had not created this creature over brunch. He was something so much bigger, older, more malevolent. We merely gave him a name, and a body.

"Come with me," he said. "I'll give you what you want. What you fear."

"Yes," I said, looking out through a ceiling hole at the purple night sky.

"It will hurt," Tom whispered, turning us around, aiming me at the city, where some unthinkable task waited for me.

"I know," I said, and I did, because for a split second I was sixteen again, when men were marvelous creatures and not monsters, panting in a hayloft as one of my father's farmhands spun me around and tugged my trousers down, whispering *It will hurt*, and I nodded my head in an ecstasy of need, because of course it will hurt, because the things we need most always do.

3. MAN
Derrick

Drinks were drunk. Jokes were told. The meeting stretched for hours, more a cordial business luncheon than a contract signing, although there was that, too. By the time I staggered out, four scotches added a slight wobble to my walk.

They weren't the Big Pharma villains I had been hoping for. Several of them were gay, and I smiled to see that our erstwhile enemies had recognized the importance of making nice with the faggots, and hired fit young lawyers for that purpose. Potted palm trees dotted the fifty-seventh floor, below a soaring, gorgeous glass ceiling built out of our blood.

Two million dollars, for the use of Tom Minniq's most iconic poem in a massive ad campaign. Subway posters and slick primetime commercials and everything in between. *Pablo would murder me for this*, I thought, as the elevator descended. But Pablo was long dead; anyway it wasn't Pablo I was trying to provoke.

And wasn't this a moment worth celebrating? Wasn't this the dawn of a new age, the one Pablo and Jakob and I had in mind when we dreamed Tom Minniq up? The cocktail. Highly Active Antiretroviral Therapy. HAART. A blend of entry inhibitors, nucleoside reverse transcriptase inhibitors, and a plethora of other inhibitors. The thing that would turn AIDS into a long-term, manageable, symptomless disease. The thing that would save all the men and women doomed by love to die.

My head cleared slightly, stepping out into the street. October cold whisked the warmth and ego-stoking away. I had lingered too long. I would never make it to Carnegie Hall in time for the start. Cab or subway? I stood there in a panic of indecision. Graffiti on a nearby door caught my eye, made my mind up, bright scarlet against rusted grey: *BURN IT DOWN*.

DOWN. The subway, it seemed to say, somehow, because I had gotten good at reading street art subtext. We all had, we survivors, we with the dubious distinction of passing untouched through a plague.

Pablo. The thought of his death sent an almost-erotic thrill through me, the horror and absurdity of it. Irresistible agony, wondering just what the hell had happened. Found drained of blood in the lobby of the very same pharma-corp building where I'd just signed away Tom Minniq's soul. How I found, on my door, that morning, a scrawl in blood: an iron, complete with electrical cord.

Oh Pablo, I thought, even before his body was found—for only someone who knew me very, very well would know to draw the symbol of my greatest hurt. Of course I didn't remember telling him about it, but we did spend a lot of time together, much of it in the company of alcohol. Maybe, drunk, I had the courage to face the story I most feared and most needed to tell.

Rich Putnam, junior year of high school, softball star and

the love of my life for six exquisite, secret weeks. The decades-gone stink of him, in the bed of his bedraggled pick-up. His exultant vigor and utter fearlessness when it came to sex; his rage and cowardice in every other moment. Culminating in the incident with the iron, the day I told him I loved him, when his anger over what he felt for me exploded, leaving the iron-shaped scar my left thigh still carries.

But in the weeks that followed Pablo's death, what started out as isolated stories—*the strangest thing happened; someone scribbled on my door in blood*—began to coalesce into a terrifying pattern. The door of every gay man in New York City, it seemed, had been marked. Never mind that there's not enough blood in ten Pablos to do that, or time in ten weeks; never mind that not even the FBI has a master list of the address of every homo, and many of the marked weren't even out. Months had passed by the time we realized what had happened. Doors were washed clean, no way to know the truth. Many of us suspected others were lying, jumping on a bizarre bandwagon by claiming a blood-smear they had not earned, and others were *definitely* lying when they claimed not to have found anything.

I walked faster, heading for the subway platform.

"*Eerily Biblical*," Jakob had said, at the funeral, "*The blood on the door? Wouldn't have pegged Pablo for a religious man.*" But Jakob, G-d bless his Judaism, could not have comprehended what religion was for Pablo. Even my own Episcopalianism was a pale shadow of Pablo's terrifying Catholicism, the Bible a big book of blood and monsters and sins not even sacrifice could cleanse. And I suspected Pablo's last act of activism was not meant to terrorize the guilty but to unify the oppressed, to prod us into an uprising against the Angel of Death.

That was when I began to wonder. What if they were right, Jakob and Pablo—what if Tom Minniq was real, a beast burped out of hell or the collective unconscious by our actions? Because whenever you talked to someone whose door had been blood-smeared, and asked what sign or symbol or word had been left for them, there was always a pause—a shifting, inside; a figuring out what to say instead—and then an answer that never felt completely honest. Not that I was honest myself. I never told anyone about the iron. Tom knew what was in our hearts, knew who was gay and who was not, and knew the symbol of our greatest shame. And used it, to kindle our anger into flames.

But why had he visited Jakob and Pablo, but never me?

So: I resolved to confront this monster, this angel. So far, he had refused to reveal himself to me; I would provoke him into it. I would sell him off.

The subway took a long time coming. I was furious with myself, for letting the hour get away from me. This was our night. It was *my* night.

Because who could have imagined another year, let alone ten? Not me, certainly, when I watched my friends walk off stage one by one and waited to be summoned into the darkness myself. Even as I wrapped my loneliness around me like a security blanket, eschewed sex and love like it could keep me alive, I still felt certain my time would come—the hate-plague in the air would claim me eventually. And yet here we were, here I was, ten years from the day *My Shattered Darlings* was published, heading for Carnegie Hall, of all places, for an anniversary commemoration. *Tom at Ten.* Imagine.

Across the platform was a poster, where two beautiful business-suited men held hands and smoldered at the camera. *LOVE & RAGE*, it said, and then: *Tom at Ten.* These ads were everywhere, the same two men smoldering in Speedos or Louis XIV frill.

We do not die, someone had etched into the glass window of the subway when it arrived. The first line of the very poem I'd just licensed away. Tom's manifesto; the source of a thousand tags and protest chants. The thing that assassinated fundamentalist politicians, kidnapped moderate liberals, burst into violence in the streets so often that dungeons shook, chains fell off. My head spun. True: it was a day for memory, but this was too much. Maybe it was the scotch and maybe it was the event I was heading for, but when I stepped off the train at 57th Street, muttering the poem under my breath—

We do not die
We don't go cold
We swell with rage/ with each fresh hurt
Each new death
Swells the flame
The heat of us/ will burn them down.

—sprinting through the eerily-empty rush-hour station, realizing I left my written remarks at my office, and that I'd arrive too late to deliver them anyway, I felt for the first time since adolescence like I was really truly losing control.

Which is when a deep voice said—

"Derrick..."

—a nightmare voice, drawing out the first syllable like a taunt, echoing down the station, and I stopped and turned, to where what I had assumed was a homeless man when I rushed past stood, and stepped forward, all black hair and jug-handle ears, and I knew that now, at the worst possible moment, what I had waited ten years for had happened.

"Derrick..."

What came toward me was no towering monster, no gilded angel. No impossible synthesis of dead beauties. Only a man, small and haggard, face deeply lined, stinking of cigarettes and wet ash.

"Tom?" I whispered. He stepped closer.

"Derrick."

I had so many questions, but I made myself wait. I wanted him to speak. My heart was a panicked bird inside me, remembering Pablo, wondering if time had stopped outside the station, if any cops or commuters could come through and save me from whatever horrible death Tom had slated for me. His eyes were jagged brown flecked with fire.

"It's silly to be mad at me," I said, finally, unable to stand the silence of his stare. "Everything I've done, I did to spread your words."

"What would I be mad at you for, Derrick?"

Profiting off your work. Not believing in you. Surviving. "The poem. Licensing it to the pharmaceutical corporation."

Tom shrugged. "There's so much to be outraged about. That seems like a pretty mild sin in the grander scheme of things."

"Then why . . . why haven't you ever come to me before? All these years . . ."

Tom raised one hand, thumb-and-finger cocked pistol-style, and reached out to touch it to my chest.

So he is going to kill me. So this is where I die. Survive a holocaust only to die in a grotty subway station.

Startling, how unconcerned I was. How little I cared. Some part of my mind scrambled backward, though physically I stood my ground even as I felt the cold of his fingers through my thin sweater. I clutched for things to hold me to the earth. Songs, food. People. The peculiar slant of October light, at twilight, in Manhattan. But I found nothing to grab on to.

"Tell me the name of one person in the last twenty years who you truly loved."

I opened my mouth, ready with the long list of friends and colleagues who filled my Rolodex, ready to tell Tom how much they meant to me, how I loved them, but it wasn't true, and there was no sense lying to a ghost. He clearly knew it already.

I shook my head.

"You survived by emptying out your heart," Tom said. His voice had an undercurrent, like wind echoing through pipes. "By caring about nothing, not even your own desires. You were a monk long before AIDS—sex might make you come to care for someone, and you couldn't take that risk."

Love is the disease. The motto of my youth, after Rich Putnam burned it out of me with a hot iron. AIDS, when it came along, years later, only proved my point, that love and sex offered far more pain than pleasure.

"You asked why I've never come to you. That's why. Jakob had hope, and Pablo had rage. They needed me. They fed me." Harsh, raw pauses grew between his words. "You. Had. Nothing."

"Then . . . why now?"

"So you can see. What you've become."

He took his fingers away. I had questions, but I didn't want to hear him speak. I didn't want to learn anything else about myself. So I turned and left, half-expecting him to sink an axe into my neck, but he let me leave.

"Derrick!" someone called, as I entered the lobby of Carnegie Hall, and there were hand-shakings and back-claps, and I turned around in a slow, dazed sort of awe, to see so many of us, all the aging editors and authors who survived the plague, all gussied up in the expensive suits that were consolation for being so old. And perhaps even more marvelous were the new ones, the young pups and bear cubs and ragged blond twinks with full heads of hair and careless charming stubble and cheeks and hands worth dying for. Squint your eyes and look at us sideways and we could have been a coffee kvetch, one last massive hurrah on my back patio, age and class and race barriers melting away in the heat of our magnificent gayness. Gender barriers preserved, but where was the harm in that?

They respected me. They fawned on me, many of them, king-maker that I was. But I didn't care about any of them. And I had spent so long trying my damnedest not to be moved by beauty that I could no longer see it, no longer take joy in the smile or ass or mind of a gorgeous man.

Intermission. I was too late for my speech, and glad of it. I took my seat and spread my coat across the two beside me, ridiculously and sentimentally clearing a space for Pablo and Jakob, but soon a dowager socialite and her sodden daughter came to claim those spots.

An Oscar-winning actress read a Tom Minniq poem. I didn't remember this one; more brash and spoken-word than most of the poems we published. From the very start, Jakob had claimed these Ghost Tom pieces as proof that divine intervention was at play, but for far too long I had dismissed them as mere bandwagonism, someone else trying to secure publication for their work or the work of their lover—or son—or brother—or father—or sister—or mother—under a famous name. Now, of course, I could see that Jakob was correct. The poem was exquisite, but I could only analyze it with a cold, officious eye.

Two men mounted the stage. One old, one young. Movie stars; out; emblems of the new Hollywood openness. They read a dialogue, a pivotal scene from a play. I knew it was genius, could marvel at it intellectually but not apprehend it emotionally. Eyes moistened all around me. Mine stayed dry.

Tom is dying, I thought, remembering his twitchy hands and the rough lines of his face. *Whatever he is, his time is past. Whatever monster or angel he was, he's a man now.*

We don't need him anymore.

We had won. Hadn't we? The fire of our rage had burned

down so much hate. Sometimes literally; Jesse Helms kidnapped and tied down and doused in gasoline and set on fire; Falwell acid-disfigured. Drug cocktails. Gay governors and Supreme Court Justices; Harvey Milk's birthday a national holiday; commitment from Congress to provide free AIDS medications to all.

The dialogue ended. The actors cleared the stage.

We had won. But I didn't feel any safer, or happier. Or less alone.

The mayor had meant to come, but been delayed by budget drama. In his stead, he sent his Deputy Mayor for LGBT Relations, a dreamy, slim-waisted, salt-and-pepper-haired creature who almost every gay man in the city was in love with, who mounted the stage with the effortless majesty of a symphony conductor and proceeded to play us like an orchestra.

"Twenty years ago, New York City was dying. We were in the grip of a plague, and no one cared. We were ruled by fear. New Yorkers were content to walk past homeless men and women every single day, like it was something natural, something other than an unspeakable injustice. We were ruled by hate—not love."

Jakob had emailed me that morning, still living it up on whatever godforsaken Maine island he and his man have built a house on. Jakob, dying, but happy, he and his man, both of them refusing the brand-new miracle-drug cocktails after years of watching friends suffer more from the medication than the disease.

"It's impossible to imagine the Housing Rights Act passing in a New York City without Tom Minniq. No other American city, through legislative or executive action, has ever made the same commitment we have, to provide housing to every single person in need of a home, regardless of their circumstances. To Tom Minniq we owe not only the lives of the men and women who are currently housed—and not only the pleasure that his prose and poetry have brought to so many of our lives—but the very soul of this city.

"Now, Tom Minniq wasn't responsible for all of that. You were. We were. His voice merely galvanized us, gave us love and beauty that served as nourishment for the fight. We're not here to celebrate him. We're here to celebrate *us*. Our strength, our survival."

Sudden shouts from the highest gallery. The flutter and snap of a canvas unfurled; I turned around too slowly to read its full message—the two men from the *Tom at Ten* subway ads, their faces X'd out in charcoal, a slogan that read in part WOMEN DIE TOO and DEATH TO GAY MISOGYNY—before security yanked it back up and escorted ten black-garbed women protesters out.

The mayor's man frowned, nodded. "It's true that our community, our city, our country, all have a long way to go. But *your* job is to hold us accountable, and I hope you won't stop."

The audience roiled and murmured. Many, men and women, echoed the banner's sentiments.

"Please," he said. "We're family, and sometimes we hate our family. But we're here to celebrate one of our own. And to celebrate ourselves. What we've achieved together."

The murmurs died down.

"I want us to give ourselves a round of applause. For having the bravery to be who we are, for living lives worthy of living. For being a family."

Scattered applause, building. I clapped, but I wasn't part of this family. I loved no one, and no one loved me.

"*Give me your hands if we be friends,*" the Deputy Mayor said, Puck's closing plea for applause in *A Midsummer Night's Dream*, and we rose, some of us with the swift verve of youth and some of us moving slow, painstaking inch by inch at the behest of failing bodies, into the ocean of applause, our hands pressing together and then separating like a repeatedly-postponed prayer, an ancient ritual, practically pagan, a spell that bound us all together in that moment and then bound that moment to all the ones that came before, stretching back to Shakespeare and far beyond, but far forward too, into unthinkable futures, rocket ships and machine mind melds, this instant, this act eternal and unchanging, a flimsy and all-too-brief immortality but one that was ours whenever we needed it. The sound of us. A shallow, mocking, momentary kind of unity. The noise we made reminded us we had each other, and so we needed neither angels nor monsters.

xiv.

"Please, man," he whispers, but that's all, because he doesn't even know what he's begging me to do. His grief is inarticulate, all-consuming.

I feel for him, this lonely man, this weird monster. But I can't help him. And I can't share the burden of the stories he has sucked up.

Slowly, carefully—lovingly, even—I pull his arms from around me. They fall to his sides. He knows he's helpless. A boxer beaten. He can't hold me.

And then I am running, away from the water, away from the dark, away from him and the horrific wonderful wild worlds he's privy to.

I don't slow down for seven long blocks. I stand on Broadway breathing heavily. I look back, afraid I'll see him, sure I won't. I lean on a tattered abandoned couch, lying like a murder victim on the sidewalk. My hands touch worn canary corduroy.

And: I see.

SUN IN AN EMPTY ROOM

THE BOY WAS BONY, full of rough angles that stabbed into my upholstery. I knew he'd be trouble from the moment he tested me out. He slumped in so hard I felt forty-seven kinds of unresolved rage and grief. His girlfriend, on the other hand, was cold and faraway and far too good for the Salvation Army. She ran her gnawed-nail fingers along my wooden frame and called my plastic dust cover tacky. Her eye was on someone else, a haughty chocolate corduroy couch who turned out to be substantially beyond their budget.

"How many people do you think owned it before us?" she asked that night, watching me warily from the door to her kitchen.

"Probably dozens," he said. "Life must be hard for a Salvation Army couch."

His jeans hung off him, barely held up by his belt and scrawny hips. The girl wore classier clothes and thick-rimmed glasses that came to points at the edges. What they had between them was all physical, spilling out in every gesture, clogging up the words when they tried to talk, transforming every moment into a potential fight or fuck.

I'd lived in eight homes in the ten years since I first got loaded onto an Army truck and dragged out onto the showroom floor. Prior to that I'd spent twenty years in the living room of a truly regal widow. Hardly anyone ever sat on me, and twice a week a woman dusted me. From Mrs. Mitnick I acquired a deep respect for good breeding, and a healthy dose of contempt for the poorer people whose living rooms I would shortly be consigned to.

"I need water," the girl moaned, during some dumb flick on some sweaty afternoon.

Three minutes passed, then she said: "Go bring me some water."

Getting up, the boy kicked over a cup of coffee she had set on the floor. The mug broke. "Why can't you watch what you're fucking doing?" she shouted. He stumbled to the kitchen, shoulders slumped, nearly bursting with things he could not say.

The families who took me in had exceedingly short shelf lives. Someone went to prison or someone cheated; someone got stabbed or someone got tired of sobbing herself to sleep and went back to her parents or ex-husband. I had seen crumbling households held together by minimum-wage jobs or heroin; I had seen relationships so fragile they were broken by a late-night phone call or a pubic hair on the toilet rim. Away from the Salvation Army, watching the spectacle of love's destruction was my one and only joy.

"My mom would disown me if she saw I had a plastic-wrapped couch in my living room," the girl said during dinner, her ass at the edge of me like I was the filthiest park bench. "So fucking kitschy."

"The couch is the least of your worries with her," he said. And belched. The girl took her dinner into the bedroom. Twelve plastic hoop bracelets clacked together on each wrist.

I did not take her dislike for me personally. We were from different generations, and couch styles had changed significantly since Mrs. Mitnick picked me out. The girl's snobbishness appealed to me, so I couldn't explain the anger that roiled my stuffing when I heard her speak or felt her body on me.

I have a high back and long arms that come down at a diagonal and then loop into a jutting spiral. I am all one piece, but folds in my upholstery give the illusion that I can be broken up into three sections. Mrs. Mitnick would describe me as *canary yellow*; the girl called me *piss-colored*.

Their apartment was small—the third floor of a four-floor house. Mismatched furniture, smudged white bare walls, a refrigerator that smelled like spoiled milk no matter how many times he scrubbed the insides with bleach. Kitchen cabinets that always seemed about to collapse, waiting for someone to place that one fatal can on their shelves. An unspeakably seedy and foul-mouthed bathroom sink. The building was on the western edge of the poorest part of that North Jersey town. No trees on the street. Only McDonald's and the liquor store were open past nine.

Mrs. Mitnick had me by the window. Her home was high up on a hill, looking down on absolutely everything. The narrow streets and inadequate parking; the buildings that had begun to sag into the slope of the hill. The unending rumble of the New Jersey Turnpike. A lovely town, once, but long since gone to shit. Curled up in a corner of me, she would dial up old friends and the few family members that dutifully kept taking her calls. She'd tell them all about the ugly things she saw from her window, reminding whoever it was how smart and lucky they had been to flee south to Florida. We were safe, she and I, an island in the sea of filth, and not once did it ever enter my mind that maybe one day I'd find myself afloat in that same sea. Not once did I stop to savor the space, the smells and heat of it, because I could not imagine anything else.

During the day, he'd drink and masturbate. Sometimes he'd scribble things in a notebook, but not for long, and it tended to end with him tossing it across the room. Loud music would thump through his cheap speakers, guitars squalling and lots of screaming, and when she came home she'd sniff and say "reliving your glory days?" Exhausted, she'd head straight for the kitchen and begin cooking the most marvelous things, complex dishes that took forever. The boy got goosebumps, eating her food. She turned down his offers of help. Every moment at the stove fed her resentment.

"You've been working out?" she asked, emerging from the bedroom with a bright red face, wearing only underwear.

Following her out, he shrugged. He had not been. But the next day he took his shirt off, did four push-ups, sat up to inspect the dust on his palms. Wiped one hand off on me. Their windows had no curtains. The boy stood in winter light and I was no longer lost in a tawdry, empty, smoke-smelling room. The sunlight, suddenly, shockingly, felt the same as Mrs. Mitnick's.

One week after they moved me in, he was banished from the bedroom altogether. He left a stack of dishes in the sink—including every single spoon they owned, so she was forced to stir sugar into her coffee with a fork. In response to her hostility, he became as quiet and empty as wood. In the evening, returning from work, she was angered by the absence of his customary interest in how her day went, and she exploded. She yelled, but he never yelled back. Which made her angrier. Finally she called up a friend to have the conversation that she could not have with him.

"Heidi, you have no idea—this man needs to get some professional help," she said, loudly, standing by the shut bedroom door. "He has some MAJOR DEPRESSION ISSUES that he needs to START WORKING ON so he doesn't need to MAKE EVERYONE AROUND HIM MISERABLE."

The boy turned on the television, and turned it up until neither he nor I could hear her.

The next morning, while she was at her job and he was at home not looking for work, he came from the kitchen with a pair of long scissors. Stood there, sizing me up. I waited for him to start stabbing. Hacking all my stuffing off. At the Salvation Army you heard stories like that. Drunks who took chainsaws to overstuffed recliners; ottomans doused in gasoline and set on fire. Crazy men and women who murdered the furniture to punish their lovers.

Instead, he dropped to his knees and ran his fingers along where the plastic tucked under the upholstery.

"Let's see," he whispered, and then pressed the scissors very delicately through the plastic, right at the seam.

I shivered. I felt sure he'd notice, but he did not.

He slit me open just enough to fit his finger in, and tugged till the corner came loose. Then, gentle and slow as a man making love, he pulled along the entire length of me. His breath was slow and heavy, smelling of coffee and toothpaste. Finished, he lifted the slip cover off and let it fall.

I expected agony, but there was none. Bliss, maybe. That filthy living room was full of sunlight, but thicker and warmer than I ever imagined it could be. Answering the prayer he could not hear me praying, he took off his shirt and lay down on me. I felt his face for the first time. Its stubble and its bushy eyebrows; its thick soft lips. I savored where his sharp points poked me. His hot, stinking armpit felt like a kiss against my velvet.

"Look!" he said when she got home. "Look how nice it looks without the plastic wrap!"

"It does, Tim," she said. "It looks brand new. And weirdly elegant."

Tim. His name was Tim.

She came behind him and wrapped her arms around his stomach, kissed the back of his neck, mumbled magnanimous forgiveness even as she bit hard at his earlobe. His hands gripped my top cushion, and his body leaned into my back. His hands were warm and gloriously alive. I felt him harden. Suddenly I was terrified she'd push him back and they'd fuck right there, right on me. I hated her. Nausea spread to my expertly-carved claw feet.

"Come on, Tim," she said, tugging at his belt.

Finally he let go of me, and turned around and took hold of her with a fierceness that made me wince. They fumbled backward for the bedroom, and their noise went on for hours.

In the morning she was herself again. She made breakfast as loudly as possible to be sure he would wake up. Then she was gone, and Tim and I were alone. Before bed something else set her off, and she was on the phone with a girlfriend:

"It's only during sex that he can really communicate what he's feeling. What he thinks about me. About us. He cries, afterward, sometimes. But outside the bed, forget it. With words he's not so good."

At night he lay atop me, sweating in the hot wind from the open windows, thinking of her. Before Tim took me in, I used to lie awake at night in the living rooms of alcoholic college students or the impoverished elderly, listening to the silence. Aching for the day when my owner's death or an eviction notice would bring me back to my Salvation Army home. When I would not have anyone weighing me down, or making demands of me. But now I held on to Tim and tried to suck him into my stuffing, tried to make him part of me, knowing that I would outlive him, knowing that someday the man I loved would vanish.

Tim would go for walks or on shopping trips, and I worried until he came home. His horrible woman might change the

locks, or call the police. Lots of lovers did that. One of my own-
ers, too stupid to see how much he needed his wife, punched
her in the face and went out to a bar for an hour and a half and
returned home to an empty house. That big man crumpled to the
floor and screamed and kicked and cried just like his two-year-
old son. Watching it happen, I had hated him for his weakness.
Now, for the first time, I could begin to imagine what he had felt.

Dinners were wordless. They watched TV with their plates
on their laps; she kept a distance of three inches between their
shoulders. How could she stand to sit so close to him, but not
touch him? If I could move, if I was physically capable of ex-
pressing what I felt, I'd grab him and never let go. Two or three
times a day they'd make love, each body desperate to suck the
other one into itself, and each time he was obliged, eventually, to
come out from inside of her.

Drunk, he dialed up friends and had long loud conversations.
About getting a band back together. About stumbling home
from a bar at closing time ten years ago, in a blizzard, and slipping on ice and lying on the sidewalk laughing hysterically and
feeling happier than they ever would again. About the depressing turns their lives had taken. About Jeremy—or Rashid—or
Gabrielle; who jumped off a bridge—or broke his neck in a car
accident—or got locked up. I could hear her in his voice, even
though he tried hard to never say her name. A tremor of hunger and pain and bliss rumbled under every word. During these
conversations, Tim's soggy voice had the energy and the clarity
that the girl was fiending for, which he could never give to her.

"I sold my guitar for the security deposit on this fucking
place," Tim said to someone. "For this fucking shithole of a
place." With his cell phone in his ear and his ear against my
skin, I could hear his friend's faraway squawk. Noontime noise
from the streets.

"That kind of shit just makes me *sad*, dude." The friend was evidently walking along a major US highway. "You were fucking phenomenal on that thing. Like—I've never heard another guitarist come close. Only reason we didn't conquer the world was because we had a half-assed drummer."

"Yeah, well, what can you do. I never played the damn thing anymore anyway. And she really wanted to move in together. Said it was 'make or break' time for us."

"Dude!" said the friend, and started in on a long coughing break. "I don't believe what I'm hearing. You used to be Joe Studbucket—never knew you to get so worked up about a girl before."

"You know how it goes," Tim said. "Sooner or later someone comes along who . . . who gets through to you. Someone who gets under your skin. In a way no one ever has before."

"It's the sex, right? The sex must just be really good."

"It's amazing," Tim said, "but that's not the only thing. She just tore down all my defenses, that's all. I'm in a bad way."

Tim turned his friend off, lay down flat along me. Sunlight turned us both to gold. That room—that house—that squalid corner of that nothing North Jersey town—the whole ugly, lonely world, of loss and needs you couldn't say out loud—everything was perfect.

She kicked him out four months after I arrived.

"You need to leave," she said. "Go sleep on your brother's couch. It's much more comfortable than this hard, bumpy thing. I need to think about things."

"If *you* need to think about things, maybe you're the one who should leave," he mumbled.

"Just go," she said, but the fact that he managed to talk back had calmed her down a little.

Missing him, she'd lie down on me and arrange her body in

more or less the same shape that he had. She'd call him, and generally spent about six minutes going from soft to violent.

"You're like a fucking brick wall!" she'd shout. "You're a goddamned emotional cripple!"

The last time I ever touched Tim was eight days later. He came while she was at work, bearing garbage bags and cardboard boxes. His brother's truck was parked downstairs. The night before, she gave him the *Come Get Your Stuff* call, and I had prayed for lightning to snake through the open window and melt her. Tim took his time, moving from room to room like a ghost.

Midway through, he stopped. Sat down on me. Cupped his hands around his face. Curled up into a ball and pushed his way into my insides like I could keep him safe. He spent a long time crying. He had to know what I was feeling—how empty the room was when he went away—how the sun and the smell of the air had changed—how I finally saw that it wasn't Mrs. Mitnick or her expensive home that had built a bubble around me. It was love. And it was gone. I felt it so hard I thought it might split my seams, but how would I know if he could feel it? And if he was feeling the same thing—how could I ever know what was in his heart?

Her friends came over every night. Monday there might be a crowd of raucous women getting drunk to Ingmar Bergman or weeping over Julia Roberts' attempts to find true love or die with dignity . . . and on Tuesday she'd host an intimate dinner for one of her fellow literary theory sweatshop workers, and break down in tears after two glasses of red wine. For Heidi she made stuffed cabbage—almost the exact same recipe Mrs. Mitnick used to make, lacking only my old mistress's quarter-pinch of cinnamon. The smell of it seeped into me, richer and denser than it had ever been before, and I ached for her to spill it all over me so that I could suck up the taste of it. How sensually stunted I had been, all those years with the plastic wrap on. How many lovely sensations dulled or deadened by the shiny armor I was so proud of. After eating she sprawled out across me and I found myself cradling her with genuine fondness. I could feel her missing him. I could chart the impressions he had left.

"This is nothing new," Heidi said. "You just have this thing for hopeless fuck-up punk-rock boys. Am I right?"

The girl shrugged.

"You fall for cute boys with mediocre hygiene and anarchist political perspectives. Guys with unresolved emotional issues who can give you what you need in bed, but whom you can run circles around intellectually. You can make them feel like shit whenever it suits you, so you can keep them at an emotional distance. You need to let your guard down, is what it is."

The girl nodded, stuck a finger at the bottom of her wine glass to get at that last drop, and forgot the words as soon as she heard them. Every single guest came with advice, almost all of it useless, so how was she to know that Heidi was telling her what she needed to hear?

I held her. I could no longer hate her, and my love for him felt like an act of youthful naiveté. Profound pity was the only appropriate response to creatures so stunted, so stuck and willfully shielded from the world they lived in. Who chose not to see the cruel horror of their world. Who looked around a room and saw only their own bodies, and the things they thought they owned. Who ignored the emptiness that surrounded them. Only the emptiness was real, and the sunlight shafting through it, and the dark that would follow.

Crummy as it was, the apartment was too expensive for her to handle on her own. The eviction notice came a month after Tim's expulsion. Within a week she was gone, leaving behind: me, a box of Tim's books, an overflowing garbage can, and a long black rug. Merciful without meaning to be, she left one window open a crack. For six whole days the sunlight brought in all the noises of that grim beautiful place, that city past its prime, those endless rows of cheap, crumbling homes, those thousands of couples screaming and fighting and fucking and laughing. Empty spaces hallowed by human sweat. And then the landlord called the Salvation Army, who sent two men to wrestle me down the stairs and onto a very familiar truck.

"I'm going to pick up my friend on the way back," the driver said to his coworker, an older heavier man. "You have to sit in the back of the truck with the stuff."

"That's not safe," the guy said.

"It's a five-minute drive," said the driver. "Just get back there."

With the door shut, there was absolutely no light in the back of the truck. The mover fumbled through the darkness until he found me, and then he sat down.

Most of the men who work for the Salvation Army are looking for salvation themselves. They're easing themselves off of addictions or out of prison, or they're just so desperate for a place to sleep that they'll put up with all the Army's shit about how they did a dreadful job of managing their own lives and now it was time to turn it over to Jesus. This guy was a recovering alcoholic, quiet and hard-working and perpetually ashamed. Whatever he did in his long drunk years, the guilt of it never left him. Even after six or seven weeks clean, his pores still had a nostalgic hint of whiskey sweat.

"Fuck," he said, to no one, about nothing. I knew exactly what he was feeling. The pain of needing something you can never have; of knowing how you want to feel but not knowing how to get there. We rattled on in darkness, heading for the mothball-smelling warehouse that was as close to heaven as either of us would ever come.

XV.

I stare at the couch in horror. Then I stare at my hands, staggered by what's in them. His gift, his curse.

I can do it too, now. Take stories, see whole worlds.

Anyone can.

ACKNOWLEDGMENTS

I STILL CAN'T BELIEVE this happened.

Any of it.

The book you hold in your hands, like my whole career, could never have been born without my broodmates in the Clarion Class of 2012 (Deborah Bailey, Eliza Blair, Lisa Bolekaja, Sadie Bruce, E. G. Cosh, Danica Cummins, Lara Elena Donnelly, Eric Esser, Jonathan Fortin, R. K. Kalaw, Chris Kammerud, Joseph Kim, Pierre Liebenberg, Sarah Mack, Carmen Maria Machado, Dan McMinn, Luke R. Pebler), as well as all our teachers (Jeffrey Ford, Delia Sherman, Ted Chiang, Walter Jon Williams, Holly Black, Cassandra Clare, and guest critic Karen Joy Fowler). Clarion rocked my world and shook me to my core, and I am so proud to be part of the ~~cult~~ family.

If Clarion birthed me, Altered Fluid raised me. I am so fortunate to belong to this incredible writing group, which in my time has included the following magnificent writers: Adanze Asante, Alaya Dawn Johnson, Alyssa Wong, D. T. Friedman, Devin Poore, E.C. Myers, Gay Partington Terry, Greer Woodward, K. Tempest Bradford, Kai Ashante Wilson, Kiini Ibura

Salaam, Kris Dikeman, Lilah Wild, Martin Cahill, Matthew Kressel, Mercurio D. Rivera, N. K. Jemisin, Paul Berger, Rajan Khanna, Rick Bowes, Theresa DeLucci, and Tom Crosshill.

Forever hugs to my agent, Seth Fishman, and Jacob Weisman and Jaymee Goh of Tachyon, and my husband Juancy Rodriguez.

Undying love to all the editors who published these stories originally—whether they edited the hell out of them or just said, "this is good to go"—I am humbled and grateful for their labor: E. Catherine Tobler, John Joseph Adams, Wendy Wagner, Neil Clarke, C. C. Finlay, John Klima, Sheila Williams, Lynne Thomas, Michael Thomas, Michi Trota. Everyone who cares about short fiction owes a profound debt to them, and to all the other incredible editors out there.

Ray Bradbury was the first writer whose short stories set me on fire, when I was a little kid checking *S is for Space* and *R is for Rocket* out of my small-town library repeatedly. Also, the framing narrative for *The Illustrated Man* might have been . . . imitated? pilfered? when I was putting together the interstitial episodes that tie this book together.

My mom, Deborah Miller, is a brilliant writer, and when I was twelve years old, she taught me how to write a cover letter, put together a self-addressed, stamped envelope, and submit stories to magazines. *Asimov's* and *the Magazine of Fantasy & Science Fiction* were two of the markets I started sending stories to; it only took me twenty-four years to get an acceptance from *Asimov's* ("Calved," included in this collection) and twenty-eight for *F&SF* ("Shucked," also here). I'm not saying that she's more proud of me for having a short story collection than for having novels published, but . . . yeah. Keep an eye out for Deborah Miller; she'll be having a short story collection of her own some day soon.

My best friend Walead Esmail Rath was the first person who

showed me how much weird, sneaky fun you can have with short stories, but he also helped me to see how other storytelling modes—from Motown to cinema—were essential to feeding the short fiction mind. To this day, my short story toolkit includes several tricks and blades and blunt objects I ~~shamelessly stole~~ learned from him.

Here's a fun story that hopefully you will agree is fun.

In 2008, I was listening to the Weakerthans' album "Reunion Tour," and the song "Sun in an Empty Room" provided the spark I needed to pull together a story idea I'd been struggling with. I named the story after the song (which is also the name of an incredible Edward Hopper painting), and started submitting it. I ended up sending it to—no joke—ninety-nine literary and spec-fic journals. Some of them still have it, a decade later. Some of them are dead now. I came close to an acceptance once—the magnificent Fran Wilde, then a slush reader at *Apex Magazine*, tried her best to get it published, but editor-in-chief Lynne M. Thomas wasn't feeling it (no hard feelings—Lynne has bought several of my craziest stories at *Uncanny Magazine* (including *The Heat of Us*, featured here), and is one of my favorite people).

All of which is just to say, being a writer can be a long, weird journey and sometimes it takes years and years for a story to see the light of day. And that you should listen to music or watch movies or play video games or whatever sparks your storytelling soul as much as possible. And that the awesome people you meet along the way—even the ones that reject you—might change your life later on. So write your weird, wild, wonderful shit.

The world needs your words.

STORY NOTES

Allosaurus Burgers

I wanted to write a story about the moment where a child realizes their parent is human, and fallible. It's such a heartbreaking and universal step, when you stop believing that your parents can answer every question and always keep you safe.

Also, I love dinosaurs. A lot. And dinosaurs make every dramatic fact about the human condition more dramatic.

Marital Easter egg: when I was a little kid, I remember sitting at the kitchen table longing for the day when I'd be tall enough for my feet to touch the ground. When my husband was a little kid, he remembers crying on the day his feet finally touched the ground, because he was so sad to not be a kid for much longer.

So I combined our experiences, here. The longing for adulthood, and the sadness at reaching it.

All my work takes place in a shared universe, so there's lots of little recurrences of events and characters—the protagonist of "Allosaurus Burgers" "grows up" to become the main character of my debut novel, *The Art of Starving.*

57 Reasons for the Slate Quarry Suicides

I legit have no idea how this story happened. Fifty-seven has always been an eerily recurrent number for me, but I can't for the life of me remember whether I started out intending to do fifty-seven reasons or that's just where it ended up. But it was my audition story when I applied to be part of the incredible Altered Fluid writers' group, and while I got a ton of great advice it was a teeny-tiny suggestion from Lilah Wild that really made the hugest difference. So, yeah. If you are a writer, you should definitely join a writer's group!

We Are the Cloud

I wrote this story in 2008; it was rooted in my work with homeless families, observing the way systems that are supposed to exist to help people (like the shelter system, and mental health supports, and foster care) often end up surveilling and stigmatizing marginalized folks and funneling them into other, even-more-toxic institutions like the prison-industrial complex. I knew a lot of guys like Sauro, who the world could only see as something to exploit, but who had the power to shake it to its core if and when they came together.

Conspicuous Plumage

This story started with a sentence: *Summer meant freedom, and freedom was terrifying.* That happens sometimes. The whole thing spins itself around a moment, a thing you see out of the corner of your eye, a curtain flapping in the summer twilight breeze, a feeling of held breath and hidden contradiction, with the whole narrative of violence and music and grief and sex and magic rushing along behind it trying to catch up.

Shattered Sidewalks of the Human Heart

Has there ever been a better monster than Kong? Or metaphor for how we are awful? At seven, I cried when Kong fell, and in a sense I am still crying. I want to live in the world where monsters are real, and they show us ourselves: how we are monsters, and how we can be better. That's why I'm a writer.

In 2018 I saw the brilliant (and sadly-short-lived) Broadway musical version of *King Kong*, which got me thinking about Kong in the context of New York—my beloved city-state of the proud and the mighty and the monstrous and the exploited, the immigrants who came here with nothing and the people who came here in chains, and what Kong might unlock in us by the example of his power and his resistance and his death. This story spun itself out of that on the subway ride home from the theater.

Shucked

It's an old story: how the rich and old exploit the poor and beautiful. How capitalism makes that harm so transactional and banal; how the damage it does is invisible, impossible to verify or quantify. How it makes us all into either victims or accomplices.

As much as I adore stories situated squarely inside of a specific genre, I also love the story where you walk away wondering, was that real? Is it supernatural, or all in their head? Or something else entirely? They're harder to find homes for, since most SF/F/H outlets want the story to really revel in the power and potential of the genres (and most lit mags don't want anything that smells even slightly of genre), but to my great joy and surprise, this was the first story of mine that was ever accepted by the venerable *Magazine of Fantasy & Science Fiction*, which I'd been submitting stories to since the age of twelve. Only took me twenty-eight years!

The Beasts We Want to Be

Sometimes the universe sends me secret messages through the "shuffle" function on my music player, providing the precise spark I need to figure out a quirk of character or plot or setting.

I was at Clarion, my head exploding every five minutes with awesome new insights and inspiration from my classmates and teachers, and I was out for a run with my headphones on—and one of my favorite songs came on—"Abel," by The National. It's about the acute pain of living on after you've lost the person who made you want to be a better person. That's Nikolai's tragedy—Apolek was his hero, his inspiration; Apolek helped him see how full of anger and hate and ignorance he still was, how far he had to go, and he came to depend upon him for help getting there. But what do you do when that person is gone? The whole story bloomed around that before I was finished with my run.

Calved

One of the most fascinating contradictions of American xeno-phobia is how U.S. imperialism and the toxic actions of American corporations have devastated the economies and environments of countries like Mexico, but then when folks come here trying to survive—because we've destroyed their countries—we treat them like shit. And put their kids in cages.

I wanted to imagine a future where the asshole Americans finally have to confront the consequences of their actions, and because of climate change become the hated refugees.

Qaanaaq would later become the setting for my novel, *Black-fish City*, and of course I had to stick in a "Calved" cameo—Thede has a short phone call with one of the POV characters.

When Your Child Strays from God

One of the reasons I am a writer is to help me better understand the things in the world I find horrifying, or incomprehensible. Human behavior being foremost among them. Frequently I find my best characters when I look at someone in the real world whose actions I find monstrous, and remind myself of Tom's mantra in *The Talented Mr. Ripley*: "Well, whatever you do, how-ever terrible, however hurtful, it all makes sense, doesn't it? In your head? No-one ever thinks that they're a bad person."

I wrote this story right after "Calved," as a kind of counter-point: both are about a parent confronted with the fact of their child growing up into something they can't understand or find terrifying, but the main characters of the two stories make very different decisions about how to handle that transformation.

Things With Beards

In 2014 I finally had the chance to see one of my favorite horror films on the big screen—*The Thing* on 35mm at BAM Cinema in Brooklyn. Talking to my brilliant buddies R.F.I. Porto and Jenny Olson (and brilliant husband Juancy Rodriguez), we debated whether or not the Things knew that they were Things. I used to think they *did* know, and were doing their best to act like humans, but how much more terrifying would it be if they *didn't* know? That got the engines turning, thinking about passing as something that you're not, masculinity and beards and gay men in a straight world and how the monsters are real, and some of them wear badges. Add to that the fact that it came out in 1982—the same year as the first documented cases of HIV/AIDS—and this whole wild, weird story of sex and monstrosity and fighting for police reform assembled itself with the eerie alacrity of a shape-shifting murder alien.

Ghosts of Home

Me, trying to understand asshole humans again. Or rather, desperate and manipulated humans whose poverty and lack of options are manipulated by asshole capitalists into harming themselves and the people who are just like them. Plus ghosts!

I love that the idea of a "home spirit" exists in so many cultures—it really captures the universal, magical relationship human beings have with the buildings they live in. But what happens to that concept in the age of late capitalism and mass evictions and massive corporations that treat housing as a commodity—not a human right, not something sacred?

The Heat of Us

Clarion changed my life. Attending the workshop in 2012 rocked my world, blew my mind open, showed me the teeming multitude of incredible worlds and writers who gather together under the umbrella of science fiction, fantasy, horror. And it gave me a crew. A community. A bunch of magnificent monsters just like me. And even though I had spent eight years as a community organizer at that point, and I should have *known* that community was a superpower, this was when I really grasped how it impacted me as a writer. "The Heat of Us" is about the power we have together, and how much bad shit we can burn down when we align ourselves.

Angel, Monster, Man

HIV/AIDS pops up a lot in my fiction—I still feel so much rage and anger, from losing loved ones to the disease and from seeing so much power and promise murdered by governmental inaction. The seed of this story came from the fantastic collection *Persistent Voices: Poetry by Writers Lost to AIDS*, edited by David Groff and Philip Clark, which got me reflecting on how much art was lost—a queer, creative revolution was murdered in its crib, and only now are we seeing a resurgence of that kind of astonishing, world-changing creativity.

Another Easter egg for the Sam J. Miller Expanded Cinematic Universe (I'm currently open to better branding)—Tom Minniq pops up again in my novel *The Blade Between*, another story about activists scheming up a fake identity and accidentally creating a vessel for a monster to come through.

Sun in an Empty Room

There's already a detailed backstory on this one in the Acknowl-edgements, but here's another tidbit: I wrote it with the title "Peel Back My Skin," a lyric from the Saves the Day song "Ups and Downs." But it wasn't quite landing. Then I was listening to the song "Sun in an Empty Room," by the Weakerthans, and the line "Now that the furniture's returning to its Goodwill home" totally captured in nine words what it took me a couple thousand to say in the story. So, yeah. Music saves the day again. Listen to music, writers! Great songs give you so much.

And go find that song. It's a killer.

These stories were written on the ancestral lands of the Mahican, Munsee Lenape, Wappinger, and Kumeyaay Nations. Indigenous sovereignty and resistance have shaped our history, but they are also our future: Native-led activism has stopped projects that would have produced 780 million metric tons of greenhouse gases every year. Learn more, including how you can support, at ienearth.org

About Sam J. Miller

Sam J. Miller is a Nebula-Award-winning author. His debut novel, *The Art of Starving*, was an *NPR* Best of the Year, and his second novel, *Blackfish City*, was a Best Book of the Year for *Vulture*, *The Washington Post*, *Barnes & Noble*, and more, as well as a "Must Read" in *Entertainment Weekly* and *O: The Oprah Winfrey Magazine*. A recipient of the Shirley Jackson Award and a graduate of the Clarion Writers' Workshop, Sam's work has been nominated for the World Fantasy, Theodore Sturgeon, John W. Campbell, and Locus Awards, and reprinted in dozens of anthologies. The last in a long line of butchers, he lives in New York City and at samjmiller.com.

About Amal El-Mohtar

Amal El-Mohtar is an award-winning writer of fiction, poetry, and criticism. Her stories and poems have appeared in many magazines such as *Tor.com*, *Fireside Fiction*, *Lightspeed*, *Uncanny*, *Strange Horizons*, *Apex*, *Stone Telling*, and *Mythic Delirium*, and several anthologies including *The Djinn Falls in Love and Other Stories* (2017), *The Starlit Wood: New Fairy Tales* (2016), *Kaleidoscope: Diverse YA Science Fiction and Fantasy Stories* (2014), and *The Thackery T. Lambshead Cabinet of Curiosities* (2011). Her short story "Seasons of Glass and Iron" won the Hugo, Nebula, and Locus Awards and was a finalist for the World Fantasy, Sturgeon, Aurora, and Eugie Awards in the same year. She is the author, with Max Gladstone, of *This Is How You Lose the Time War*, a queer, epistolary, spy-vs-spy love story, and *The Honey Month*, a collection of poetry and prose written to the taste of twenty-eight different kinds of honey. She reviews books for *NPR* and is the science-fiction and fantasy columnist for the *New York Times Book Review*. She lives in Ottawa with her spouse and two cats.